Into the Hurricane with a Cheap Umbrella

Eunice Barnes

Text © 2023 Eunice Barnes

Editor: Allister Thompson

Cover design by Anthony Bennett

All rights reserved. No part of this publication may be reproduced, stored in a retrieval system or transmitted, in any form or by any means, digital, mechanical, photocopying, recording or otherwise, without the prior consent of the publisher, except for the use of brief quotations in a book review.

This is a work of fiction. Unless otherwise indicated, all the names, characters, businesses, places, events and incidents in this book are either the product of the author's imagination or used in a fictitious manner. Any resemblance to actual persons, living or dead, or actual events is purely coincidental.

ISBN-13: 9798397532655

To my mother, the most interesting person I know, who taught me a thing or two about being frugal.

One

It was 10:20 a.m. I placed my empty coffee cup in the sink and was about to check my tablet for emails when I heard my phone ring. That could only mean one of two things: it was a scammer or someone who didn't text. Which didn't leave many people. My heart jumped when I looked at the display. Mom. I hadn't heard from her in over nine years. "Hello," I answered warily.

She was hysterical. "He's having a heart attack! Your father!" She let out a blood-curdling scream. "He's turning blue! Rachel, Rachel!" She screamed again. My heart pounded as I panicked along with her.

"Mom, Mom! Calm down. Call 911," I said, attempting to sound reassuring, wanting to help her regain composure.

"I *did* call 911. What do you think I am? An idiot? They're on the way." *Good old Mom*, I thought. Certainly not an idiot. Occasionally slightly vitriolic, often sarcastic, but never an idiot. Sharp as a tack, my mother.

"Good. Things will be fine. They'll be there soon."

"I need you! You need to get over here."

"I can't this very second. Just keep doing chest compressions. He'll be fine."

"He won't be fine. He's not breathing. Breathe, damn it! John, breathe!" she screamed. Then she hung up.

My mother was right. He wasn't fine. My father died twenty minutes after arriving at the hospital.

It was the first Monday in the month of May when my father died and left my mother all alone. The first Monday in the month of May my husband too left me. Though my husband had departed a year before.

Positively uncanny. Was Dad's dying a cruel joke? No. My father left, not for another woman or another life, but because he suffered a myocardial infarction, more simply known as a heart attack. While he had no choice, my husband's exit was strictly by choice, as was his means, the front door, which he slammed loudly on his way out.

Another major difference was that when my father left my mother, he left her with a four-million-dollar home, two luxury cars in the garage, a beautiful summer home in Muskoka, stocks and bonds, full bank accounts, and a very generous life insurance payout. She did not want for anything.

My husband left me with $20,000 in credit card debt, two months of overdue rent, and a five-year-old son to raise as a twenty-nine-year-old single mom with a low-paying job in a company that was in the process of filing for bankruptcy. And don't let me even get started on my daycare issues.

My father's heart attack occurring at the same time, one year after my husband's exit, was definitely unplanned. Why would one plan a heart attack, if that were even possible? And what was more, my parents did not know my husband was gone, because I hadn't told them.

Why not? So I wouldn't be inundated with humiliating comments such as, "I told you so. Did you change the locks? Have you cancelled your bank accounts? Did he hit you? Was he on drugs? Were there other women? Have you been tested for STDs?" I didn't want or need their overwhelming concern, however justified under the circumstances, so I simply chose not to tell them.

It was true. They had warned me that if I married Alex, I

would have nothing but trouble, and like many a young person, I didn't listen.

I was in love, or so I thought. He was my first love. We attended the same high school and were in several classes together. He was bright, funny, articulate, and very good-looking. A real charmer. His family was from Ecuador. And man, could he dance! At lunch, he would play Spanish music from his phone: salsa, bachata, and merengue. He would scoop me into his arms, spin me, and dip me. I was in seventh heaven.

The other thing he did in the hallways at lunch was gamble. Sometimes a card game, sometimes dice. That never bothered me. It should have.

After a pregnancy scare, following graduation we decided to get married to raise our nonexistent child with two parents. After all, we were in love. And isn't love all you need?

My parents were incensed. They pleaded with me, told me they could help me raise the baby, if that was what I wanted. *Anything, but please don't marry Alex*, they begged. But I had made up my mind. They, in turn, refused to attend my wedding, which was both painful and embarrassing. After the wedding, I stopped talking to them and they made no effort to reconcile. Four years later, I became pregnant for real and gave birth to Daniel.

They had expected more from me and were disappointed. My father was head of the civil engineering department at the university, and my mother had received a business degree, after which she was the first woman appointed chief financial officer of one of Canada's Fortune 500 companies, remaining there until her company merged with another, making her position redundant. She retired with a very substantial severance. My parents were the epitome of success, extremely wealthy, highly intelligent. Then there was me, their failure of a daughter, no university, not even college, pregnant and marrying an immigrant boy who worked in construction.

The snubbing became mutual. Since they didn't accept Alex, in effect, they did not accept the person I had become. I made no effort to reconnect and we became strangers. My mother's call about my father's heart attack was the first time I had heard her voice in almost ten years.

I turned to my six-year-old son, Daniel, my life, sitting on the couch, happily playing a video game. Just looking at him warmed my heart and steadied my racing pulse. A sweet little boy whose father's departure, thankfully, had little to no effect on him. Probably because Alex was absent more than he was home, and when home, he spent most of his time on his phone. I did my utmost not to fight with him. Growing up, my parents didn't fight around me, and I did not intend to bring my son up with constant fighting. My concerns were always discussed quietly when Daniel was either at school or in bed. Eventually, since it appeared change was not on the horizon, we stopped talking. Alex remained a stranger to his own son.

I coughed to get his attention. "Daniel." His eyes remained on his game.

"Daniel" I said, louder this time.

"What?"

"That was your grandmother on the phone."

"Lita?" He got excited at the mention of his grandmother, the only one he knew, Alex's mother.

"No, Daniel, you have another grandmother. My mother."

"Your mother? I didn't know you had a mother." He sounded genuinely confused and more than a little disappointed. After all, who was she to him? His love was for Lita, whom he hadn't seen since Alex walked out. I knew Daniel missed her, but awkwardness made me stay away because being divorced from her son, I didn't know how to act around her.

"Well, I do have a mother," I said rather abruptly, surprising even myself with my angry tone. Then came the lies. "She's lived too far away. That's why you haven't seen her. Anyway, Daniel, she called to tell me your grandfather, my father, has had a heart attack and is very sick. We need to go over there."

"Doesn't she live too far away?" he asked, never missing a beat.

"Not any more. Let's go, turn your game off," I said, getting frustrated.

"Can I finish first?"

"Nope, sorry kiddo, no time today." I walked to the machine and flipped the switch to *off*.

*

I pulled my rusted twelve-year-old sedan into the large, circular driveway of my parents' house, which was devoid of all vehicles. Their two luxury vehicles and my dad's beloved classic 1958 Thunderbird stayed in the garage, away from possible thieves. "One cannot be too safe," my dad always remarked.

I glanced at my son, who was silently looking out the window. "Daniel, you stay in your seat. I'll be right back. I'm just going to be at the door. You can watch me."

"Can I play my GameBoy while I wait?" he asked, barely six years old and already addicted to electronics.

"No," I shot back, perhaps a little too abruptly. His bottom lip pouted, and he looked as if he might cry, so I softly added, "I won't be long."

I walked up the path to the oversized front doors and banged the large brass knocker. Suddenly I had a sweet memory of my father carrying me on his shoulders into the house. "Duck your head," he had said, and I laid my head on top of his, taking in the scent of his wonderful hair. Standing at the door, twenty years later, I swore I could smell it. After dad and I went in, he put me down, then my older brother by two years, Tommy, cried out joyfully, "Carry me, carry me on your shoulders too, Dad!"

"You're going to have to catch me first," Dad said. A game of tag erupted, only to end with the two of them wrestling on the floor, the dog barking, and my mother standing over them on the stairs, laughing. I saw it all as if it were yesterday.

I waited briefly at the door and was about to return to my car when the next-door neighbor, Mrs. Doyle, called from the other side of our neatly manicured hedge, arms waving frantically to catch my attention. The moment I looked at her, she rushed to my side.

This woman has not changed in almost ten years, I thought. She wore the same hairstyle and style of clothes, and until she came close, I didn't think she had aged at all. Then I saw deep lines etched in the corners of her eyes and mouth.

While I was slightly taken aback, with her it was the opposite. "Look at you, Rachel, look at you!" she exclaimed, throwing her arms around me and hugging me tightly. Holding me at arm's length, taking me in, she squeezed my shoulders and said, "Now aren't you a beauty. I can't believe it's been so many years. Time's been very good to you, I see," she said in her slightly diminished Irish accent. "But your poor dear da is in a bad way. They just took him away in an ambulance. He had a heart attack. But I suppose you know that."

"Where did they take him, Mrs. Boyle, did you find out?"

"Oh, yes, I did indeed. I asked your mum as they were leaving." She looked quite proud of herself. "Humber Memorial Hospital. You hurry on, dear. You'll find him there. And it was lovely seeing you again. And don't be a stranger now, you hear?" she cried out to me as I was hurrying to my car.

"I won't, I won't," I answered distractedly, getting into my car.

At the hospital, I was directed to a small room in the

emergency department, where I found my mother sitting in a chair across from my father's prone form. My heart pounded as I heard myself gasp. My mother's hand was resting on his forearm. I had Daniel's little hand grasped tightly in mine, and I didn't know who was more frightened, him or me. I could've put bets on me. In fact, Daniel barely seemed fazed at all. And why would he have been? The two people in the room with us were unknown to him.

I approached my mother, gently touching her shoulder. "I'm here now, Mom." I tried to avoid looking at my father.

She turned her head slowly and looked up at me, and it was as if she didn't recognize me. Suddenly, tears streaming down her face, she threw her arms around my hips, buried her head in my lap, and sobbed. After a few moments, she pulled away and said, "Rachel, Rachel, thank God you're here." She noticed the now frightened Daniel standing beside me, and, laughing through her tears, she said, "Daniel, oh my goodness. I hope I'm not scaring you. You're such a little man. I can't believe it; I've missed so much."

"Hey, Mom, yes, we're here now. Let me drive you home. Let's get out of here," I said.

"I can't leave your father here. I can't just leave. He needs..." And her voice trailed off as she looked at my father and realized he didn't need her anymore.

I put my arms around her shoulders and told her I would take care of everything with the hospital and that we just needed to go home. Reluctantly, she agreed and walked ahead of me, holding Daniel's hand while I stopped at the nurse's desk to ask questions.

On the drive home, my mother turned at a ninety-degree angle, looked straight at me, and announced, "Rachel, I've been thinking. You need to ask Alexander to come to the funeral."

For a moment, I was thrown. Alexander? Who was she

talking about? Then I remembered that Alex, my ex, to my very proper mother was Alexander. She never shortened anyone's name. My friends Matt and Mikey were Matthew and Michael, and Kat was Katherine. Even my brother, whom I always called Tommy, remained Thomas.

Poor, poor Thomas who died so young. One day, tragedy struck, and he drowned in the neighbors' swimming pool. "Tommy! Tommy, my baby Tommy," my mother cried. The one and only time she shortened a name.

"I've been thinking about us. A lot," she continued. "We've wasted too many years already, and we need to be a family. We *are* family. We just need to act like family. And, Rachel, I'm sorry we didn't come to your wedding. That was all my fault." I knew that. Without actually knowing. "I told your dad that we shouldn't go. I told him that maybe, just maybe, if we didn't come to the wedding, you wouldn't go through with it. But you did, and now you're happy and we can't waste any more years apart."

"Mom, Alex won't be coming to the funeral. We're divorced. It's been six months now, and I don't even know where he is."

There it was, now I waited to hear the "I told you so." But much to my relief, she looked at me with her puffy, swollen, tear-filled eyes, and as if taking in the enormity of the situation, proclaimed, "Alexander's gone? Well then, you're moving in with me. There is no need for you to pay for somewhere to live while I live alone in the big house. It's settled, and I won't take no for an answer."

I was trying to come up with some excuse but was caught off-guard, and while I stumbled for words, she added, "It makes perfect sense."

I had no reply, because it *did* make perfect sense. I was about to become unemployed, was completely broke, in debt with no way of getting out of it, and my landlord was threatening to call the cops to have me evicted. And my mother, although I didn't see it at the time, needed a diversion, a project — me — so she wouldn't have to mourn my father, just as my father was her project when Tommy died.

Two

My father's funeral was attended by no fewer than a thousand people. Mourners were standing in the back aisles, spilling out the door down to the street. I had never witnessed anything close to that before. Flower arrangements, from the delicate daisy to some that reached as high as the ceiling, adorned the room. It was an extravaganza extraordinaire. Everyone from neighbors, students, former students, to colleagues of both my father and mother and a few dignitaries from city hall. I had no idea my father was so important. He always hated crowds and would have loathed this.

Following the ceremony, my father's inconsolable elderly mother was held up by his two brothers, who helped her join his sister, my mother, and me to form a receiving line to accept condolences. My mother's eighty-five-year-old father sat in the front row, scowling at my mother. I learned later that when his driver's licence was revoked, he refused to stop driving. Subsequently, my father removed his car from his driveway and sold it. My father gave the money to my grandfather, who threw it back at my father and spat on him. Grandpa remained venomous toward my mother to this day. Not one word of sympathy came from him, and everyone was surprised he even showed up for the funeral.

One by one, the guests walked past us. The ones who knew my father well extolled his virtues and heaped praise. One would have thought the man an angel incarnate. Did he never do anything wrong? Of course, he did. But there is a time and place for everything, and a funeral is the time and place for compliments only. Never speak ill of the dead.

A middle-aged man stopped directly in front of me; staring intently into my eyes, he said, "Rachel, your father spoke highly of you, but he failed to tell me how beautiful you turned out to be. It's really quite unnerving. You're a sultry combination of the Mona Lisa and Marilyn Monroe. Innocence, vivaciousness, and sensuality all combined the most appealing mixture. Yes, indeed." He winked then turned abruptly and talked to my mother. My face was now a deep shade of scarlet, and had he remained by me, I would have told him my opinion of him, which lay somewhere between a common lech and a super lech. Maybe it was better he left. My mother also looked none too pleased.

After the funeral, my mother, Daniel, and I went back to mom's house. Sitting on her couch, with Daniel now asleep, head on my lap, we finally had a chance to talk. I said, "What's with that man? What an inappropriate display he made. Who is he, Mom? Do you know?"

"Oh yes, him I know, and all his scandalous ways. Marcel Mancy. He was a fellow engineering professor with your dad in his department. He was one of your father's favorite subjects. Your father used to remark that Marcel reminded him of an ice cream shop owner who always had a flavor of the month. But always young and fresh. Kind of like you. And you know what is really sad is that he and I are the same age, but me he walked by with barely a word. I think he did say sorry or some pitiful form of it. Beelined straight for you. And at a funeral of all places. Disgusting!" She sighed deeply.

"I'll say!" I agreed wholeheartedly.

She shook her head as if in disbelief at what was happening and said, "What a horrible day. Rachel, I just want your dad back. I need him. This wasn't supposed to happen. We were going to grow old together. We had so many things planned." My mother buried her face in her hands and sobbed.

I sat by helplessly, watching her cry. Why wasn't I crying? Was I dead inside? Empty of emotion from the death of my marriage? And everything that preceded it? I truly hoped not. But somehow, I couldn't relate to my father's death. I felt detached, as if I was some stranger watching the whole thing. I couldn't put it in any proper perspective. I hadn't seen my father in over ten years, and now he was gone. Permanently. Because he was gone from my life before he died, in some way it seemed as if he never had existed at all. It was really messed up.

I timidly said, "Mom?" and when she didn't hear me, I repeated myself a little louder.

She took her hands away from her eyes and stared at me. "Yes, Rachel?" she asked, reaching for a tissue and blowing her nose.

"Did you mean it when you said I should move back?"

"Of course, I meant it. Anytime, the sooner the better."

"There are two of us now. But Daniel is a good boy; he won't cause any trouble. He's very sweet and obedient. And he will soon be school all day, so he won't get underfoot."

"Perfect, so then I take it you want to come back."

Want to? Well, not exactly, but I was not about to tell her that. *Need to* was more like it. Temporarily, until I had a bit of money and a place. "I'd love to," I answered with as much gusto as I could muster.

The move back to Mrs. Deborah Armstrong's house was a breeze consisting of just four baskets containing freshly laundered clothes, toys, and bedding straight from the laundromat. Everything else I owned was thrown into the huge bins behind my old apartment building. I had no intention of bringing the cockroaches that lived in our old apartment, well aware they'd hitch a ride in our couch, dressers, mattresses, or anything else. Seeing my diminutive haul, my mother raised an eyebrow, asked me if that was all I had, and when I answered yes, she thankfully pried no further. I had forgotten how considerate she could be — when she chose.

Daniel loved the house, the yard, and his room. And he especially loved my mother's dog, Luna, a gentle Border Collie who seemed to love him equally in return.

Sitting in the backyard, enjoying a cup of afternoon tea and watching Daniel throw a ball to an enthusiastic Luna, I turned to my mom and said, "They seem to be made for each other. Finally, I don't have to throw ball for him."

"I wasn't too fond of it myself," my mom said. "When your dad was away on business and Thomas would drag me out to play ball, I would try to get out of it, but there was no way. I just didn't get it. Throw, catch, throw, catch. I mean, I would have rather played dodgeball. At least you're throwing at something."

"You're not throwing at something; you're throwing at *someone*! That's your evil side, Mom. You wanted to throw a ball at Tommy?" I was laughing at the thought. I looked over at my mom, and her eyes were filled with tears. She pulled a tissue from her sleeve, where she kept one permanently these days, and wiped her eyes.

Feeling stupid for being so insensitive, I sat with eyes fixed on Daniel and Luna. I dared not speak lest I made another thoughtless remark.

"I can't believe they're both gone, Rachel. What did I do to deserve this? Do you think God hates me?"

"No, I don't think God hates you. I think life just sucks sometimes." And after a long moment of silence interrupted by sniffling, both hers and mine, I added, "But you have us now, Mom, you have us."

"Yes, I do. Thank goodness for that." She gave me a weak

smile while waving back at smiling Daniel. "If I call him Thomas, please forgive me. He reminds me so much of him. Sometimes when I am looking at Daniel, I think I am seeing Thomas again."

"That's perfectly understandable. I would be honored if you made that mistake. I loved Tommy too." My mother and I sighed in unison and then laughed. Grief can make you a little kooky, to be sure.

Three

A few days later, the first of many gifts arrived by UPS courier. One was addressed to my mother and the other to me. Both were from the same man, Marcel Mancy. He sent two small succulent plants in beautiful handcrafted clay pots, one for each of us. A little attached card read, *Wishing you nothing but comfort and strength. Marcel.*

The next day, UPS pulled into our driveway delivering two packages to our door. Again, we received the same gifts, only different colors. Super-soft herringbone throws, my mother's in soft blue, mine mint green. Same card.

Third day, it was Swarovski crystal flower stud earrings, mine with a navy center, my mother's yellow. Same card.

The fourth day, we both got silk scarves, mom's in mauve, mine aqua. Same card.

The fifth day, he sent two crystal wine glasses and a bottle of 2016 Ritual Monster Block Pinot Noir. Same card. My mother said, "Mmmm. Good choice."

Sixth day, he sent us gift baskets with white cotton robes, slippers, bath salts, and bubble bath. Same card once more.

And while we were finding this all slightly weird, we were, admittedly, starting to look forward to UPS pulling into the driveway. And the seventh day, we were not disappointed. Same time of day, UPS arrived with our gifts, which were large envelopes. My mother opened hers to find a gift certificate to spa, and my envelope contained a gift certificate for a very expensive restaurant. Her card read, as did all the previous cards: *Wishing you nothing but comfort and strength, Marcel.* However, this time, mine read, *May I join you to redeem the restaurant gift certificate? Marcel 647-454-3790.*

I showed the card to my mom. She rolled her eyes and said, "I should have known he was up to something. I guess that means no more gifts. Well, it was fun while it lasted."

"Argh. Why didn't you warn me? What should I do, Mom? He has been kind of nice. Would it be rude not to call him and just go with you and Daniel?"

"Well, what do *you* want to do? If he wants to take you to dinner, you know what that means. It is a date. And Rachel, the night your dad died I made a promise to myself that I would never interfere in your life again. I couldn't risk losing you and Daniel like I did after you married Alexander. But I have to tell you, I intensely dislike Marcel Mancy. He is a delusional egomaniac who preys on younger woman, and I fear that's what he is doing with you. I would strongly advise you against going out with that man. But, having said that, it's solely your decision. I can't make it for you."

Wow, that was quite the warning. I mulled it over. He was almost twice my age, fifty-two to my twenty-nine. With a very bad reputation. Plus, my mother hated him and would probably never let me live it down it something went wrong. On the other hand, he didn't look fifty-two, and I was almost thirty. From what I remembered, he was sort of good-looking, in an older guy kind of way. He wasn't bald or overweight, and he had style. I tried to look beyond the negative and recalled the things I kind of liked. Or at least didn't hate. And he did have an imagination, as the gifts indicated. Plus, his intelligence was appealing. While Alex could fix a car or change a light switch, he wasn't exactly book smart. I was always correcting his grammar, which he hated, but I couldn't help myself. He resented my educated parents and knew that I held back partly because of him. Although not intended, I made him feel insecure. Well, it certainly wouldn't be the case if I did see Marcel Mancy. And what would just one dinner mean anyway? It was already paid for, and it could be my way to say thank-you for the gifts. Plus, I was bored and it was something to do.

However, each time I went to my phone to key in the numbers, it was as if something was holding me back. I'd get a sick feeling at the pit of my stomach. I should have paid more attention to it. My intuition was working, but I ignored it. It took three days of attempts till I finally called his number.

"Hello," he answered on the fourth ring. A man in control, I would find out. Let the person on the other end wait. But not too long, lest they hang up.

"Hello, Marcel, this is Rachel." I didn't state a last name. He knew who I was.

"How are you, Rachel? I'm so glad you finally called me. I was beginning to think you wouldn't. Did you like the gifts? And your mom, did she enjoy them as well?"

"We did. They really lifted our spirits. Especially my mother's. She's still in shock, a bundle of nerves. But they helped. We were actually looking forward to UPS coming everyday. I think she's sorry it's stopped now that you've asked me to dinner. Or is it me asking you, seeing as I'm the one with the gift certificate."

He laughed heartily. A nice laugh that made me smile. "You're right. I planned that, you know, you asking me out. It's called rejection avoidance or some such nonsense. I don't have to come right out and ask you and hear you say no. Which you would have, I'm sure."

"Yes, I would have. You are my father's age." I had to be honest now that he brought it into the open. "Even now I'm not sure how I feel about going out with you. But seeing as I've already asked you, I think I did, didn't I? Anyway, let's have dinner," I said, perhaps a little too cheerily, attempting to convince myself it was a good idea.

Friday evening, with reservations for eight, at seven he arrived at my door. I opened to him standing there smiling and immediately felt disappointment. I wish I could say I was pleasantly surprised and that he looked younger than I had remembered. But he didn't. I wanted to tell him I had changed my mind, but how unkind and foolish that would make me appear. Better to have the dinner and tell him after. Not put him on the spot, embarrass him in front of my mother, who was standing in the background, glaring. And Daniel, who was clueless.

The restaurant was outstanding. It claimed to have a five-star rating by many restaurant critics, and I could see why. Marcel ordered for us both. He wanted to, and I let him, seeing as he'd been there numerous times and knew what they prepared best. He had a calm and easy manner, and I felt comfortable around him. He didn't act as if it was a date; it felt more like he was an older friend. Someone I had known for a long time.

He spent a little time telling me about where he was from: born in Poland, immigrated when he was nine, where he went to school, Toronto, and when he started teaching at the university, sixteen years ago. He told me a bit about his family and that he had never married because he never found the right girl but thought that maybe he might want to some day, if the right girl appeared. "And maybe she has," he said and smiled mischievously.

I half smiled in return.

"What's your story?" Marcel asked.

"Well, it's not too exciting. I married my high school boyfriend. I was young and in love, and he could dance really well. Isn't that stupid?"

"I've heard of worse reasons."

"Yeah, I guess. Anyway, life was kind of tough. Dancing doesn't pay the bills, plus he loved to gamble but didn't love working, so we were always broke, and then the cheating started, so I hardly saw him; he was always at one of his girlfriends' places. It was pretty lonely. So now I'm divorced. But if it wasn't for Alex, I wouldn't have the love of my life, my sweet little boy Daniel. So, I guess it was all worth it."

"That little boy at the door is your son?" His smile disappeared.

"Yes, whose son did you think he was?" I asked incredulously.

"Honestly, I thought he was your brother. So many of my friends' wives are having babies later in life, in their forties. I thought your mother had another child. I did wonder why John never told me about it. But we didn't talk that often, and when we did it was usually about the university and its politics, so I just figured it slipped his mind."

I eyed him suspiciously, thinking that our conversation had just about dried up, when the female bartender walked toward our table. She was about my age and was wearing a skin-tight low-cut black dress that left little to the imagination but guaranteed good tips.

"Hello, Marcel, how are you?" A seething anger undermined her forced cheerfulness. Plus, she seemed extremely nervous.

"Angeline, what a surprise. I didn't know you worked here. How are you?" He flashed his biggest smile, but his eyes remained cold.

"Marcel, I believe we have some unfinished business to talk about. Can you call me?" she asked, looking as if she was about to burst into tears.

"We don't have any thing to discuss, Angeline. We've said it all already. And it looks like Robert is looking for you." He waved Robert, the owner, over to our table. As he was walking toward us, Angeline made a quick exit back to the bar.

I watched her take her station, dab her eyes with tissue, then smile broadly while taking orders from the businessmen at the bar. Robert approached our table and said, "Good evening, Mr. Mancy, so nice to have you at our establishment once again. Anything I can do for you?"

"I just wanted to congratulate you on another outstanding dinner. It's never a miscalculation coming here."

On the drive back home, Marcel brought the conversation back to Daniel. "Rachel, I think it is wonderful you have a little boy. In fact, I was wondering if I could take you and Daniel to Cirque du Soleil? It's coming in two weeks, and I would love to watch it through the eyes of a child."

I didn't answer right away. I took a minute to glance over at him and ponder. In the car, the evening darkness with only streetlights to illuminate us, he looked younger. He was still handsome. And he liked to do things, go out and have fun. It had been so long since someone had spent any money on me and taken me to nice places that I was starting to feel confused. Maybe it wasn't such a stretch to start seeing this man. Plus, he had included Daniel in our plans. *Maybe he really likes kids*, I thought.

I must have been staring at him longer than I realized, because when he turned and smiled at me, he caught me off guard. I felt foolish. But his smile was warm, and his manner the whole evening had been relaxed, as if nothing fazed him. He had it all under control. What a difference from Alex, who was young and exciting but always left my head spinning when he never had any money. Or when he left me for days on end while he cheated. And then he started borrowing on my credit card, and creditors were calling with threats. Yes, I did it for love, once, and look how that turned out. Maybe stability had something going for it, too.

"Okay," I said.

"Okay? We're going to the circus?" he asked happily.

"Yes, that would be fine. But I have a question for you."

"Shoot."

"Who is Angeline?"

"Oh, I thought you might ask me about her." He snickered then continued, "I was seeing her last year. We dated for a few months, but then she became a little unhinged and began stalking me."

"Why would she do that?" I asked. In my opinion, from observation and personal experience, women don't just become "unhinged" for no reason. They are, in almost one hundred percent of the cases, pushed that way. Driven crazy. However, I wanted to hear him explain it.

"Because I told her it wasn't working for us. At first it was great, and I wanted what was best for her. To improve her lot in life, get her degree and become independent. But instead she became clingy and dependent. She needed me to help her make every decision, no matter how small, and she just wanted to be around me all the time. I was starting to feel smothered."

"How did you meet her?" I was almost afraid to ask, knowing the answer.

"She was a student." Just what I thought. He continued, "A top student. Her drive and thirst for knowledge were outstanding. She could have been anything she wanted, and then she just decided that school wasn't for her any longer. She thought I would support her. We just had nothing in common. So, I told her I thought it best for both of us if we called it quits."

I was sure that if I asked Angeline I would hear another side and decided to file that away in the recesses of my mind and revisit the idea in the future if it became necessary. A thought did come to mind, however, and I asked, "Marcel, you know I have no postsecondary education. If it is so important to you, why would you want to start seeing me?"

"Have you looked in a mirror?" he asked. And then he flashed another smile.

I rolled my eyes. Did he just say that? I shook my head in disbelief. "Not the answer I was looking for. But at least you're honest. I'll give you that."

"No, I was joking. Kind of. Truth is, aside from your beauty, your dad was one of the best around. And from what I know of your mom, she is good folk too. Honest, generous, and loyal people. Excellent qualities that you have inherited. But really, Rachel, your father, John Armstrong, was hands-down the smartest man I knew. And that is in the university setting! And your mother wasn't far behind him, from what I hear. So, you can get an education if and when you want. And I can help you. I've got connections, you know. You'd have a degree in no time when you decide what you want to study."

When he pulled in my driveway, he turned off the car, got out to open my door, and walked me to the house. I felt my mother watching us, and I am sure he did too, because at the door he just leaned over and kissed my cheek and told me he would let me know about the circus after he made the reservations. I was relieved. Everything seemed to be happening too fast, and I really didn't know how I would have reacted had he tried to kiss my lips.

Four

I got inside to find my mother in the hallway leaning against a doorway with her arms folded on her chest.

"Hi, Mom, did Daniel go to sleep okay?"

"Yes, he did. Cried a bit for you, but I read him some stories, and he fell asleep during story number four. So, what happened? How was your *date*?" she asked, drawing out the word, making it sound dirty.

"It was fine, Mother." I was cross. I was a twenty-nine-year-old woman who had been married and had a child. I did not need the third degree from her.

"I don't trust that man. And don't you either, Rachel. Your dad seldom had a good word to say about him. He's a womanizer. That is the god's honest truth." Hadn't this same woman given me the okay to have dinner with him? I attempted to hide my frustration.

"Okay, Mom. Don't you think I can see that? I'm not a teenage girl any longer. I'm aware of the consequences of my decisions. I'm just getting to know him. That's all. And he wants to settle down now, or at least that's what he said, so maybe the womanizing is in his past. But it's fine, don't worry. I will listen to your opinion. This time, I'll be cautious." I wished I could tell her it was just one dinner with him, but I had agreed to go out again.

She looked at me, and her bottom lip turned out, tears filled her eyes, and she started sobbing. "Don't listen to me, Rachel. Don't! I'm such a mess. And it has been a horrible night. Your grandpa took a cab over here and started pounding on the door. Luna was barking and scared the life out of me. Luckily, Daniel stayed asleep. When I opened the door, he was screaming at me to give him his car back. He forgot we sold it. He accused your dad and I of being thieves and stealing his car. I had to sit him down and go over with him what happened. Ten times, and then I even had to get the announcement from the funeral to prove that your dad had died. He was so awful."

"Why didn't you call me? I would have come home to help." I felt horrible now as well.

"I didn't want to bother you while you were having a night out, and anyway, he finally seemed to get it and let me call him a cab to take him home. It was heartbreaking to see him like that. He's so confused. And when I saw the announcement again, it was as if learning your dad died for the first time all over again. I think my heart almost failed. I don't know how I'm going to survive. I just miss your dad so much. I can't believe he's not here. I've never been without him in thirty years. What am I going to do?" She started sobbing uncontrollably, and I walked over, put an arm gently around her shoulders, and led her to a chair before she fell.

Somehow, I didn't think my mother, in the state she was, would to try to interfere too much in my life. For now.

*

For the circus, Marcel bought VIP tickets that included a meet-and-greet with the performers and the animals to be held at the conclusion of the show in a huge tent set up for the event. We entered an enormous room filled with Cirque du Soleil artistes and their delighted, star-struck fans. Me included. Daniel was dumbstruck. We had never done anything like this before.

"Daniel, is there anyone you see here that you would like to talk to?" Marcel asked him kindly. Daniel just shook his head, so in awe, he was unable to speak. "Okay, just follow me."

We both tagged along behind Marcel until he noticed I wasn't at his side and gently put his hand around my waist, pulling me forward. With his other hand, he grasped Daniel's hand. All three of us made the rounds, greeting and complimenting each performer. Many of them crouched down to Daniel's eye level and whispered in his ear, sharing a secret or two about performing in the circus. The room was vibrant and alive, buzzing with excitement. Daniel was beside himself, and so was I.

Then, as if things couldn't get any better, Marcel bought Daniel a Cirque du Soleil t-shirt to remember the evening by. And what an evening! On the ride home I reflected on the evening while Daniel and Marcel chatted enthusiastically about everything they had experienced. The two of them were at the same level of extreme exuberance.

Marcel had been great with Daniel, and it was heart-warming to watch the interaction. In his short six years of life, Daniel hadn't had much attention from men, and I noticed how he became braver when Marcel asked him to do something. It was wonderful to observe. He wouldn't say no, from patting the animals to saying hello to the clown. With Marcel, he was not scared of the world, afraid of anything new, like he was with just me. *Maybe I'm not making a mistake*, I thought. *Maybe I'm making the best decision of my life.*

The next few weeks with Marcel were mostly enjoyable. He always had original and entertaining events planned, from live theater to farmer's markets, and he was open and charming with everyone, from the ticket girl at the theater booth to the transit driver taking our fare. He was very witty, and I laughed constantly. Also, he was quite knowledgeable about Toronto, so

I learned a lot from him.

"Toronto history is my hobby," he told me. "And I have quite the collection of Toronto memorabilia. You'll have to come to my place to see it sometime." He gave me a wink.

I returned, "We'll see about that." Being uncertain about us, I was going to take it *real* slow with him. Plus, I was continually having second thoughts; his age was not sitting well with me. To his credit, he seemed to understand when I explained that our relationship was on a trial basis. I had never dated someone older before and did not wish to rush anything. From experiencing regret in the past, I knew it was not my favorite emotion. In fact, I hated it. This, I decided, would be an observation period. Some of what I observed was not great.

Sometimes we did things just us two, but there were times when we included Daniel. I was beginning to notice that while Marcel enjoyed Daniel for the most part, at times his nerves seemed slightly on edge around him, and he didn't really understand Daniel's behavior. Once, when we were walking along the sidewalk on a downtown trip to Chinatown, Daniel hopped on a half wall to walk along its edge. He was skipping and chattering nonstop. Marcel quickly became annoyed and told him, harshly, to get down. Daniel obeyed, but his feelings were hurt. He darted to my side, which was farthest from Marcel, took my hand, and stopped talking.

"Why did you tell him to get down?" I said, squeezing Daniel's hand so tightly, he cried out in pain. "Oh, sorry, baby." I loosened my grip.

"Why does he always act so childish?" he retorted.

"Maybe because he is a child." Was he seriously asking me such a stupid question? "Weren't you a child once too? Or don't you remember?" I stopped myself before adding, "Because it was such a long time ago."

"You're right, Rachel. I'm sorry. I can be such a jerk

sometimes. Please forgive me. I'm really trying to work on being more patient. And it's been so long since I've been around a young child, although the older children I teach are sometimes more immature than Daniel." He attempted a joke; I didn't crack a smile. However, he seemed genuinely remorseful.

"I'm not the one you need to apologize to," I said flatly.

He apologized to Daniel, bought him an ice cream, and Daniel seemed to forget all about it. Oh, to be five years old, when everything is made right again by an ice cream cone.

Bringing Daniel along on our dates was my way of making them get acquainted and form a friendship. I knew this was of the utmost importance if Marcel and I were to have a future, and I believed that Daniel should be included more often, but I had run into another roadblock. My mother dreaded being alone, and Daniel's company transformed her from a wilted flower to a blooming orchid. Hence, I left him with her most of the times I saw Marcel. Anyway, I needed to know Marcel, and maybe being on our own was best. Plus, I didn't want Daniel to get too attached to him and then have it fall apart, only to see another man exit his life. Those were the reasons I didn't bring Daniel on our dates. It wasn't because Marcel didn't really like kids. At least that was what I told myself.

My grandpa was also making himself more visible at my mother's house, showing up by taxi at least two or three times a week, demanding to have his car back and not being placated until my mother showed proof that not only was his car not around, but my dad was not there either. At least she was not falling apart at doing that any longer. She also found the receipt from the sale of the car and made photocopies of it, sticking it with magnets on his fridge so my grandpa would have it at home to remind him. It didn't help much.

Sometimes I was there to witness the scene, and I would try to intervene to help smooth things over. My grandpa did not have a clue who I was. It was so sad. I thought it best not to go out with Marcel as often so I could be around, but my mother told me that I deserved to have some fun and didn't want me to be a homebody just for her.

"I'll figure it out, Rachel. I think it's time to get him live-in care," she said after one particular trying visit. "I've been talking with a few agencies. I should have something worked out soon."

The evenings Marcel and I did not see each other, he would text at least three or four times, asking how I was, telling me he missed me, and recounting his day and what students were keeping him most busy and what colleagues were irritating him most. He seldom asked about my day, which did bother me somewhat, but I assumed it was because he knew I didn't have much going on besides supporting my mother, taking care of Daniel, and dealing with someone in the throes of dementia. My life was something he knew very little about, couldn't relate to, or it wasn't a high priority to him. Since he never asked, I never offered information, although I took note of his indifference. However, I was more interested in hearing what happened during his day, any altercations or annoyances he had experienced, and how he handled them. After witnessing him lash out at Daniel for a perceived misbehavior, this became important. I wanted to make sure it wasn't a pattern and that he was able to handle situations appropriately.

A couple of months into our relationship, he stopped calling or texting me. I'd guessed it was because things were moving a little too slowly for him on the physical plane. Still, I was miffed and a little bewildered, since he had seemed serious. At least he said he was and was constantly showering me with gifts and expensive dinners, which led me to believe what we had was serious. Nonetheless, he disappeared. Mostly I was relieved and felt vindicated at taking things slow. *Maybe I am maturing*, I thought. Well, experience is the best teacher, and I had learned from my first marriage. The hard way.

My mother didn't even ask about Marcel. Not once. But I did notice her countenance brighten immediately when I told her that we weren't seeing each other. I think she was relieved that he was out of the picture. In fact, I'm sure she was. She was probably inwardly celebrating.

Five

The changes in my life, from getting divorced to losing my father and moving back home, were happening at breakneck speed, so I took the breakup with Marcel as a sign to apply the brakes. Keep the status quo, help my mother through her grief and come to terms with my own, since my dad was popping into my mind unexpectedly and appearing in my dreams almost every night. Plus, I intended to spend as much time as possible with Daniel, the sweetest little boy on Earth. And my grandpa was still a going concern. But now in another area.

My mother had found a live-in caregiver for him, a woman named Delores from one of the Caribbean islands, and upon meeting her, both of us agreed she was perfect. She waited on my grandpa hand and foot, never lost her temper or became frazzled. And my grandpa loved her too, which was why it shouldn't have come as much of a surprise when he announced, three weeks after she moved in, that the two of them were getting married.

We had dropped in unexpectedly one afternoon coming home from a children's program at the library when he dropped the bombshell.

"I'm so happy the three of you dropped in today. Isn't it a beautiful day out there?" he practically sang.

"You're awfully chipper today, Dad. Glad to see you in such good spirits."

"Well, why wouldn't I be? The sun is out, flowers are blooming, birds are singing, and I'm in love," he answered cheerfully.

We looked over to catch Delores's attention, but she seemed to have slunk out of the picture. I ran to the front window to see her walking down the street. My mother stayed by my grandpa's side, grilling him.

"What do you mean you're in love? With whom? Don't tell me it's Delores." Her eyes rolled exaggeratedly.

It was. From that point on, mom and I became investigators, until our investigation led to involving the police, since Delores was not the person she purported to be and had done this type of thing before to older men, moving into their houses as caregivers and somehow duping them into giving her everything. My mother managed to put a stop to it and get her arrested, but by then my grandpa had lost his zest for life. When my mother suggested he move into a retirement home, he put up no argument other than after the move he never wanted to see my mother again. She was devastated. Another blow.

*

So, three months in from her husband's death, her own father disowned her. She became even more despondent and moped about for most of the day. Around noon, she would finally get out of her nightgown and get dressed, only to come downstairs to the kitchen table and sit dejectedly with her chin resting in her hands. I decided to make her my project. And it worked.

As I started focusing more attention on her, she started paying more attention to the house and began noticing the things that were falling apart. And what particularly caught her eye was the yard. Previously, she never had to given it more than a second glance; it was my father's domain, and he maintained it all, from painting the fence to pulling the weeds.

"We need to have the deck repaired and refinished, Rachel. Your dad would strip it and put new varnish every few years. Look at the broken boards. I guess we need to find a company to do that."

After searching the web and looking at reviews for various deck companies, I found one that promised excellent results at reasonable rates. It also had four-star ratings from over one hundred customers and promised to look at it the next day. And so arrived Justin.

He walked the yard with my mother and me, blowing us away with his knowledge of horticulture. He listed the tasks that needed attention and gave us pointers on how best to prune our overgrown garden and what fertilizers worked best. My mother left Justin and me in the garden while she took a call, and in conversation we discovered that we had attended neighboring high schools and knew the same people from the same hangouts. It was so much fun reminiscing. And it didn't hurt that he was so cute.

When I told him I was married to Alex Moreno, his jaw dropped. He immediately attempted to change the subject. I suspected why. "You didn't like him, I gather."

"Honestly, the guy was a weasel. Sorry," he quickly added.

"Don't worry about it," I said. "There's a reason I'm not married to him anymore. And there is nothing you can tell me I don't already know."

"Yeah, I guess. I remember when he told us he was getting married. I thought, I pity the girl that gets him. I knew the guys he would gamble with and then renege on paying. And I knew about all the beatings he received. And some he gave."

"Yup," I added decisively. Maybe there were things I didn't know about him but were better left that way. "Well, enough about him. I was pretty young and foolish. Not anymore, though. That marriage was a learning experience I don't intend to repeat." I suddenly got a sick feeling in the pit of my stomach and was glad Daniel wasn't around to hear our conversation. He beat up people? What next? He robbed a bank?

"I'm sorry. I can see I upset you. Let me just look at this job and figure out a price before I put my size-twelve foot in my equally as big mouth again. Then I can give you a price and get out of your hair. And you won't have to hear my stupidity again."

"Won't you be back to do the work?" I asked.

"No, I'm the owner. I quote the prices. I'll send my guys to do the work. If you like the price, that is."

"Oh, too bad. This was fun talking about school and people. Other than Alex, of course."

He looked at me, and his expression changed, as if seeing me for the first time. "Well, we could always go out and talk."

I hadn't meant I wanted to *see* him when I said that, or had I? Now, I wasn't sure. But then why *had* I said that? I had a sinking feeling I was about to screw up again. But it had been enjoyable talking to him, and we seemed to hit it off, so I agreed.

I smiled broadly at him and said, "Okay, Justin. I really could use a friend right now. I've lost touch with so many people, and it's just my mom, Daniel, and me these days, all day, every day, so it would be great to spend time with someone of my generation."

We arranged to meet at a restaurant midway between our houses. That way it seemed less formal. We had agreed we would be going Dutch. I was so happy, because I was about to have someone my age to talk to. Not because he was really good-looking. And built. And nice. I didn't even think about those things. At least, not constantly.

Friday afternoon, I broke the news to my mom that I had an arrangement to meet a friend that evening. "Would it be okay if Daniel stayed here with you tonight so I can go out and meet a friend for supper?"

"Of course, you don't even need to ask. I'm glad you have someone besides me to spend time with. Who is it?"

I was hoping she wouldn't ask. But she did, so to be truthful I told her it was the fence guy. I braced myself, ready for a full-blown lecture about dating so soon after seeing Marcel and being reminded that I should take time to be a single mature woman, strong in my own right. And how would it look to neighbors and others if I was always dating someone different? After all, didn't I have a son now? Responsibilities? I waited for the tongue-lashing.

Mom said, "That's nice, Rachel. He did seem like such a responsible young man."

I could not believe it. I thought of getting her wallet to check her ID. Had someone come in our house and stolen the original Deborah Armstrong, who was always opinionated and in control? The woman whose reputation as the pant-wearer in the family was infamous. She had never approved of any decisions I made growing up. Why was she fine with this one? *I* wasn't even convinced it was the right thing to do. I was secretly hoping she would try to talk me out of it.

As it stood, I was meeting Justin. Also, I kind of liked this new Deborah Armstrong, even if she was an alien. Now, we wouldn't butt heads constantly, leaving me free to decide what I wished, when I wished, and the consequences, good or bad — mostly good, I hoped — would be entirely my own to live with. The alien mother would probably depart one of these days, and the one I knew oh too well would be back. By then, maybe I would have my act together, and Daniel and I would be on our own.

I walked onto the patio of Arizona's Bar and Grill near the airport at six Friday evening. We had agreed to meet there because we could watch the planes fly over; we both loved watching planes, and the place had great chicken wings. And beer.

He was sitting at a table for two, and when he saw me walk

in, he smiled and stood up. He looked even better than he had when he walked around my backyard, measuring our deck. Well, if I was going to have a new guy friend, why not a gorgeous one? Easy on the eyes was good. As I approached the table, he walked toward me and kissed my cheek. I flushed.

We sat down, and I saw he already had a beer. After we ordered some food and a beer for me, we talked a bit about the garden and mundane stuff. Wanting to surprise him, I said, "I brought something." I pulled my high school yearbook from my bag and handed it to him. Immediately he started paging through it, laughing and nodding as he looked at the faces he remembered. Until he came to one that made him stop and stare and not say a word. After a moment, he pointed to a face on the page and said, "Gavin Webster. Did you know him?"

"No, I don't remember him. Why what about him?"

"He died last year from a drug overdose. He was my best friend in middle school. I loved that guy. He was so crazy, always making me laugh. I heard that when his parents divorced, he got some bad friends and started using drugs. His mom called me once, a few years ago, to see if I could talk to him, but I didn't know what I could say or do to help. So, I never did. I still feel so bad. Maybe I could have helped." I saw a tear come to his eye, and he wiped it with the back of his hand.

Man, did I feel like a jerk. "I'm sorry I brought this book, Justin. I feel awful."

"No, Rachel, don't. I'm glad you did. At the funeral, his mom said to me, begged me to promise not to forget Gavin. And I *was* forgetting Gavin. So, you helped remind me." He smiled at me through more tears, and we were silent for a moment longer, and then he lifted his beer, took a drink, returned it to the table, and said, "So, what's a nice girl like you doing in a place like this?"

*

The following Friday evening, we met at Arizona's once more. He had already ordered the wings just as I like them, medium spice with extra sauce on the side. Conversation turned to our childhoods. Justin started.

"I had a pretty decent childhood. My dad was a super-smart guy who was fantastic with numbers, and because of it he kind of controlled every dollar spent by my mom. And he never paid a cent more for anything than required. I remember he made a cashier take the sales tax away from a BBQ chicken at the grocery store. He told her he was buying it to make lunches, and so it wasn't a luxury purchase and therefore shouldn't be taxed. My mom used to be so embarrassed. I thought he was kind of cool until I figured out he was just super cheap. And from then on, I refused to go anywhere with him that involved money." He stopped and laughed.

"My dad never questioned my mom about how she spent money. But then again, she had a high-paying job, so how could he? I had a really happy childhood until my older brother died."

Justin immediately said he was sorry and that I didn't have to talk about it.

"No, that's all right. To tell you the truth, I don't remember too much after he died. I know before that we were always laughing and having fun. We went on awesome vacations to Disney World and other places. Those things just kind of stopped. And our house got a lot quieter, but we were still happy. My dad adored my mom."

The next Friday when I arrived, he had ordered our wings, and to mix things up a bit, a plate of nachos and cheese, which was fine because I was starving. When we both reached for the same wing, I withdrew my hand immediately. He picked it up and handed it to me. It was a very sweet gesture. I took it and blushed. And then picked one up to hand him. And that became our tradition. We picked each other's wings. It was silly. But fun. And strangely intimate.

Justin and I met every Friday at Arizona's for wings, beer, and airplanes and sometimes nachos. Sometimes we stayed and danced to the DJ. Soon, it became hard for us to say goodbye. We started sitting in his car to spend more time together. We'd talk a bit, then we'd kiss a bit. Soon the kissing started to replace the talking altogether. We had a very delightful romance happening. But only a Friday romance. He never asked to see me on a Saturday, Sunday, or any other day of the week. He only texted me sporadically. And we had many days where we didn't talk at all. I was definitely confused but didn't want to appear pushy, so I didn't bring it up. At first.

In our conversations, I would I happily and openly describe in detail how I filled all my evenings and days. But I started to realize that he was somewhat evasive, not as forthright, as if holding back something, so on the sixth Friday we met, I decided to confront him. We were sitting in his car, and he reached for me to pull me close. I stopped him.

"Justin, I have to ask you something. I don't understand why we never see each on days other than Friday. You know I'm available. But you don't seem to be, and I haven't wanted to appear pushy, but I need to know why. What is going on?" His answer couldn't have shocked me more.

"I don't know how to say this, Rachel, so I'll just come out and tell you. I'm engaged. I'm getting married in October." Four months away. I just looked at him, agape. A lump formed in my throat. I couldn't have spoken had I wanted to.

"I'm so sorry. Serena works on Friday at Chapters. So that's my night I have free. For you." I still didn't talk, so he continued. "We don't have to stop seeing each other. Even when I'm married. I mean, if you're okay with that. I don't want to stop seeing you. You mean so much to me. I'm falling in love with you, but I'm committed to Serena now. I have to marry her. Our families are involved. There is just so much to it, I can't explain it to you. I'm so sorry, I didn't think I would fall for you like this. It's just that you're so—"

"What?" I interrupted, finding my voice. "What am I, Justin? Gullible? Naive? Or stupid? Yes, that's it. I'm so stupid. Stupid, stupid, stupid." I pressed the heels of my hands to my temples and closed my eyes. I opened them again and looking at him said, "This is the last time you will see me. Congratulations, and I wish you all the luck in your marriage. You're going to need it!"

I jumped out of his car, slammed the door, and ran across the parking lot to my car. Driving home in the pouring rain, it was difficult distinguishing the rain on the windshield from my tears. At one point, driving became impossible and dangerous, so I pulled over to let myself cry and regain my composure. The phone rang, and my Bluetooth showed it was Justin, so before I could give myself time to change my mind, I blocked then deleted his number from my phone. I took my hairbrush from my purse, brushed my hair, applied some lipstick, then drove home to face my mother, who was oblivious. Thank goodness.

Six

I must say, the Justin episode affected me more than I expected it would. I had added a new emotion to my repertoire besides regret: guilt. I was the other woman. All the times I had cursed in my mind the women who had lured away my Alex. Now *I* was that woman. I hated myself.

But more, I hated myself because I missed Justin, and Friday night just didn't seem the same. I decided to get a part-time job, something to help get my mind off him. I didn't tell my mother exactly what happened, just that we broke up and I was feeling bummed, so she agreed a job might be a good idea. Besides, she and Daniel were getting along swimmingly; in fact, he didn't seem to miss me at all when I wasn't around or notice when I was.

The two of them did everything together. If she was out in the garden pulling weeds or watering flowers, he was right beside her with his little trowel or watering can. They watched TV together, played games, and ate every meal by each other's side. He was good medicine for my mom; she was constantly laughing at things he would say and do, and he loved being the center of attention. But I was starting to feel jealous, especially when he preferred being with her over me. Plus, I was worried about my mother's emotional state. I had caught her calling Daniel Thomas more than once. The third time I heard it, I brought it to her attention. She shrugged it off. I thought she might be losing her grasp on reality, and that raised my concern for them both.

However, a Friday-night job appeared out of the blue. *Perfect,* I thought, *someone must be looking out for me.* It was at a liquor store in a nearby mall, to be a brand ambassador for a wine/beer company. Imagine, me an ambassador! Maybe not a highly distinguished ambassador representing a country, but an ambassador all the same. Plus, I loved beer and liked white wine. I had not acquired a taste for red wine, and while everyone told me that one day I would, I knew I would not. Ever. Horrid stuff, as far as I was concerned. Unless mixed with ginger ale. However, that would be my little secret. The company didn't need to know my tastes, and neither did the public. If I was selling it, then it had to be good. I supposed that made me a hypocrite, but I didn't care. I needed to be out of the house on Friday nights. Being a hypocrite was the least of my worries. Calling Justin again was my first.

The job was awful! I hated every minute of it. I hated that people avoided eye contact with me, making a large arc around me as if I had the plague. Some were more polite and would saunter over, as if doing me a favor, to sip wine from a dollar-store plastic shot glass. A few actually wanted a sample to help them choose what to buy. Some just wanted the cheese because they were hungry, which was fine. On the job, the time dragged, and although I wasn't with Justin in body, he was constantly on my mind. I persevered, however, because I wished the weeks to fly by, knowing he would fade from my memory as time went on.

My third Friday night on the job, I looked up at the customer walking into the store and was about to paste a smile on my face and offer a sample when I saw who it was: Marcel. By himself. He looked good, and it was actually nice to see him again. But then again, at that job, any familiar face was something of a godsend. Something about him seemed different. And then I noticed he had colored his hair blond. It was an improvement, actually. He did look somewhat younger. And he seemed genuinely pleased to see me as well. And a bit sheepish. Rightfully so.

"Well, fancy seeing you here," he said, peering down at my display of a bunch of fake grapes, a plate of cheese, and plastic wine glasses. "What are you selling?" he asked cheerfully.

I wasn't in the mood to be friendly to him, so my answer was succinct. "Red wine."

"Oh, c'mon. You have to do better than that. You have to sell me. Rachel, tell me what are you selling?" He winked at me conspiratorially, as if I actually knew anything about wine. Was he going to make me do a pitch? But it wasn't as if I could walk away, and he was a customer.

Okay, I thought, *here goes. For what it's worth, I memorized it, so let's see what I remember.* "I have a Pelee Island Cabernet Sauvignon. It has plum and blackberry aromas with a smoky note. It's dry, medium-bodied, and it's dark fruit-flavored with a hint of vanilla."

"Hmmm, I'm impressed. Tannins?"

"Soft tannins, good finish." I couldn't believe I remembered all that. I was impressing myself.

"What does it pair with?" he asked with a grin.

"Any red meat, a nice filet mignon or lamb. And it's great in sauces." Finally, I was having fun at the job, using my knowledge.

"You try it?" he asked suspiciously.

"Um...no," I answered a little guiltily. "But I've been told it's good."

He laughed. "How can you sell a red wine when you won't drink it yourself? Why don't you pour me a sample? Please?"

I poured him an ounce of wine then offered him a piece of cheese to go along with it. He declined because of a dairy allergy. I had forgotten about that. Or maybe I didn't know in the first place. He took the wine into his mouth and swished it around and then waited to swallow it. I always found that kind of gross. Finally, he drank it.

"It's a little young. But not bad for an Ontario red. I'll take two bottles. One to age, and the other I'll use for sauce. You're a great salesperson, Rachel, seeing as you hate red wine."

"Shhhh," I said, holding a finger to my lips. "Nobody knows that, and they don't need to either."

"Okay, it will be our little secret. I'm going to go now and pick up a few groceries before I head home. But I am so glad I saw you here. I've been thinking a lot about you lately, and I want to apologize for the way I stopped calling you. I'm not going to give you any excuses, because I know you are too smart to believe any of them. I just want to tell you that it was pretty thoughtless of me, and you didn't deserve that. And I guess I see that even more from the way you've treated me here today. You could have given me the cold shoulder, but you were absolutely lovely, as you have always been. I'm pretty thick-headed, aren't I?"

"Meh, don't worry about it. I'm sure we have all wronged people at some point in our lives. And I'm fine. Seriously. Besides, I needed to pay more attention to my mother anyway. That's why I moved back with her. She needed and still does need my help." I could have told him that I wasn't upset about our break up because I didn't feel much, if anything for him. I was trying him on like a pair of shoes to see if they would fit. And he did fit, but was never very comfortable. Maybe had I walked in them longer, they would have broken in. But he had exited, and I was fine with it. And still was. Justin, on the other hand, fit too well. He left me barefoot and broken-hearted, like a country song.

He took my hand and kissed it. I felt my face flush from embarrassment, like I felt the time I met him at my father's funeral. He was so impudent and bold. I laughed awkwardly, to which he laughed and said, "Adios, senorita."

"Bye, Marcel. Enjoy the wine. Oh, and one more thing, you can use it for a marinade." I gave him a wink. He laughed again and breezed out of the store.

When I got home that evening, the house was empty. My mother never went anywhere and especially this late. She always put Daniel to bed by eight. I called her phone, and she picked up on the first ring.

"Hi, Rachel, you home now?" she asked, sounding unusually calm.

"Yeah, but you're not. And neither is Daniel. Where are you?" I asked, definitely not calm.

"I'm literally three blocks away from the house. I'll be there in less than a minute."

"Okay, fine." I hung up, and sure enough, as I looked out the front window, her car pulled onto our street. I opened the front door and stood, hand on hip, waiting for her. She got out and then opened the back door for Daniel. Out he came with Rexy, his toy dinosaur, in one hand and the other hand in a cast. His eyes were red from crying.

I threw my arms around him, squeezing him tight. Soon I was crying. A deluge of tears was streaming from my eyes. A stockpile of tears. As if all my life pains, Alex, Dad, and Justin, were surfacing, along with the fear that overwhelmed me at the thought of Daniel injured. Daniel just let me hold him tight for the longest time until I could talk again, then I looked at my mom.

"What happened? How did he break his arm?" I asked, calmer now. She looked so afraid to face me. My poor mom, she'd been through so much. Had I truly been a help for her? How helpful had it been leaving her with the responsibility of caring for a six-year-old? All I had been thinking about was myself and the stupid guys in my life. That was it: I was swearing off men. For the time being, anyway. And I was quitting that dumb job.

"Hey, babe. You all right? Does it hurt?" Daniel looked more fearful of me, a blubbery mess, than anything else.

"Yes, Mommy, I'm okay. Grandma brought my Gameboy to the hospital and let me play it, even though it wasn't my game time. She said you wouldn't mind. Under the circumstances."

"No, of course, Daniel. Grandma was absolutely right. I don't mind at all. I'm sorry I haven't been here for you." I almost started crying again at the thought of my little boy saying "under the circumstances," like an adult. But stopped myself lest he think his mother had totally lost it.

With my crying finished, my mom explained, "He was in the backyard with me, and I went back into the house for just a moment, and next thing I know I heard him screaming. He had climbed the chestnut tree in that short of a time and then fallen out of it. I'm sorry, Rachel, you got that little job expecting I would take care of Daniel, and I let him get hurt."

"No, I'm sorry. It was selfish of me to take that job and leave Daniel with you. A six-year-old boy is super active, and I knew that. I just wasn't thinking straight. It won't happen again. He will not be solely your responsibility again. All right? Don't feel bad. I mean it."

"Okay, thanks, Rachel."

"Nope, no thanks required. Listen, I brought a bottle of wine home. A red that I was sampling tonight, and people actually liked it, so I thought time for me to grow up and drink red wine. Do you want a glass?"

"That sounds wonderful. Let me put Daniel to bed first."

"No, you go relax. I'll get him to bed."

Seven

The next few weeks were mostly spent planning for much needed home improvements. Each of the four bedrooms had the same wallpaper from when I was a little girl. And although the house had been painted, the colors remained basically unchanged. Beige was changed to cream, light blue to lighter blue. My mom and I spent a lot of time looking at professionally decorated homes on decorating sites and Pinterest, and then we signed up for a Do It Herself workshop, designed just for women, at the Home Depot around the corner. I was a little insulted at first and thought the concept somewhat sexist. Did they think we learned differently? Last I looked we had two arms, just like men, and an equal brain. But it was free, and we would learn to use power tools, so who was I to complain? Plus I had the perfect babysitter for Daniel.

I had been wanting to reconnect with Alex's mother, whom I adored, to give her a chance to see Daniel again. Now I had the perfect reason. But first I would have to eat some humble pie. After Alex walked out, I refused see her or even take her calls. I knew it was wrong and rather vindictive. She didn't deserve that treatment, plus she had the right to see Daniel, but I was seething, and if I couldn't punish Alex, I could punish his mother knowing that it would get back to him, and if anything it would guilt him somewhat, since he seemed nonplussed by what he did to me. But now, a year later, I had lost most of the animosity I had harbored against Alex and had a longing to see the woman who had been like a mother to me for so many years. I just hoped she felt the same. I would approach her, requiring her help. Marguerita never refused anyone who needed help; she was the kindest woman I knew. And when she found out the help needed was having her grandson to herself on a Saturday morning, I was absolutely positive she wouldn't refuse. If she wasn't too cross with me for avoiding her for a year.

The Wednesday evening before the course was to start, I announced to Daniel that we were going to visit Lita. I didn't have to say it twice. He ran to put on his shoes and then waited for me to do the laces. Any progress we had made at getting him to conquer lace tying had taken a slide since he broke his arm. Thankfully, it was summer, and we didn't have to struggle with coats. I had sent Marguerita a text that afternoon and asked her if she still wanted to see Daniel and me. When she answered *YES*, followed by five exclamation marks, all my misgivings disappeared.

Over supper, I told my mother where Daniel and I were going that evening, and rather than be happy about the idea of Daniel being taken care of by his other grandmother, who loved him equally, if not more than her, she became withdrawn and sulky.

She began clearing the table without a word. I tried to make conversation, but she ignored me and gave me the cold shoulder. What the heck? Well, if I had been worried that the old Deborah had disappeared, it seemed like she was making a comeback.

"Something wrong?" I asked and waited for an answer to what possibly could have set her off.

"Why didn't you tell me you were taking Daniel to his other grandmother?"

"What difference does it make, Mom? She has a right to see him, and I've left her out of the picture long enough. Over a year. We were close when I was married, and I would like to see her too. You should be happy someone that loves Daniel will watch him while we do our workshop. Listen, come over with us tonight. I'll introduce you. I think you'll like her. She's very smart and was an architect when she lived in Ecuador. And Daniel adores her. I shouldn't punish him any longer by keeping him away from her. That's not right. You know that." I appealed to her reasonable side.

"What do you think she will say when she sees he has a broken arm? And that he was with his other grandmother when it happened. What will she think of me? That I can't even take care of a little boy?" Her eyes were getting larger and larger. She looked fearful.

"Mom, that's ridiculous. She will think that these things happen. She had boys too. Three, in fact, and as a single mom I'm sure she went through her share of broken bones and injuries. She won't think less of you. Bones mend. Three more weeks and the cast is coming off. You'll see what I mean when you meet her. You have nothing to worry about. She's not like that."

"What if Daniel tells her it happened when I went into the house to get a glass of wine?" she asked timidly.

I eyed her suspiciously. "And why would he tell her that? Is that what happened? He fell when you went into the house to get a glass of wine?"

She didn't reply. She didn't need to; the answer was written all over her face. "Was it just one glass?" I asked, afraid to hear the answer.

"It was after supper, and I had one glass of wine in the garden watching him play and went to get a second when he fell. I was only going to have two glasses. And I was only in the house for a minute. But I know it doesn't look good, and they questioned me at the hospital as if I was some kind of drunk. But I wasn't drunk. And once they established that, everything was fine at the hospital. They fixed him up wonderfully. And then we came home. And that was why I didn't tell you about it, because there was no need to." As much as she tried to appear calm, she looked mortified.

"Well, I don't know about that. I think it's something you might have mentioned. Kind of important." I sighed deeply and continued, wishing to put her at ease. "But really, Mom, don't worry about Marguerita. Daniel won't say anything. He probably forgot how it happened already. You know the attention span of a six-year-old. It's pretty short. He'll have so much to tell her, that would be the last thing, I'm sure." I sounded convincing and only hoped I was right.

"I don't even know why you're in such a hurry to fix up the house anyway. Your father and I lived quite happily with it this way. Or at least you could have waited to do this workshop thing. Or let me have stayed home with Daniel, and you could have done the workshop on your own."

I was starting to fume at this point; fixing up the house was supposed to make *her* happy. I was doing it, in part, for her. I had forgotten how difficult she was to please.

"No, I didn't want to go on my own. You need to get out of the house and have fun too. Now stop worrying. You and I are going to have a riot at the workshop; Daniel and I are going to reunite with Marguerita, plus you might make a friend. The way I see it, it's a win-win situation. So, go get ready. I want to be back for Daniel's bedtime. Please." She didn't have much to say to that; sometimes I impressed even myself with such logic.

My mother, Daniel, and I stood at Marguerita's front door, and while I took a deep breath to steady my nerves and prepare myself for what was to come, Daniel leapt to the forefront and rang the bell. So much for that. Marguerita opened the door wide, and Daniel rushed in, straight for her open arms. They embraced, arms locked around each other with her head resting on his, for what seemed an eternity. The reunion between Daniel and his Lita was so touching, I felt as though I was part of a Hallmark movie. I appreciated then how truly heartless I'd been in keeping those two apart. Both of them were bawling. Soon I was too.

After Marguerita tore herself away from Daniel, she straightened up and looked me in the eye, hands on hips, not saying a word. "I'm so sorry, Marguerita. I'm so sorry." Next thing I know we were embracing, shoulders wetted by tears.

"Don't say you're sorry. It's not necessary. You don't need to apologize."

"Yes, I do. I do. It was not fair of me to punish you because of Alex. And Daniel too. I'm wicked."

"Well, maybe a little. But what can we do about that now? It doesn't matter. And it wasn't only Daniel I came to love; it was you as well, *mi amor*. I missed you too. Never do that again, understand? Especially for that *mentiroso* son of mine. Okay?"

I wiped the tears from my eyes with the back of my hand and promised. Then I introduced my mother, who had been standing sheepishly in the background. Marguerita scooped her into an awkward embrace. My mother, not accustomed to such displays of affection, especially from a stranger, appeared somewhat stricken, plus she towered over Marguerita by close to a foot.

When all the crying and hugging had stopped, I explained to Marguerita that she would have an opportunity to make up for lost time on Saturday morning, if she was willing to babysit. Marguerita jumped at the opportunity and said he could stay the whole day, if needed.

"Maybe, once the actual work on the house starts, I'll take you up on the offer." I showed her pictures of the improvements I intended to do to the house, along with old pictures of my father that I found on my phone. Even though she never knew him, Marguerita was broken-hearted about my dad. Every picture that came up she would look sadly at my mother, which made my mom tear up again. Marguerita put her arms gently around my mother's shoulders and had a little cry with her. I determined to try to imitate her compassion and be a little more kind toward my mother, who, from all our time in close quarters, was starting to wear my patience thin. We said our goodnights, not staying long and wanting to get Daniel home to bed.

*

Mom and I were first to arrive for the workshop, and while the class filled and waited for the teacher, we got acquainted, writing our names on sticky labels then pasting them on our chests. Half an hour later, not one, but two women teachers arrived, frazzled and apologetic for being late. There had been an accident on the 401, and all vehicles had been diverted off to side streets, which were jammed and extremely slow. We told them not to worry about it, that we had all gotten to know each other while waiting and thus could skip introductions.

Our workshop project was building an end table. I was just happy to be operating the power tools. Nothing beats hands-on experience, not even YouTube. Especially when using something with the potential to take off a finger or thumb. The teacher started the class by telling us that in the United States about 400,000 emergency room visits are made yearly due to misusing power tools and not working safely. She was big on safety. Couldn't tell us enough to keep our work place clean, make sure we didn't have on loose clothing or jewelry and always wear protective clothing like leather gloves and safety glasses. I watched, amused, as the teacher singled out my mother and some other women, telling them to remove long necklaces and bracelets. It was funny until she called my name and told me to tie my hair back.

Then we got busy. I couldn't believe how my mother took to carpentry. She was a natural. And I wasn't too shabby either.

Now that we had mastered the use of the power drill, saw, and staple gun, we were ready to shop for supplies. Thankfully, we didn't have to buy tools; my dad had loved to dabble in carpentry and was always building something, and so he had a complete workshop in the basement. All top quality, because as loved to say, "Buy cheap, buy dear."

I had carefully measured each room we were to work on and had brought the list of needed materials. The upstairs hallway was getting a chair rail and all door handles were being replaced, since they were old and mostly not working. I was excited. I left my mother in the door handle section while I went to get a cart. When I came back, she was happily chatting away with a very handsome man close to her age. On seeing me, the conversation stopped abruptly and my mother's smile disappeared. I felt like an intruder.

The man introduced himself as Carlos and said, "Your mother told me about your undertaking. I think that is wonderful. Women can do almost anything a man can. You both should be very proud of yourselves. Anyway, I won't hold you up any longer. Happy house renovations." He was walking down the aisle when he turned, walked back to my mother, then said, "I really enjoyed talking to you, Deborah. Would you like to get a coffee sometime?"

Her face turned scarlet and she said, "Oh, no, no, no. Thank you anyway, but no, I can't do that." She was so flustered, I almost laughed. Thankfully, I didn't.

He said, "Well, that's too bad. But it was nice meeting you. And you too, Rachel." Then he left for good.

On our drive home, I asked what had been on my mind since we left the store. "Why didn't you want to have a coffee with Carlos, Mom?"

"Because I didn't want to, now drop it," she answered matter-of-factly.

I wasn't buying it. "Didn't look that way to me. Looked like you were enjoying yourself very much talking to him." I gave her a smirk.

Deadpan, she turned to me and said, "I said I didn't want to. Now drop it."

So I did.

Eight

A text from Marguerita appeared on my phone. She was inviting us to stay for lunch when we came to pick up Daniel. My mother said no, she didn't want to, and I said too bad, because I had already answered yes. She gave me stink-eye.

"Rachel, that is so disrespectful to answer for me. I really don't want to stay for lunch. Why don't you drop me at home first? Tell her I had a headache or something."

"I don't think so. And you two hit it off. So why wouldn't you want to have lunch? I'm not lying for you, and besides, we would be the disrespectful ones just picking up Daniel and taking off. She is showing hospitality, and we are going." Then I added, enunciating carefully, "Mother."

"Well, I want to let you know that I don't really feel comfortable around her. I know she was nice and pleasant toward me. But seriously, I think it might have been an act and she probably hates me. Not coming to your wedding, not being around when Daniel was growing up and ignoring her son and now letting Daniel break his arm. What else could she think of me? Our first meeting was emotional, but now she'll probably have thought of all those things. I know I sure have. I don't think I should be around her. And she'd probably be just as happy if you did drop me off at home first. You two could catch up all on your own."

"Mom, I know you're going to hate me for saying this, but you are overthinking things and quite frankly need to get over yourself. You can't change the things you did in the past; all you can do is try to make up for them. And she is giving us an opportunity to do that. And I am saying 'us,' because remember, I ignored her for the last year, so she has reason to be angry with me too. I've kept her grandson away from her. That's pretty despicable. And so I am not going to be rude and refuse lunch. And neither are you."

"Well, all I can say is I hope you are right."

I was. Lunch was amazing. We had a lovely time. And as I knew they would, Marguerita and my mother hit it off tremendously. Their first point in common was their love of the TV series *The Crown* and their crush they shared equally on Helena Bonham Carter.

"I know she doesn't look even the tiniest bit like Princess Margaret, but I just love watching her. She's perfect. What I wouldn't do to look like her," my mom said. "She's always been my favorite actress."

"You do look like her," Marguerita said.

"Oh, c'mon," my mom answered, obviously delighted. "As if."

"Doesn't your mom look like her, Rachel?" I had to admit that I didn't know what Helena Bonham Carter looked like, having never watched The Crown. They both chastised me for missing such quality television, and then Marguerita googled a picture of the actor. I agreed with my mother. I saw no resemblance, other than maybe the dark hair.

"Well, you are a very beautiful woman, Deborah. I wish I looked like you. I would love some of your height, at least."

"You would hate it. I always towered over all the boys in school, and it made me very self-conscious growing up. But I'd give you a couple of inches if I could. And anyway, you're just the right height. You don't need to change a thing." What in the world was I witnessing? A mutual admiration society?

But soon they talked about other things, such as what type of architecture Marguerita studied in Colombia and why she never pursued it in Canada. And my mother told her the joys and challenges she experienced in her high-powered job as a woman in a predominantly men's field. The only thing that interrupted their nonstop conversation was when Marguerita served us lunch, which was delicious. Marguerita was an excellent cook, and we ate every bite, including Daniel, who lately would only eat peanut butter on crackers and blueberries. Occasionally he would have a banana or orange, but getting him to eat anything else was like pulling teeth. I figured he was at least getting protein from peanut butter and wouldn't starve.

Our lunch visit turned into an entire afternoon of laughter and conversation between my mother and Marguerita. And me, once or twice. Which didn't bother me in the least; in fact, I was so pleased by the outcome, I almost shed a tear of joy. Then again, it didn't help that I was hormonal at the time. Before leaving, Marguerita and my mother embraced each other warmly and exchanged numbers, promising to call. We arranged to bring Daniel back the following Saturday for the entire day. We were going to get busy and fix the house. On the drive back, Daniel fell asleep, and my mother and I were enjoying singing along to oldies when I received a text. I pulled in to our driveway and parked, then looked to see who sent it.

It was Marcel. *An amazing chef made an excellent Cabernet sauce for my lamb dinner last night from your wine. Just thought I would let you know.* Followed by a chef man emoji.

Hmmm, I thought. *What's he up to?* I supposed he wanted me to respond by asking who the amazing chef was, but I responded, *Good job*, no emojis. No encouragement. Whatever he was up to, I was not playing his game.

Two days later, another text came from him asking how my day was going. I was tempted to say *fine till now*, but instead I decided to reassess the situation before giving him a reply. He obviously wanted to connect with me again. And honestly, I wasn't angry with him, or hurt or anything. I wasn't that into him to begin with and had only dated him to see where things would go. He had a lot to offer, plus he said he wanted to help me. Maybe I was being a little selfish, but all that sounded fantastic. Then he ghosted me before I made any decision about my feelings toward him. I determined not to respond to his text to see if he would persist.

The next day, he sent another text and then another the following day. He started getting more creative in the messages, sending memes and other silly stuff. Finally, the third day, I texted him back. *I'm glad you liked the wine for making sauce.*

What are you selling this week?

Nada, I quit that job. Contrary to what it may have appeared, I am really bad at sales. He didn't require the real reason.

Besides, it was true; I couldn't sell if my life depended on it. That job gave me a new respect for salespeople. It really is a skill. The other aspect of that job was that it helped me gain a new perspective as I watched how customers would avoid me. From that point on, I would not feel guilty passing a perfume salesperson or hanging up on a telemarketer, knowing they aren't taking it personally, and once you are gone, they look for their next target and move on.

Marcel's response was instant and direct. *Would you like to go out with me again? I'm very sorry for the way I treated you.*

I'm not sure. I'll get back to you. But thank you for asking, I texted back.

Yes, of course. Take all the time you need. I'll be waiting. No emojis, thank goodness.

That night, after putting Daniel to bed, I sat up with my mother for a heart-to-heart. I knew how she felt about Marcel.

She had told me repeatedly in no uncertain terms her true feelings of contempt, but what I mostly needed to know was her feelings about me now that I was living with her. We had never actually had that talk. Daily living seemed to have gotten in the way.

Sitting in our deck chairs in the backyard, watching the sun set a beautiful purple-pink in the evening sky, I looked over at her and said, "Hey, Mom, do you want to talk? We never just talk, do we?"

"About what, Rachel?" She sounded sad.

"Stuff, just stuff. How you're feeling and, I don't know, life, I guess. And us. Oh, and Marcel, he's been texting me. But not right away. I don't want to talk about him now. I want to know how you are. Really are."

"Truthfully? I'm surviving. Which is no fun. Surviving is just existing, coping but not very well. I miss your dad so damn much. Sometimes I feel so alone. You can be right beside me in a room and Daniel playing in front of me, and I still feel so alone. And it hasn't gotten any better, not really. The pain has dulled somewhat, but it is still there all the time. The only time I am not in pain is when I am sleeping. And I don't want to take medication, but sometimes I feel like I need too."

I didn't know what to say. That I missed him too? Because I did. But my pain in comparison to hers was minuscule, so I didn't say it. Instead, I decided to ask her what she missed most about Dad.

Mom's face lit up, and she looked so happy, and I saw, as if for the first time, how much she loved him. "Oh, let's see. I miss the way he would make the coffee Saturday morning and then call me to wake up and smell the coffee. It wasn't really funny, but it was, if you know what I mean. And especially because I'm not a morning person, so getting me to smile first thing was quite the feat."

The first tear came to her eye, and she continued, "I miss the way he would insist on using his old-fashioned hedge shears, clipping away for hours because he hated the noise from the power tools. He'd clip away, all the while whistling at the top of his lungs. He'd see me watching from the kitchen window, and he'd wave at me, so happy. I guess that's what I miss most, how happy he was all the time. Except about you. He missed you but wanted to wait till you came around. He never liked to force anything on anyone. Maybe that was one thing he did wrong. Listen to me. Because it was me that was holding a grudge."

"Mom, stop. I don't want to talk about that. I want to know all the great things he did that made you so happy. Just think about those things now."

"Okay, let's see, there are so many. I miss our cocktail hour. Five o'clock, after he'd arrived home and showered. I'd make him a John Collins — he'd insist I make it, since mine tasted better than when he made it, he said. Not true, but I did it anyway, he was so grateful. I loved watching his face taking that first sip and hearing the mmm sound he made. Then he would say, 'just what the doctor ordered.' Every time. I'd say it along with him in my mind. Never out loud, never once. I loved listening to him say that. Do you want me to go on?"

"Of course. I feel like I'm learning about him in ways I never knew."

"I miss how much he cared about people. If he knew a neighbor was having difficulties with something, such as, oh let's see..." She seemed to be searching her memory. "Oh yes, the time the Bondars across the road needed to find a tree-cutting company for their overgrown poplar tree, your dad helped find a good company and stayed around to make sure they did a proper job." She sighed deeply. "And that is why I didn't want to have coffee with that man, Rachel. I could never find someone like your father again."

I digested what she told me and thought, *Now that's true love*. I felt sorry for being a blight on that beautiful arrangement. True, my mom had been the instigator in keeping us apart, and my dad her accomplice by not standing up to her, but I could have done my part to reconcile with them. I had missed so much by remaining angry and staying away, and I was sorry Daniel never got a chance to know or even meet my dad. And I would never get to say goodbye. Soon the two of us sat there silently weeping.

I put my arms around my mother as she began sobbing. After the longest time she stopped and then wiped her eyes with the back of her hand before asking, "Now, what did you want to tell me about that scoundrel Marcel?"

"What do you think?" I asked.

"He wants to start seeing you again."

"Yes, he does. Mom, I need to know how you feel about the decisions I choose to make. Specifically, who I date or not. Meaning Marcel. Would you really be that disappointed in me if I did try it a second time? I mean, I did like him; he was funny, and he is successful and established, and he said he wanted to help me get enrolled in university so I can get a degree. So, he seems to genuinely care for my well-being."

"Are you trying to convince me or yourself?" She was very perceptive at times.

"Hahaha, very good, Mom. I'm not sure. Maybe both of us?"

"And you know very well that you can get into university without his help. But Rachel, to answer the question about your decisions, I learned a hard lesson when I tried to stop your marriage. It cost your dad and me dearly. I am not going to interfere again. I'm not crazy about Marcel, you know that, and even though, for the most part, personality traits are very difficult to change, they're not impossible to change. I mean, don't hardened criminals get reformed? At least I think they do.

Not sure of the success rate, but anyway, you get my point. It's up to you. I'll be here for you and Daniel no matter what you choose to do."

"Thanks, Mom. I'll decide over the next couple of days. I'll think about it for a while before I answer him."

"That's a wise thing to do. It's never good to make rash decisions. And Rachel, thanks for asking me to talk about your dad. I can't tell you how much lighter my heart feels. Nobody has asked that. I think everyone is afraid to bring him up in case I have a meltdown or something, but it was so good for me, and like he used to say, it was just what the doctor ordered." She smiled sadly, and we gathered our dishes and went inside for the night.

After a couple of days, I sent Marcel a text to say I would be busy working on the house with my mom and would get in touch with him after that. I gave him no time frame, and he didn't ask for one. Quite judicious indeed.

Throughout the next couple of weeks, the relationship between my mother and me plunged deeply. We argued constantly and mostly about trivial things, from how I put flowers in a vase to what time Daniel went to bed, along with his bedtime routine. I liked to read him stories, and she felt he was old enough to learn to fall asleep on his own. But how could I miss what would be the best part of the day?

Eight o'clock in the evening after his bath and changed into pajamas, Daniel would sit in bed and wait for me to come into his room.

I'd peek my head in then ask, "Ready for story time?" He'd nod enthusiastically. Then we'd have a picking-a-story routine. I'd go to his shelf and pull out the first book, *Green Eggs and Ham*.

He'd say, "Not that one."

"*The Cat in the Hat*."

"Nope."

After naming three or four different stories, I'd say, "Okay, mister, I can't read your mind, you know. What story would you like me to read to you?"

"Um, I would like..." Long pause. "*Green Eggs and Ham.*" To which I would throw myself on him, tickling him into a laughing fit. Then I would read *Green Eggs and Ham* plus every other story I had picked up. I loved it. He loved it. What was not to love?

After the stories were read, I'd turn out his lamp, lean over to whisper goodnight, and kiss his cheek. Daniel never failed to wrap his arms around my neck, generously kiss me in return, and say, "I love you, Mommy." *I love you too, my sweet little angel.*

I was not giving up our bedtime routine, no matter how much my mother complained. Which was a lot. She was growing increasingly critical, and I was probably too sensitive. Not a good match. Either way, I was beginning to feel smothered, so I suggested we start working on the house. Hopefully, that would bring about a respite from the arguing. And indeed, for the most part, it did.

The renovations were mostly a breeze. We sustained a few injuries like bruised thumbs from hammers to wood splinters, but the skills we learned from our classes and watching YouTube tutorials served us well. Working together, conversation flowed and we had zero arguing. Mom told me stories about her childhood, going to school under the nuns and how much she hated it and what her own parents were like, and I told her about some of the things she missed while we were apart.

One thing she had been dying to ask me, she said, was about Daniel's birth. I proceeded to tell her, as if it was yesterday. Who can forget a painful ordeal like that?

"It's really much too long a tale, so I'm going to give you the shortened version. I planned for Daniel to be born in a cozy birthing center by a midwife. It was to be the perfect birth. First miscalculation. I didn't know the likelihood of having a perfect birth is next to none."

"You were a perfect birth. Not so much Thomas," Mom interjected.

"Well, Daniel was certainly not. My water broke at home at 1:00 a.m., but I wasn't in actual labor, and nothing went as planned. After a long, non-progressive twenty-four-hour labor, the doctor gave orders for the delivery room to be prepared for my Caesarean section, but thankfully Daniel changed his mind and decided to come out after all. Naturally, with no surgery."

"I wish I was there for you. Not that I would have been much help, because I'm not good when people are in pain. Or bleeding."

"Or crying. Or sad. Or begging. You hate beggars. Or has that changed?"

"Nope not really. I'm sorry, but my compassion falls short for people asking for handouts."

"Mom, why would you say that? You're not sorry. You never liked poor people asking for money." What was wrong with me? I was goading her. Was I looking for a fight? Or testing her, to see how much she had or had not changed in our years apart. Or maybe it was me who had changed, for the worse.

"To a degree, Rachel, I am sorry. I donate to charities that take care of the poor. Quite a bit, if you must know. I want to make sure the money is used responsibly. If I hand money to someone on the street, they would probably, or at least might, use it to buy drugs or alcohol, so I'm not doing that." She said this in that tone that said *discussion over*, but I wasn't finished.

"You don't know that, Mom. They might also use it to take care of someone in their family who's sick. Who knows? Anyway, at least you're doing something good by giving to charities, which is a lot more than me at the moment."

I felt stupid and told myself to stop being a jerk, instigating arguments out of nothing. Maybe our close quarters were getting to *me*. A little too much familiarity, breeding grounds for unneeded and unwanted contempt. Thankfully, a reprieve was on the way.

Nine

My mother spent the next morning on the phone to my Aunt Giselle. Giselle was my dad's younger sister, the youngest in the family, and the only girl. She grew up learning how to fight, climb trees, and play football. I loved her. When I was a child, whenever she visited, she'd come right to my room to sit and talk. I think she viewed me more as the little sister she never had, and she was actually only ten years older than me, more like an older sister than an aunt.

The summer I turned fourteen and entered high school, she took me shopping to buy some really great clothes. Looking back, my parents must have asked Giselle to take me shopping, since going with my mother always turned into a battle. Mom usually hated everything I liked, and vice versa.

Giselle had worked as and still did work as a talent agent and manager for a rock band and was the coolest person I knew. And she was beautiful. Men were constantly finding excuses to talk to her or stealing glances at her from the corner of their eyes. She just laughed it off, very gracious and never rude to anyone. I wished to grow up to be exactly like her. We drifted apart through my high school years as Alex became the most important person in my life and everyone else took a back seat. I was happy to hear it was Giselle talking with my mother and that they had remained close.

I was in the backyard pushing Daniel on the swing when my

mother came up from behind me to hand me the phone, but not before I jumped three feet in the air.

"What the heck, Mom?" I practically yelled. "You can't just sneak up on people like that. You almost gave me a heart attack."

She laughed so hard, she held her stomach all the way to the bench, plopping down while doubling over in hysterics.

"Very funny. Is it still Giselle on the phone? I'm presuming it is." She was laughing so hard she could only nod a yes.

I took the phone, pressed *mute*, and said, "Mom, do you think you could laugh and push Daniel on the swing at the same time?" I hit *unmute*. "Hey, Giselle. How are you, my coolest auntie in the world?" My mom was still laughing, but it was starting to fizzle out a bit.

"Good, kiddo. I'm dying to get over there and see you and your adorable boy. Your mom has been telling me how lovely it has been to have you both there, especially since John died. I'm glad you are there for her too. Takes a load off. I didn't think she would survive his death."

We chatted a little more, then she came to the point of her call.

"Rachel, I was planning a trip with my good, or at least used to be, good friend. In two weeks, we were supposed to be leaving for a three-week cruise through Scandinavia, and I have till today to book. This morning she calls me and tells me about this guy she has been dating that she met online and how great it's going and how he's the right one and all that other bull. Then, the bombshell, she says that she's scared if she goes away for three weeks now, he might forget her while she's gone and move on."

"Seriously? If she thinks he could do that, well then, it doesn't sound like he's Mr. Right to me."

"Yup, I said exactly the same thing. But you know, love is blind and all that, so there is no changing her mind. She just better not even think about asking me to be her bridesmaid if it does work out, which I highly doubt. And I have three weeks booked off work and want to go on this amazing cruise. So, I thought of asking your mom because she doesn't have a job to book off, and it would be good for her to get away."

"What did she say?" I asked.

"She said she'd like to but wanted me to run it by you. See if you're okay staying at the house without her."

"Of course. I lived on my own for over nine years. I swear, sometimes she thinks I'm a little kid again. Actually, it would be great to have a break from each other. Please, take her away," I said and then looked around, hoping she wasn't behind me again. She wasn't.

"Great! I'm so excited. I'm going to phone the travel agent now; she's been holding the booking for me with just a deposit. Can you put your mom back on so I can get her details? And when we're back, I'll come by to hang out and catch up."

For the next week, my mother was busy organizing her things to take away. I sat on her bed, and while Daniel looked through her jewelry box, I watched her take her clothes from her drawers to pack in her suitcase. As she put her neatly folded clothes into the suitcase, I started to notice a pattern. Every item was at least ten years old.

"Mom, I remember that striped green sweater from when I used to live here. And those beige pants — didn't you wear them to my grade eight graduation? With that black blouse with the ties?" I pointed at it in the suitcase.

"Yes, I love black and beige together, and I am exactly the same weight and can still wear them. There are not too many women my age that can boast they have maintained their ideal weight throughout their adult life." She looked proud of herself, and although I hated to burst her bubble, I couldn't help myself.

"And I doubt there are many women who hang on to the

same clothes for over twenty years just because they fit. Mom, these make you look like you never left the nineties. You look great, but when you wear this stuff, you look like an old lady. With no style."

"Thanks a bunch. The clothes are high-quality, and there is nothing wrong with any of them. Why should I get rid of them? Care what others say?" Oh, to have such misplaced confidence.

"It's not because you care what others say — well, at least not entirely. But you should care what Giselle says, or at least feels, because she won't say anything. She's too nice. You know that she's cool and has amazing style, so you've got to meet her halfway and get some new clothes. You'll be going out to dinner at really nice places, and I'm sure the cruise is fancy. Plus, you will feel like a million dollars when you have new fantastic outfits to wear, and you're so slim you'll pull off anything spectacularly."

"Okay already, I'm sold. When can we go shopping? I only have five days before I leave."

"Today, I think. Let me make a phone call," I said.

I called Marguerita, and soon we were dropping off Daniel then on our way to the mall. We found a really good parking spot close to an entrance. I took that as a favorable sign.

As if. Shopping for my mom was more complicated than I thought it would be. It felt like when we used to shop for clothes for me, but reversed. She hated most things I picked out, and the clothes she liked looked like copies of what she already owned. This time I was the mother and her the difficult daughter.

At our fourth clothing store, a sales woman asked if she could help, and I could tell we might finally get somewhere. My mother liked her instantly. I think it was because the woman was close to her age, and there was a connection. I explained what our shopping experience had been like so far. She laughed cheerfully and said, "Don't worry, I'll take care of your mother."

The saleslady presented her with clothes almost exactly like the ones I had tried to give her, only my mother took them happily from her then tried them on. And bought most of them too. It dawned on me that she didn't really respect me and would always see me as a little girl. And that stung. I felt the steam coming from my ears, but I said nothing and tried to stay calm.

Finally on the drive home, I could remain quiet no longer. I calmly asked, "Why did you do that, Mom?"

"What?" she asked, oblivious to my irritation. I was skillful at hiding my emotions, and she didn't even know I was upset.

"You hated every item of clothing I suggested you try, but when the saleswoman brought them to you, you loved them all. And they were almost exactly like the stuff I was showing you. In fact, a few of the items were the same."

"You must be imagining things, Rachel. They were completely different. You were always too sensitive." And it became about me. How did she turn a conversation so effortlessly? Did I do that too? I sure hoped not. I was grateful Giselle was taking her away for three weeks. We needed the break.

*

Five days later, Giselle arrived in her Uber minivan to pick up my mom with her suitcase full of snazzy new clothes. She stepped out to help, and on seeing me, she ran toward me and hugged me so tight, I could hardly breathe. Then she hugged Daniel. She made me promises of long, leisurely visits once she returned.

Turning to my mom, she said, "So, Deborah, ready to have some fun? Did you remember how crazy I am?"

My mom looked somewhat perplexed, as if not quite sure what she was doing. Probably wondering what she had got herself into. She had never been anywhere without my father, and now here she was going off with his baby sister to another continent.

"As ready as I'll every be. You better take me now before I change my mind," she said.

"Oh, you're not going to change your mind. Don't worry, we'll have a great time. I'm not really crazy. I just need to say that to keep my reputation. Because I manage a rock band, you know." She gave me a wink. "I'm probably older than you in so many ways. I'm usually in bed by nine thirty, although don't spread it around. When on holiday, however, I sometimes stay up to eleven. But come on, let's go; I don't need this Uber guy giving me a bad review."

My mother reached over and gave me a warm hug and kiss on the cheek but then turned all her attention to Daniel.

"Okay, little man, Grandma is going away. Just for three weeks, but I'm sure it will seem longer for me. I'm going to miss you so much. You are the best thing in my life. I love you very much," she said with eyes full of tears.

"I love you too, Grandma," Daniel replied, then added, "Have fun on the big ship and take lots of pictures."

My mom and I looked at each other then burst out laughing. He sounded so grown up. He must have heard someone say that before.

"I will, I will. And I'm going to bring you a very special present. Okay? Now take care of Mommy and Luna, and I'll see you soon." She gave me another quick hug, and I watched as they got into the minivan while the driver put the cases in the back.

I stood in the driveway holding Daniel's hand, and we both waved as they drove away.

Ten

The first week without my mother in the house was heaven. I hadn't realized how much she was making me feel like a child by doing everything for me, from cooking to laundry, and also how much I had been taking advantage of her kindness. Or her need to be in control. Either way, it wasn't good for us. I needed to think seriously about leaving, but in any case, when she got back, I would do much more around the house. Besides, I rather enjoyed domesticity.

Daily, after lunch I'd leaf through recipe books of supper dishes to prepare. Then Daniel and I would take the ten-minute walk to the Loblaws and buy what we needed. In the evening after supper when all the dishes were done, we would play out back with Luna till Daniel's bedtime. Daniel would get five stories read to him, since there was no one telling me that was too many, and afterward I would watch a movie or read.

The first Friday night sitting in the quiet house, with Daniel sleeping peacefully and a glass of white wine in my hand, my mind involuntarily wandered back to Justin and our Friday nights together. I wondered what he was doing. I thought how easy it would be to call him. All I had to do was look up his business. All business calls went right to him.

I gave my head a shake, made a mock smack gesture to my cheek, and picked up the remote, finding anything but a romance movie on TV. I did not have a second glass of wine and went to bed immediately following *Young Frankenstein*.

We spent Sunday at Marguerita's. Sitting at her kitchen table, I tried to pay attention as she described her week, but my mind kept wandering back to how close I came to calling Justin. To avoid a repeat, I decided to look up some old girlfriends from high school and see if any of them wanted to get together next Friday. Marguerita suspected my mind was elsewhere and that she had been talking into the wind.

She took the seat across from me, looking me in the eye, said, "Okay, Rachel, I can tell you haven't been hearing a word I have spoken in the last ten minutes. What is wrong?"

"Oh, nothing, nothing. I'm just thinking about what I will cook all week." A lie, of course, but I couldn't tell her about Justin. I had divorced her son, after all, even though he was a no-good rotter.

The following week, Daniel's and my routine stayed basically the same, except for a little excitement on the Wednesday afternoon when I was in the laundry room and came back to where I had left Daniel watching TV to find an empty chair. Knowing how much he loved to hide and seek, after counting to ten I called to him that I was coming to find him. I knew he was a good little hider, but after twenty minutes of searching, I started to panic. Had someone come into the house and snatched him away? I read about things like that happening all the time. I was about to call 911 when I looked at Luna and thought, *Of course, Luna would have barked.*

Looking at her asleep in her bed, I said, "Luna, wake up, go find Daniel." She sat up, perked her ears, and looked at her treat jar. "No treats, Luna. Where is Daniel?" I kept repeating, "Where's Daniel, where's Daniel?" till she finally got it and led me to where he was fast asleep on my mother's bed, tucked behind her numerous decorative cushions. Not one of them was out of place. I had no idea how he got back there like that.

I woke Daniel and embraced him so tightly that he begged me to stop, because not only was he having trouble breathing, but also, "Mommy, your tears are getting me wet."

Then, wiping the tears from my face, I said, "Let's go give Luna a treat. She deserves one."

On Thursday, I joined a Facebook group of people that went to my high school. Then I made Facebook friends with six girls that I knew. I asked them all if they were still in the neighborhood and if any were free that Friday evening to go out. Three of them who had remained close after school till now said yes, they were planning to go clubbing, and I was welcome to come along. I called Marguerita to ask if Daniel could stay the night because I would be out late, and she said, yes, of course, although she didn't like the idea of me clubbing and someone putting the "rape date" drug in my drink. I said not to worry; my drink would not leave my hand.

I didn't correct her language, either. I enjoyed listening to her broken English, and not just because it sounded funny. It was mainly because it brought back fond memories of when Alex and I were dating and hanging at his house. He would kid his mother about her broken English until she would say, "You think you big man, so smart because you're born in Canada and speak English? I still can beat you with a wooden spoon, Chico. Don't shove me." And we'd laugh, knowing she meant to say *don't push me*. But Alex didn't dare correct her lest she chase him around the kitchen with a wooden spoon.

Friday night at seven thirty, Daniel knocked on Marguerita's door. She must have been standing there waiting, because the door opened before we knocked again. She picked up Daniel, smothering him in kisses while I gave her the rundown of his bedtime routine and handed her his overnight bag complete with pajamas, toothbrush, and favorite dinosaur. And, of course, his blankie, which he needed to fall asleep.

As I was explaining what I did to help him fall asleep, Margucrita put a hand up to stop me and said, "Just get out of here. Don't worry about him. Go have fun." She kissed my cheek, and then I gave Daniel a kiss and left. Somehow, I didn't feel like going out and having fun. I wanted to stay there with them. It was the first time I had been away from Daniel.

But I put on a brave face, smiling broadly as I pulled out of the driveway, beeping the horn and waving as I drove away.

I came back home to a wagging Luna at the door and no one else. The house felt strange. I walked past the family room, and I could swear I saw my dad sitting in his favorite chair. I didn't think of him often, but whenever I did, he seemed so real. Like I *could* reach out and touch him. I wished I could reach out and touch him. Right there and then. It wasn't fair he was taken so early. But what about my poor brother Thomas, who never even reached ten? I guess life just isn't fair sometimes. No wonder my mother, who lost so much, could be such a jerk at times. I resolved to cut her some slack before it was me who became the real jerk.

I went through my clothes and found my nicest jeans to wear with black pumps and an off-the-shoulder black lace top. I put the hot curlers on and did my makeup. I even applied false eyelashes, after three attempts, that is. I was never good with those things. It had been years since I had dressed up to go out to a club, but from what I remembered, you had to look the part. Lots of makeup, the faker the better. It was kind of fun getting done up and being someone other than Daniel's mother. I played dance music and had a glass of wine while getting ready, and by nine I was done.

Lara had said we were taking an Uber downtown to a club called Fiction, and since I lived closest to the club, I would be picked up last after her, Candice, and Sophie. Shortly after nine, I sat at my front room window, watching for a car. When they hadn't arrived by ten, I texted Lara and was told they would get me at ten thirty.

Why so late? I texted back. I was pissed.

Nothing starts happening till 11.

I wished she had told me the night didn't start till practically the next day. But then I hadn't asked. I had just assumed we would go at a normal time. How late did they plan on staying out if we didn't even get there till eleven? I didn't have a good feeling about the evening. Besides which, I hadn't really liked Lara, Candice, and Sophie in high school. I was staring at my phone, debating whether I should text Lara and cancel, when she sent me a text.

Uber is early, we're on our way. Party time! Followed by a wine glass emoji and three kissy faces.

They pulled into the driveway, and when they saw me walking toward the car, Lara jumped out, hugged, and kissed me as if we were the closest friends in the world.

"Wow, Rachel, you look so hot! I can't believe you have a child. You're so buff. Are you on the keto diet?"

"No, just my genes, I guess. You look great too." But something about her looked different. Kind of weird. I tried not to stare, then realized her lips were humungous, obviously from implants. Stifling a laugh, I quickly peered into the car window in order to avert my gaze from her and said to Sophie and Candice, "All of you look amazing. I guess I sit in the front?"

I listened to them talking and soon became distracted by how often they used the word "like." So many times, I decided to keep count. Over seventy times in a little less than thirty-five minutes. We arrived at the club then joined the line-up. I noticed Sophie hardly said a word. She just kept looking at her phone.

"Everything all right, Sophie?" I asked.

"Nope," was all she said, then looked away, ready to cry.

Candice said, "Oh, it's her jerk boyfriend. He hasn't called her in like a week, and someone told her he's, like, cheating with a girl from his work. So, she's, like, really bummed out. We're going to get her like so drunk tonight she won't even be able to walk, right, Lara?"

"Oh yeah, party!" She threw her arms in the air. I think she'd had a few drinks already. Suddenly, I felt as though I didn't belong there and was having some serious reservations.

The guy manning the door came up and told us that good-looking women didn't have wait. He pulled us out of line, and we marched to the door in front of all the other people who weren't what he considered good-looking. What kind of world did we live in? One where good looks ruled, obviously. Especially when it came to clubs. *Great,* I thought. I felt like apologizing to the people we passed. But at least it wasn't cold.

When we entered Fiction, I immediately regretted coming out. I wished I could have changed places with the people in the line. The music was loud and consisted mainly of beats. Not rhythm, just beats. There was no dance floor, and some people were dancing on the spot, while others just looked around, attempting to be cool. People occupied every inch of space. I dreaded to think what would happen if a fire ever broke out.

I followed Lara, Sophie, and Candice to what I thought would be good spot off to the side, but instead they stopped dead center in a room full of bodies. We got a lot of comments from guys as we walked by, like "Nice. Hot. Fine." But mostly the guys looked bored, and the girls looked like they were trying too hard.

The waitresses walked around, wearing next to nothing; the guys loved it and the tips flowed. My companions ordered a bottle of vodka with four shot glasses, and I told them I was having a beer and didn't need a shot glass. The waitress gave me stinkeye knowing that no tips would be coming from me. She read me like a book. I returned the look.

Lara and Candice started pouring Sophie two to one shots

on them, and soon Sophie was holding the bottle upside down and pouring the vodka straight into her mouth. Some guy came up behind me and pushed his groin into my rear and started to grind. *Are you kidding me?* I turned around and yelled, "Stop." I think he got the idea and walked away. Soon he returned with a few of his friends, and they all started dirty dancing with my friends. Behind me, a girl threw up on the floor. I had been there a little less than half an hour but made my way to the exit, ordered an Uber, and went home. I texted Lara to let her know I had left. I was sure she didn't care.

Walking into the quiet, empty house, I reflected on my pathetic life. I had a child, and I didn't fit in with people my age anymore. And from what I had observed that night, I wasn't sure I wanted to. I didn't regret having Daniel, not for one second, but I regretted my failed marriage and that Daniel didn't have a father. And then there was Justin. How did I let that happen? What stupid thing would I do next?

I opened my iPad and read an email from my mother. She said she was having a wonderful time and looking forward to seeing me next Saturday. She attached some spectacular pictures of the Scandinavian landscape and a cute selfie of her and Giselle. Well, at least she was having a good time. I think she would have been proud of me tonight, to see how dignified I was when everyone around me was anything but. I sent her a reply that said *come back safe*, then went to bed.

Ten o'clock the following morning, I drove to pick up Daniel. He was sprawled out on the couch watching *Paw Patrol* and barely gave me a sideways glance when I walked into the house. My mother-in-law, or should I say former mother-in-law, I could never figure that out, was in the kitchen with her sister Rosa. She invited me to sit down and tell her tell them about my evening.

After I finished the rundown of my disappointing night out and my encounter with that grinding creep, Rosa said, "I'd love some guy to try that on me. I'm a black belt in karate. He wouldn't be left standing if he did."

"Seriously, Rosa? I didn't know that. Oh man, would that have been great to see."

"It doesn't surprise me that you didn't enjoy yourself, Rachel," Marguerita said. "You never were like those *chicas*. What are they called, 'high-maintenance?' That is why even though you and Alex married young, I thought you had a good chance at success. You were mature. Even at nineteen."

"Thanks, I think," I said. "Now I feel so old at twenty-nine. But I guess that has its advantages considering that Daniel deserves a good mother, if he doesn't have a father around. Speaking of which, how is Alex doing?"

"Ugh," she said, throwing her hands in the air in disgust. "I'm sorry he is such a deadbeat, Rachel. I hardly see him myself. I can't keep up with him and the women he goes through. He's had three since you split. I think he is living with someone now, but Rachel, I don't even ask. I hate what he did to you and Daniel. That was not how I raised him. His brothers are so much better. You married the wrong son. I don't know where I went wrong with him."

"Raising kids is hard, little sister. Especially sons without a father. You tried your best, that's all you could do," Rosa said, patting Marguerita's hand.

I thought about Daniel not having a father, felt slightly dejected, then added, "You raised all three, and if two are good then it seems to me Alex made his own choices, and you are not to blame. He knew what he was doing when he gambled and when he cheated." Immediately I remembered Justin, and my face burned.

"Let's change the subject. What can we do today?" Marguerita asked brightly. "You are going to stay a bit, yes? Let's do something."

"That would be nice," I said.

Rosa said, "Well, I have to be going. But I'm so happy to see you again, my love, and especially your darling little boy." She kissed me on the cheek, then smothered Daniel with a million kisses, so many that he squirmed away from her, shouting "stop" but laughing with delight. The she left.

We decided to take Daniel to Woodbine Mall, where he could get a pass for the indoor amusement park. Marguerita was beside herself watching him on every ride and waving frantically, trying to take pictures before he disappeared from sight. Daniel had done each ride twice, and when I asked him if he wanted to go on any more, he gave a resounding "No way." We went for lunch in the food court, and I had Thai, which was surprisingly delicious for food court fare.

Daniel was eating French fries when I turned to him and said, "Well, you've had a lot of fun this morning. Do you think you could cooperate and sit and rest in a cart while Lita and I have some big-girl fun shopping?" He agreed that was fair.

We walked through the mall, and since fifty percent of the stores were vacant, we decided to head to The Bay. First, we looked at jewelry and watches then walked through the perfume aisles, guiltily avoiding the ladies with their bottles in hand ready to give you a spritz, going to the counter to sample one of our own picking. We perused the bedding department and ran our hands across the luscious towels. Marguerita commented that it was a shame they couldn't keep that velvety feel. I agreed. When I saw they were forty percent off, I bought a set of hand towels for my mother in Tiffany blue, her favorite color. We looked at the furniture, and I picked out some that I'd buy when I got my own place, which was a long way off, I knew, seeing as I was broke and didn't have either a good job or an education. One can always dream.

Daniel was now asleep, out like a light, head dangling to the side, so I lowered the back of the seat, and we headed to the clothes department. We looked at some dresses, which were very beautiful, but both of us agreed that we had nowhere to wear a nice dress, so why would we buy one or even try one on? Then we went to the hat department for a few laughs. I tried on a straw hat with a brim that was a good twenty-four inches wide. After Marguerita stopped laughing, she asked me how much it was because she wanted to buy it for me.

"Ha, ha, ha," I said. "You couldn't even pay me to wear that."

"It would certainly protect you from the sun." True, true. That was the only thing it had going for it.

From the corner of my eye, I saw the department that made Marguerita swoon: the shoes. Her weakness. Alex had told me that when they were little and Marguerita got a job in a shoe store, she would come home with only half her paycheck after buying new shoes each time. Then she'd cry and cry and feel so guilty and plead with her boss to let her return them until the third time, when the boss told her it was either stop buying shoes or look for another job. She looked for another job. That was the easier decision.

My mother, too, loved shoes, as did Giselle. Me, well, not quite. I do like nice shoes. I just don't *love* shoes. I like leather because it lets my feet breathe, and a nice heel, not too high, but high enough to look feminine and attractive, but if I have a couple of pairs that go well with numerous outfits, I'm happy. Maybe I'm not normal, I wonder, not sharing this obsession with shoes, or handbags, for that matter. Just give me a nice one for winter and another for summer and I'm good to go. Oh well.

Marguerita approached the new arrivals section, her eyes landing on a pair of Marc Jacob patent leather slingbacks with a bow. She held the shoe in her hands and said, "Isn't this beautiful?"

I thought *meh* but said, "Yes, it is." Beauty is in the eye of the beholder. To Marguerita they were beautiful

"Try them on," I said.

"No, there is no point. I can't afford these. They are forty percent off, though. No, no I can't afford them." She placed the shoe back.

I called over the very bored-looking, gum-chewing sales girl and said, "Do you have those in size seven? It is size seven, isn't it?" Marguerita nodded shyly.

You would have thought the sales clerk would be happy to have something to do to help her day go faster, but instead she sighed audibly then walked off to find them. Marguerita and I both had a chuckle over that, then all of a sudden Marguerita turned serious and said, "What are you doing to me, tempting me like that? You know I can't afford those shoes." And then as if talking to herself, she continued, "Oh well, no harm, I suppose, I'll just see what they look like, but I have no money with me, and I got rid of my credit cards, so I won't be able to buy them anyway."

The bored-looking girl came back, sans the gum — someone must have told her to spit it out — but she held the box of shoes, and Marguerita's face lit up like a kid in a candy store. She gently removed them from the box, took them from the paper wrapping, and then placed them on her feet. I felt like I was witnessing Dorothy putting on the ruby shoes, or maybe Cinderella.

"What do you think?" she asked, and before I even answered, she had walked over to the mirror.

I said, "Tap your heels together three times." She looked at me blankly before cluing in and then laughing.

Looking at them in the mirror, her face became dead serious, and she put her hands over her mouth and gushed, "Oh, I love them." She then quickly walked back to the chair, took them off, and called the girl. "Take them away. Please."

"Please take them to the cash register. We'll take them," I said to the girl.

"What are you doing? I'm not letting you buy them," Marguerita snapped.

"Too late. I already told the sales clerk we are, and what's more, I want to. Money is not an issue. When my mother left for her holiday, she put money in an envelope and left it on the table with a note that said to have fun. I've hardly spent any of it, and I want to do this. It's fun. You wouldn't want to disappoint my mother, now would you, by taking away my fun?"

She threw her arms around my waist and said, "*Muchas gracias, mi amor.*"

"*De nada,*" I said. "You deserve it."

Eleven

Daniel and I returned to the house shortly after five to an excitable Luna greeting us at the door with spins.

"Oh, my goodness, Luna, I'm sorry I forgot all about you. I'm not used to having a dog yet." Luna ran straight to the back door, and I let her out to do her business. I thought the stream emitting from her would never end. Poor thing, holding it all day.

I turned to my sweet little boy. "So, Daniel, what should we do tonight? It's been a long day. Want to order a pizza and play some Snakes and Ladders and then watch a movie?" I asked, expecting him to jump up and down in excitement.

Instead, he asked if he could play on his iPad. I couldn't believe it; he preferred electronics to having fun with me. He looked so cute standing there waiting for a yes, so I said, "Let's take Luna for a walk, and then you can play on the iPad while we wait for the pizza to be delivered, but it's off after that." He agreed to that, but I knew he knew he would pressure me for more iPad time when I told him to turn it off. I needed to be firmer. Let my no mean no. Set up some rules before he became an expert at wearing me down. It didn't help that my mother absolutely loved spoiling him. I decided the new rule would be no electronics after supper, and I would make sure to tell her when she got home.

Pizza arrived, and we only had one minor crying episode

when I told him to shut off the iPad, because he was actually quite hungry and wanted to eat. After eating, we didn't play Snakes and Ladders because I didn't feel like it and Daniel didn't remember. Did I feel guilty? Not in the least; he'd had a lot of fun that day. Instead, I made buttered popcorn, took it to the couch, and popped my favorite Disney movie, *Emperor's New Groove*, into the DVD player. I plopped myself down beside my little man for some well-earned cuddles and chuckles.

I heard the notification sound of my phone, which annoyed me, but still I got up to see who had texted. Of course, I couldn't find it. I looked in my purse, my jacket pockets, and the hall table. I found it on the bathroom counter, the first room I went to when I got home. I was getting so forgetful. *Maybe something is wrong with me,* I thought. But twenty-nine was too young to get Alzheimer's, although not a brain tumor. I worried for a split second, then looked at my screen.

Hey there, I hope you haven't forgotten about me.

It was Marcel. And I had forgotten. But I wasn't about to say that. I had manners, after all.

No, just been really busy. My mother is on a cruise, so I've been busy with Daniel. Having a kid was great if you needed an excuse to cover over a big fat lie.

Truth was, I *had* been giving him some thought. I thought about his many good qualities and that I had enjoyed his company but reconsidered answering him. Mostly because of the way he had stopped contacting me out of the blue and for no reason. That was inexcusable. I also thought he was too old for me. In addition, his reputation as a womanizer preceded him, and that episode with Angeline in the restaurant still didn't sit well with me. Plus I wasn't convinced he really liked kids. The negatives definitely outnumbered the positives.

But the real reason I used my manners and gave him an excuse, not blowing him off entirely, was I had one more Friday night to endure before my mother came back. So I decided that he could take Daniel and me out to dinner, if he wanted. If he really had changed his ways, he wouldn't object to having Daniel along.

Would you like to go out sometime? he texted.
Daniel and I are available Friday for supper if you like.
Perfect. I'll pick you up at five.

Kudos for knowing kids eat earlier. I guessed he'd learned a few things from our time together.

Friday afternoon at four, I told Daniel our plans for the evening. He screwed up his face into a scowl. Not what I expected.

"Do you we have to go out with Marcel?" he whined, which I hated.

"What's wrong, Daniel? Don't you want to have supper with Marcel? He's going to take us somewhere nice." I'd hoped more than nice — kid-friendly too.

"Where is he taking us?" he asked. *Smart kid. Just like Mom*, I thought.

"It's a surprise!" I said gleefully. "Now let's get washed up and dressed in something clean. Nothing off the floor. Upstairs, young man. March, one, two, three." He always liked marching, and it was the easiest way to get him to follow along.

Five o'clock on the dot, Marcel pulled into the driveway and we went out to meet him. He looked so happy to see me; I was taken slightly aback. It had been months, and I hadn't really given him more than a fleeting thought. I figured he felt the same about me, especially since he was the one who had ended things between us. I came to the conclusion that I really didn't understand men.

I opened the back door to get Daniel belted in the back seat when I noticed an addition to the car. Marcel had bought a booster seat and had it installed. Now I was certainly taken aback.

"You bought a booster seat? For Daniel?" I asked incredulously as I secured the straps around him.

"Yup," he said cheerfully, his body turned with arm resting on the passenger chair in order to watch me strap Daniel in.

Getting into the front seat beside him, I asked, "Why would you buy him a seat just to take him to the restaurant? I mean, it's nice but unnecessary. Well, maybe not exactly, I hope unnecessary, though. Anyway, what I mean is, you didn't have to do that. But thanks."

"From what I understand, a booster seat is necessary for a child under four-foot-nine, less than eighty pounds, and younger than eight years old. That seems to fit Daniel."

"Yes, but only if it is the parent's car or guardian. Not a car he just rides occasionally." I was beginning to wonder if Marcel was only book-smart.

"I know that. I wanted to wait to tell you, but seeing as you're grilling me now, I might as well tell you now, I want to give you this car. As a gift." He looked over at me, my mouth agape, and added, "Free."

"What are you talking about?" My antennas were going up. Nobody gives away cars. Was accepting it a way of obligating myself to him? Putting me under some unspoken debt?

"I just bought a new Tesla. I know you think this car is expensive and fancy and all that, but it really isn't. It's a lower-end BMW. They were going to give me very little on a trade-in, so I thought why bother? I knew you drove that old Kia, and it probably wouldn't give you many more miles before it cost you money, so rather than get a pittance on a trade-in, I wanted you to have it. That is, if you want old Rosalyn. That's my name for her." Then he flashed me that warm smile, and I relaxed. Somewhat.

But he was right; my car was on its last legs. I was going to need a replacement soon. And as much as I didn't want anything from Marcel, I equally didn't want to be indebted to my mother. I needed to seriously consider obtaining a degree or diploma in something that could enable me to support Daniel and myself. Still, I was suspicious of a gift so grand. Especially from someone who had recently broken off with me so abruptly.

"Well, that's *really* nice of you. Really nice of you. Are you sure I can't pay you something for it? At least what they were going to offer you for the trade-in." I didn't have a penny to my name and didn't know how I could pay him if he said yes.

"No, I know you don't have any money. And I just came back from the Bahamas, where I did some consulting, and got paid handsomely. So, I don't want a penny from you. I'm glad to see the car go to someone I know and like. Like you." He smiled warmly again, and as if reading my mind, before I could protest, he added that he wouldn't hear another word about it.

I looked around the car, at the leather seats, sunroof, and beautiful dashboard, then smiled. It was a fine car. A little voice in my head was saying *don't accept it* and *if anything is too good to be true, it's not* and there would be strings attached. I told it to shut up and leave me alone. I wanted this car. And he wanted to give it to me, so all was good. I hoped.

Marcel took us to restaurant in Port Credit with a patio overlooking Lake Ontario, and Daniel had fun watching the sailboats while Marcel explained how to sail a boat and what weather conditions to look for and things like that.

"I'll take you and your mommy sailing next week, if you want. On my boat."

Immediately, Daniel started begging me, "Can we go, Mommy, please, can we?"

"Be quiet," I reprimanded him. Turning to Marcel, I asked, "You have a sailboat?"

He pointed at the docked boats and said, "The third one in is mine. When we finish eating, we can go see it, if you like." I felt something at work here. I was being swept along with Marcel's plan. He was doing his utmost to make an impression. And against my better judgment, it was working. It was as if I was a little fish on the end of his line, and he was slowly pulling me in.

He paid for our meal, and we walked to his boat for a look. Like the car, it was fine, too. I guessed older guys did have their advantages. I agreed Daniel and I would go sailing with him on Monday.

When he stopped the car to drop us off, it was almost nine o'clock. Daniel was in the car seat, rubbing his eyes. Which was good. His bedtime was one of my favorite time of the day. Then I got some peace.

Marcel said, "Thanks for coming out with me tonight. I really enjoyed being with you again. I've missed you." I didn't believe that but said nothing. I was sure I had been replaced by someone else in my absence. We made arrangements to be picked up at eight on Monday, and I said goodnight. I kissed him on the cheek; after all, he had promised to give me a car. Marcel liked that, even saying thank you.

The next day, my mother arrived home, pulling up in an Uber minivan with Giselle in the passenger side. I ran to the car and gave Giselle a quick embrace through the unrolled window then went to my mom, now standing outside the van, to give her a warm embrace. She reciprocated lovingly, but on seeing Daniel, she swept him into her arms and hugged him tight. I couldn't really blame her; after all, he was adorable. Giselle promised to be in touch, and then her driver drove away.

"Boy, it's good to be home," Mom said, looking around her house and the front garden. "Have you been watering my plants? They look a little dry." They were fine. I had been watering. Every day. But we were not going to start arguing the minute she got home, so I just said yes, of course. Arguing could wait till tomorrow.

She got in the house and picked up her mail piled on the hall table. "Junk, junk, and more junk," she said as she sorted through it and tossed it back down. "Oh wait, a bill. And another. Whew, lucky me. I thought I was only going to get junk."

"So, how was the trip?" I asked.

"As soon as I get settled and have a bath, I'm going to show you and Daniel and all my pictures and give you your presents. But Rachel, it was wonderful." She broke into an enormous smile and with a faraway look in her eyes continued, "It really was smart thinking on Giselle's part to ask me to go away. It seems to have cleared my head. Of course, I still miss your dad; I don't think I will ever stop missing him, but new surroundings gave me something different to consider. New cultures and climate, food, and music. I don't know how to describe it; maybe like a reboot would be accurate. But I'm glad you're here, and I'm not coming back to an empty house. And you too, Luna." She patted the dog.

After my mother's bath, we decided to order Ethiopian food for delivery. She wanted us to wait till after we ate to see our gifts, but Daniel was much too excited to do that. He tried his best to remain calm but kept circling the luggage and peering at it as if he could see through it just by staring. She could take it no more and asked him, "Would you like your present now?" A pointless question.

"Yes, yes! Please, Grandma, can I have it now? Please, please, *please*?"

"*May* I have it," she corrected, "and yes you may."

She had bought Daniel a wooden labyrinth game and me a bottle of my favorite perfume, Lancôme Hypnose, from the duty-free. I don't know who was more thrilled. Daniel loves toys, and my weakness is French perfumes. We sat there watching Daniel try to beat the labyrinth, his little tongue sticking out the corner of his mouth as he turned the board, trying to maneuver the little ball to its destination.

We were chuckling away at his faces, and he looked only too pleased to be amusing us, regardless of the reason, when my mother said, as if having an epiphany, "Rachel, you have to enroll Daniel in school soon. We're already in the first week of August."

"What? You're kidding." I had lost my sense of time. Not wanting my mother to be aware of my blunder, I said, "Of course we are." What had happened? Best I could figure was though I had settled into living at my mother's, it still didn't feel like mine, and so all normal routines like preparing for a new school year had completely slipped by the wayside.

"Time has gone by so quickly since I've arrived, Mom. Do you want me to stay for another year? I wasn't sure if it was just a temporary arrangement to help you get through the first few months after Dad died."

"Rachel, what am I going to do with this big house all by myself? I want you to stay as long as you like, forever if you want. I'll never ask you to leave. Seeing you two everyday makes me feel alive. Gives me a reason to get up."

"Thanks, Mom, that's nice. And believe me, I really appreciate it. But you do know that I will want to get on my own again. I know it's impossible now — I don't even have a job — but I want to try to work towards that. It's wonderful living here, but I think we both know it can't be permanent."

"Well, what about trying to get a degree or diploma in something? While you're living here. And I can watch Daniel so that would free you up to attend school, be it university or for a college degree."

I knew she meant well and was right, but somehow the idea of living here with her for a few more years wasn't sitting well with me. Before she went away, we were constantly arguing over the littlest things, and I was beginning to think moving away sooner than later might be best. Our time apart only confirmed it. It was the freedom and independence I had been missing.

While she was away, I had told Marguerita my feelings. She let me know that she had made good money cleaning houses, and she was thinking of cutting down her work. She would train me and give me her contracts. I was thinking of taking her up on it. The money was decent, and I liked the idea of having a job that kept me physically active and in shape. But I knew if I told my mom that, she would lose it. A degree in something, anything, would provide more security in the future, in her opinion, and justifiably so. And I hadn't made up my mind. I told Marguerita that I would think about it. And remained mum as regards to my mom.

My mother sat across from me, arms folded at her chest and foot tapping the floor. She awaited my reply. "I'm not sure what I want to do, that's the problem," I told her, and it was the truth.

"Well, in the meantime, on Monday let's walk over to Rivercrest Junior School and see if they are open for registration." She turned to Daniel. "For you, young man, are going into grade one."

Daniel looked up briefly, nodded in acknowledgement, then quickly got back to his labyrinth. Brilliant toy, I thought. He was completely absorbed, intent on beating it. This was the first time I'd seen anything other than an electronic game hold his attention for so long. And according to the claims on the box, once he beat it, the challenge remained to beat it again, only faster.

"How does that sound, Rachel? Should we go over after breakfast?"

"Monday isn't good for me. Mom; Marcel wants to take Daniel and me sailing."

On hearing that, she screwed up her mouth. "So, I take it you decided on seeing that man again."

Seemed to me she had said she would support me whatever I decided. Or had she forgotten? But there was no point in lying either to her or myself. I was seeing him again because he had a lot to offer. Why not? I was at a crossroads. I had decisions to make that I really did not wish to make at all. School, housekeeping, living with Mom. So why not add one more? Date Marcel to see if he was serious and worth it. If he turned out to be a timewaster, then I could strike him off my list for good.

"Did you want to come with us?" I asked.

"No thank you," was all she said. Very plainly. And rather coldly.

Twelve

Fifteen minutes before Marcel was to arrive on Monday morning, Daniel and I had a showdown over sunscreen. He hated me applying it on him, but if I left the job to him, he missed too many spots. Finally, he agreed to let my mother do it. I ran around finding his hat, extra shoes, and clothes in case the ones he was wearing got wet, plus lots of fruit, granola bars, and nuts for snacks. Marcel said he always kept drinks on board, water and beer and wine, plus he'd bought juice boxes for Daniel.

He pulled into the driveway, and my mother didn't even come out to say hello. She walked to the backyard with Luna. Marcel didn't care; he didn't even ask about her. He jumped out of his car with a huge smile on his face and handed me the keys.

"It's going to be yours soon, so you might as well get used to driving it," he said cheerily.

With our stuff packed away in the trunk and Daniel safely strapped in his seat, I was about to drive away when I happened to glance at the front room window. My mom was there, waving at us and blowing kisses. She had a huge smile, but in her eyes I saw only sadness. I unrolled Daniel's window so he could shout goodbye to her. I blew her a kiss too. That woman was breaking my heart. Maybe she needed another trip. Ha, fat chance of that. Maybe there was an association for widows and widowers she could join. I'd research finding one when I got back.

The sailboat was more a yacht, but Marcel assured me that

it was indeed a sailboat, and once we used the motor to steer it into open waters, he would hoist the sails and shut the motor off.

About a mile out into Lake Ontario, the sails were open and we skimmed water as calm as skaters on smooth ice. The winds were light, so the sailing was smooth, which was fine with me as I nervously tried to hold on to Daniel, even though we hardly suffered a bump. Daniel, on the other hand, was fearlessly running to the front of the boat, holding on to the railing and shouting joyfully. I remained behind him every step, holding his life jacket from the back. Marcel thought it all too funny, which I did not appreciate.

"Rachel, stop worrying so much. I wouldn't let anything happen to Daniel. We have a perfect day for sailing. I wouldn't have taken you both out if I thought it was dangerous and the water was too rough. I'm going to go down to the fridge to see what I can find to eat."

He brought up a basket of fresh buns, cheese, and different meats. He also had cut up celery, carrots, and peppers with a dip. I went to prepare Daniels's bun for him, but Marcel suggested I let Daniel do it himself. Daniel looked so proud when Marcel asked him if he wanted to make up his own bun. I wanted to cry; it was as if I was watching Daniel grow up before my very eyes. He very carefully put his cheese then the meat together and sat eating while watching the birds circle around. When he caught me looking at him, he smiled and wordlessly pointed to the birds.

"Those are cormorants, Daniel. If you keep watching them, every now and then they dive down into the water and come up with a fish." And sure enough, that was what happened. Daniel was so excited, he started jumping up and down, and I panicked again, yelled at him to sit down, afraid he would choke on his food.

"You're a fantastic mother, Rachel," Marcel said.

This time it was me who was proud as I looked around to find Daniel's sunhat and put it back on his head.

Our sailing expedition lasted a couple hours, then we headed back to land just before suppertime. Daniel repeatedly asked Marcel when we could come again, and I repeatedly told him to stop, but he was far too excited.

"When we have the perfect sailing weather, like today, I'd be more than happy to take you and your mom out again." And he looked over at me and gave me a wink.

A wink! I felt like I was being hoodwinked. Was he endeavoring to win me over through my son? I feared so. But my goodness, I started to think, what was really that bad about being won over to enjoy some of these finer things of life? If I put the age difference out of my mind, that is. Which I was starting to do.

Marcel drove home, thankfully. I felt a little wind-blown and quite exhausted from all that fresh air. Plus, Marcel had me helping him when we left port and when we docked. All in all, it had been an enjoyable but tiring day.

When I got in the house, my mother wasn't home. She never went anywhere. I mean, *never*, so I was baffled. I shot her a text, and she responded immediately.

I'm at Marguerita's. Will be home soon.

Great, I thought. That's what I got for ignoring Marguerita's text earlier that day. She wanted my mom and Daniel and me to come over and spend the day, but I didn't want to tell her what I was doing or lie to her, so I just ignored it. She wouldn't know why I didn't respond, I figured. I could have a low battery or misplaced my phone or any number of reasons. I didn't want to tell her about Marcel. I didn't figure on her inviting my mom directly. But she must have, and now she would find out about Marcel.

I knew Marguerita would not like it. I just knew it. *Argh*. I could only imagine what my mother might be telling her. But I was hoping somehow my mother would show a little discernment and not tell Marguerita anything. Oh well; I guessed I wouldn't have long to find out if she did or not.

Daniel's bedtime consisted of three stories and four songs, and even then he wasn't tired. He was still wired from sailing, and he wanted to know everything there was to know about boats. I looked up nautical terms on Wikipedia and started to rhyme them off, starting with A. But first I made an agreement with him: he was not allowed to stop me to ask what terms meant, because I didn't have a clue. He wisely agreed.

"*Aback*: A sail is aback when the wind fills it from the opposite side to the one normally used to move the vessel forward. The purpose may be to reduce speed, to heave to, or to assist moving the ship's head through the eye of the wind when tacking. A sudden wind shift can cause a square-rigged vessel to be 'caught aback' with all sails aback. This is a dangerous situation."

I continued reading the meanings of "abaft" and then "abaft the beam," and when I looked over at him, he was sound asleep. The next term was "abandon ship," which of course I knew, but reading it sounded downright scary.

"*Abandon ship*: An imperative to leave the vessel immediately, usually in the face of some imminent overwhelming danger."

Okay then. I thought I had better stop before I read enough never to want to go on that beautiful boat again. I leaned over my sweet little boy to kiss his forehead, place blankets over him, then turn out his light and leave his room.

I heard the front door and went downstairs to find my mother standing in the front foyer, texting someone.

Noticing me, she said, "I'm texting Marguerita to let her know I got home safely." She put down her phone, but not before laughing at Marguerita's reply. "You were right, Rachel, she's a wonderful woman. And such a colorful life. I couldn't get over some of the challenges she had to overcome, both in Ecuador and here in Canada. And she is so funny. Even with everything she's been through, she has kept her sense of humor. Inspiring, really."

"I knew you would like her. Did she ask you where I was?" Which was a stupid question. I really wanted to say, *Did you tell her who I was with?* But that made me sound as if I felt guilty. Which I did not. Or did I? No, I did not.

"Yes, I told her you and Daniel went sailing with a man you are seeing." I looked at my mother, eyebrows raised, waiting for her to elaborate. But she teasingly did not. Instead, she walked into the kitchen, putting dishes in the dishwasher.

"And?" I asked, following her.

"And what?" She was good at this game. I took three steps and blocked access to the dishwasher. I crossed my arms in front of me and glared. "All right, all right." She laughed. "Of course, Marguerita wanted to know all about him. She really does love you and Daniel. But I told her just enough for her to know. I told her he was a little older and was a professor but that he had a good reputation."

"Really?" I asked incredulously.

"Well, he does, academically. So, it wasn't exactly a lie. Maybe a lie of omission. But what she doesn't know won't hurt her; in fact, if she knew his past, that would probably hurt her more. Because then she would worry."

"Well, that's good," I said, and then added, "Thanks. And anyway, we've just been out twice. It doesn't mean it's permanent." I didn't tell her he was giving me his car.

"Exactly." Then under her breath she muttered, "Hopefully." Which I ignored.

The next day after breakfast, we all walked over to the school to register Daniel for September, which was approaching quickly.

After filling out forms and showing proper identification, we walked through the halls to find his classroom, room number twelve. At the desk at the front of the classroom was Mrs. Beck, the same teacher who had taught me in grade one. I felt six years old all over again. She looked exactly the same. Maybe a couple of fine lines around her eyes and grooves at the sides of her lips, but other than that she was identical.

Mrs. Beck recognized me immediately, and I was so happy to see her, I thought I might cry. And she was going to be my son's teacher! I knew then he was going to have a wonderful year. I'd loved school each and every day when she was my teacher. She made everything seem fun. She had a gift. A natural teacher.

"This is your little boy?" she asked. And looking at Daniel, she said, "I'm going to enjoy having you in my class, Daniel, just like I enjoyed having your mom." She remembered my mother too, but Mom, I could tell, was drawing a blank and doing her best to feign recognition. I was pretty sure she was fooling no one, but Mrs. Beck was far too gracious to call her out.

We walked back home, where I saw an unfamiliar car in the driveway.

"Do you know who that is, Mom?" She did not. I walked up to the driver's window to see a woman's head bent over her phone. I gently tapped, and Lara turned to me, startled.

"Oh, you scared the crap out of me," she said, laughing.

"I could say the same for you, Lara. Do you want to come in?"

I made tea for Lara and I. My mom said she needed to finish her laundry from the trip. We went out the back to sit in the garden. Something about Lara looked different. Better. I knew I was staring, but I couldn't help it. Finally, I said, "Lara, you look different."

"Oh yeah." She chuckled. "My lips are normal. I went to a stupid Girls Night Out Party where I got talked into having injections on my lips. Anyway, I hated them. And you saw me when they were at their fullest. Like sausage lips. Oh, man, they were awful. Thank goodness they've gone back to normal. I looked like a freak. I'm surprised you didn't laugh at me."

"Well, to tell the truth, I almost did. I had to turn away from looking at you."

"How do you think I felt every time I looked in a mirror? What a joke. Don't ever do injections. Anyway, you don't need them. You have perfect lips."

"Yeah, right, regardless, I have no intention of doing anything to my body. No nips, tucks, injections, or burning. Of anything. I hate pain. And self-inflicted pain is something I just don't get. Now, maybe when I start getting wrinkles, I might think differently, but right now I'm okay with things the way they are. Besides, I'd be too afraid something would go wrong and I'd be permanently scarred or worse."

"I know. I really don't know why I went along with it. Maybe it was the three glasses of Champagne." She started laughing.

"You're crazy," I said, and soon we were both chuckling.

After the spontaneous laughter subsided, Lara looked around the yard and said, "This is a beautiful yard. But don't you just hate this time of year?"

"No, it's perfect outside. I love summer. You don't like it?" I was befuddled. Who didn't love summer?

"No, I love summer too. It's just that we're so close to September now, and then it's all over again. Do you know I actually saw some leaves turning color already? And it's getting darker earlier again. Ugh. I hate thinking about it. Soon we will have to go through those miserable winter months stuck inside. And that is why I hate the last days of summer, because I can't put the thought out of my head that it's going to be over soon. Isn't that crazy?" She laughed again.

"Yup, that it is. It's still summer. So enjoy it. And even fall can be nice."

"I know, I know. It's more like a love/hate thing. Silly me."

"So, what's up? What made you come by today? Not that I'm not glad you did. Because I am."

"I don't know. Nothing really, I was driving by your house and wanted to say hi, so I stopped. Also, I want to apologize."

"For what?" I asked, puzzled.

"For the awful time you had when you came out with us. I knew you were upset when you left, and I felt bad. Like it's my fault. I chose the place. We go there all the time, but you have to be into that kind of thing. So, if you were upset, I'm sorry."

"I was more upset at the guys that came up to us and the one that got behind me. I really didn't like that. If he did that on the street, he'd be charged with assault."

"Yeah, those guys are there every week. They always do things like that. It's just dancing."

"Not my kind of dancing. Anyway, it's not your fault. I let you pick the place. I just felt uncomfortable there, so I left. No harm done. For real."

"That's good. I was thinking, if you like, for something different we could catch a movie and have dinner sometime? You didn't know this, but I recently moved back into my parents' house too, which is taking some getting used to. I got renovicted. You heard of that?"

"Yeah! It's disgusting. Landlords evict tenants under the guise of renovating the apartment, but it's really just an excuse to jack up the rents. How awful for you."

"No kidding. Anyway, I'm making the best of it and thought now that you're back in the neighborhood too, we should do something. How does that sound?"

"Sounds great, now that I'm back. Although I hope I'm not back for good. I really need to be independent again and not living with my mother. Did you know I was married and have a six-year-old boy?"

"No, I didn't know that. Who did you marry? Was it that guy who was your boyfriend all through high school, um, let's see don't tell me, Alex, uh, Alex Moreno? That's it, right?" She was very pleased with herself for remembering.

"Yup, the one and only. And now I am living to regret it. We're divorced."

"Well, he was hot. Everyone was jealous of you. But everyone knew that you two were going to stay together. You made the perfect couple."

"The problem was he didn't grow up after high school. And when we had Daniel, he needed to mature and settle down, but he couldn't do it. And because we had a child, I didn't have a choice. I had to leave him. And here I am." I held up my arms to encompass our surroundings.

"Well, I'm glad you're here," she added sincerely.

My mom joined us, and we spent the afternoon talking about people we knew from the neighborhood. My mother asked Lara about her family, where they lived, and what she did for work.

"Oh, I'm a paralegal. It's great! It only took two years at college, unless you want to specialize. You can do other courses. It's really interesting. Right now, I'm assisting lawyers in preparation for family mediation cases. I love it! I'm never bored."

"Why don't you look into that, Rachel?" my mother asked.

And why don't you let me make my own decisions? I wanted to say. And maybe, just maybe, I had thought about studying law. Which was something I thought my mother might expect from me. But it looked as if she had lowered her expectations. Anyway, this was not the time to discuss my future, so instead I said, "Possibly."

Lara turned to look up at the house behind us and remarked how beautiful it was, so my mother suggested a tour.

We started in the basement. It was typical, with a large open-concept area containing a big sectional couch and a sixty-five-inch television above a gas fireplace. Behind the couch was a pool table, and behind the pool table was a bar. My mind drifted back to my parents playing pool and having drinks with their best friends.

"Mom, I remember you and Dad playing pool down here with Robert and Natalie every first Friday night of the month. You guys were always laughing and joking around."

"Except when your dad was losing; he was such a sore loser. If Robert and Natalie beat us, he would always insist on a rematch. Sometimes it seemed as if the game would never end. But it was fun," she said wistfully.

"What happened to them? Do you ever talk to them?"

"Right around the time you moved out, they got divorced. I heard that Robert left Natalie for someone else, but I didn't ask your dad about it. He would have known because he still golfed with Robert. But you know your dad, he hated gossip, so he never told me. And I think Natalie is still around, but we've lost touch."

"That's a shame. They always seemed so happy."

"Yeah, it didn't make much sense, really. But then again, divorce seldom does."

She was right about that.

Next, we showed Lara around the main floor, the remodeled eat-in kitchen with the huge six-burner gas stove and double oven, perfect for a house in which neither woman liked to cook, and at five Daniel was too young to learn. I would have to wait at least two years to expect anything from him. From the kitchen ceiling hung beautiful copper utensils. All for show. Also, on the main floor was a family room where there was another sixty-five-inch TV that Daniel was parked in front of, and we had a separate formal living room and a dining room. Another room had an upright piano, which my mother played beautifully and I too had learned to play. In that room were framed family photos completely covering one wall. I walked over and looked at the pictures of my dad and then Tommy. Mom was gazing at the pictures too, so I put my arms around her shoulders and walked her out of the room before either of us had a chance to break down.

Upstairs were four bedrooms, each with their own bathroom. My mother's bedroom was massive and had two balcony rail windows overlooking the back garden. The hallway had a skylight that would bring the natural light down from the roof of the second floor to the front hall through the central spiral stairway. It really was quite lovely, and in fact, my parents had designed it themselves and had it custom-built to their exact specifications. It was a work of love.

When we got back downstairs, Lara commented that it was getting on, and she was going to head home. I walked with her to her car.

"I'm on holidays this week and am just staying around, so you should come to my place and bring Daniel and your mom. We have a swimming pool, and they would love it," she said while getting in her car.

"That sounds really good. It's so freakin' hot, I could jump in a pool right now."

"You could come later if you like." When I didn't answer, she said, "Okay, I'll text you my address, and if you want to come, you're welcome. Just shoot me a text. Or any day this week, I'm completely open."

Then, to my complete surprise, she gave me a hug and said, "I'm really glad I stopped by today. I've been thinking about you ever since that night at the club. You're super nice. I'd be happy to have a friend like you."

After she left and back in the house, my mother said, "What a lovely girl. Were you friends with her in school?"

"Not really. Mom, how would you feel about going to her place this week with Daniel and me to swim in her pool? She invited all of us. What do you think? Would it be too much for you, with everything that's happened?"

"I think that would be lovely."

"Me too. She's so nice. It's going to be good having a friend."

Thirteen

After supper, Marcel called and we chatted for a while. He asked about my day, and I told him about enrolling Daniel in school and about Lara coming over, then he told me all about his day spent organizing his fall schedule and taking care of doctor's appointments and things he needed to do before school started again.

"Guess what's happening tomorrow?" he asked.

"Your new car is ready." I guessed correctly. He was silent for a moment. I had stolen his thunder, and he was a little miffed. I mean, what else would it have been that I would have been interested in?

"Yes," he answered dejectedly. "Anyway, I'll come and get you about ten to drive over there, and then after I take it home, we can go over to the Ministry of Transportation and I'll transfer the Beemer to you. Oh, and do you think you can leave Daniel home with your mother? It would just make it easier. We'll have paperwork to do, and it would be better to do it all uninterrupted."

My back went up immediately when he said that. I wasn't sure why. It was true that children could be distracting, but Daniel was very well behaved and wouldn't have been any trouble. And had Marcel not said anything, I probably would have left him with my mother. However, I saw this as a subtle hint that Daniel, although part of my life, was not part of his. I should have seen it for what it really was, a foregleam of what was to come. A warning. An older man who had never married or had children was that way by choice. And can a leopard change his spots? Why didn't I remember that they can't?

But Marcel was doing something generous and kind, so how could I object to this simple request? I put him on hold, confirmed with my mother that she was available to babysit, then said of course he could pick me up at ten, and I thanked him.

Getting off the phone, I also informed my mother that as of tomorrow I would be driving an older BMW, a gift from Marcel.

"Why is he giving you that? That's quite the gift, isn't it?" she asked sardonically.

I told her the reason for giving me the car, that it wasn't worth much on trade-in. She wasn't buying it.

"Ha! When were you born, yesterday?"

"No! I believe him. I know they don't give much for trade-ins. And if he thought the car would be put to better use by me, he was right. My old car is going to need lots of work soon. And I don't have a job to buy a new one or even fix it. So, I'm not overthinking it, Mom, and neither should you."

"Well, I am. That is an awfully expensive gift, and maybe the only thing you are seeing right now is a shiny, expensive automobile. If a car was what you wanted, you could have had one from here, in our garage. I think you're making a huge mistake taking that from him. He's going to expect something back from you. Don't forget, I know his past."

"Yeah, yeah, and you're not going to let me forget it either, I know." But she was right; I did want that car. It was sweet. I just didn't want to hear it from her.

She rolled her eyes at me, and I responded like any other mature woman of twenty-nine would: I stuck my tongue out at her. Then she stuck her tongue out at me, and I was about to make a gesture I don't normally make but stopped myself because this whole thing was getting too comical. Then, to my surprise and delight, my mother walked to my side, put both arms around me, and held me close. I rested my head on her shoulder and breathed in her lovely perfume.

"I only want you to be happy, Rachel. Nothing else. If Marcel will make you happy, then I am not going to stand in your way."

"I know, Mom," I said. "I get it. You're just doing your job as a parent. I suppose I'll be critical of every girl Daniel brings around when he's old enough to date."

"Maybe you will, maybe you won't. We only hope our kids make the right choices and they don't have to pay for their mistakes. Parents just want their kids to be happy."

"Mom, how did you know with Dad? That he was the right one." I wanted to know the formula, considering my dismal record.

"I saw the way he treated other people. And his family. He was very polite and good-natured. And he always acquiesced if the situation allowed. I watched the way his mom and dad interacted. They really loved each other, always speaking kindly and with respect. So they were an excellent example for their children. Also, we discussed the important things, like where we wanted to live and if we both wanted children, to see if we were on the same page. And we were. And then of course he was very good-looking."

"Oh, of course, wouldn't want to leave that out," I joked. "Maybe you were just lucky."

"No, I don't think so. Even my dad, who hated every guy that came around, approved of your father. I think that was the clincher for me. He saw something in him, something good. He even told me, 'Deborah, I like this one.' My dad was not a man of many words, so if he said that, he meant it. And I loved my dad. And I put stock in what he told me. I think it was after his nod of approval for your dad that I looked at him seriously. As if through a new lens, so when he asked me to marry him, I was convinced I was doing the right thing saying yes."

"Well, I'm glad you did. And he was a great father, from what I remember, but it seems so long ago now. I remember him and Tommy always laughing and wrestling. What about me, Mom? Did he play a lot with me? Sometimes I have difficulty remembering how we were together."

Her face went kind of blank, and I knew I had hit a sour note. It always hurt her to remember Tommy. "Of course, he loved you, Rachel. He loved all of us."

I was about to say that she didn't answer my question but knew it was pointless. That period in our lives was better left untouched, I could see. I just said, "Anyway, now that I have Daniel, I'm glad I married Alex. Even if he wasn't the greatest husband. And I want to give Marcel a chance. Even though he's old, no offense meant," I quickly added.

"None taken. He's old, not me."

"Ha, ha. But seriously, I want to see where this will go. He seems to care very much for me, and I really do have a good time when I'm with him. He doesn't act like an old man. He wants to have fun, and he seems to have a lot of energy. He handled that sailboat as if it were a rubber dingy. A lot of young guys I know aren't even in as good a shape; they just spend all their time gaming, getting fat."

"He cares for you, and I can see why. You're his type: young and beautiful. But what about Daniel? Will he care about him?" she asked wisely.

"Well, we come as a package, so he'd better. And I think he does. He seems to. And Daniel certainly likes him."

"Daniel is six years old, so I don't think he is the best judge of character. He'd like most men who he could look up to as a father figure as long as they bought him an ice cream cone once in a while or an occasional toy."

I had had enough of this conversation and where it was heading, especially since she was right. I didn't want to hear her logic. Marcel's attitude toward Daniel nagged at me, but I had time to figure that out. It wasn't as if we were getting married. We would go out for a while. I could get to know him, slowly, see the real him. I hoped.

We said goodnight and went to our rooms. Lara texted and asked if I wanted to come over the next day to swim, and I said I was free in the afternoon. After I got my car. Which I was stupidly happy about.

Marcel drove into the driveway at 9:55 the next morning, and when I approached the car he got out to take the passenger seat and let me drive. My mom stood in the doorway, arms crossed at her chest, while Daniel, tears streaming down his face, waved goodbye. He had wanted to come with us, crying for half an hour nonstop. I felt terrible leaving him and really didn't understand why he had to be excluded, but I promised him an afternoon of swimming at Lara's, and he reduced the waterworks slightly. I promised the same to my mother, but she took a pass. She was proving a point — she thought.

On the drive to get his new car, Marcel was boyishly excited. "You know, Rachel, I'm so excited to be buying an electric car. Zero emissions. A big fat zero! Declared world green car of the year. And it is beautiful." He sounded each syllable as if a separate word. He looked so happy, I couldn't help but smile along with him, until he said, "I can't figure out why everyone doesn't buy an electric car and do their part for the environment. Look at that pickup truck in front of us. I can literally smell the oil it's burning. Where is a cop when you need him to take that vehicle off the road? People are just so inconsiderate of others and the environment."

Okay, Marcel, I thought. *Everyone should have that kind*

of money, like you do, to buy a Tesla. Or any new car, for that matter, which is costly. And the poor guy who is trying to eke out a living, driving whatever gets him from point A to B, should be taken off the road. Who will buy him a new clean-driving vehicle? You, Marcel?

Was he that oblivious to the plight of the working class? Having lived it gave me fresh perspective, and while it wasn't desirable, poor people certainly didn't deserve the disdain they received from the more privileged.

"Marcel, maybe that is all the guy can afford to drive. Maybe he's on his way to the garage to get it fixed because he can't afford a new truck. Where is your empathy?"

"You're so good for me, Rachel. I need you around to keep me grounded. That's why I love you." He threw that out there, easily, then laughed heartily.

I hoped he was just spewing clichés, because he did not love me, and I didn't love him. Maybe acquiring a sparkly new car was making him slightly giddy.

At the Tesla dealership, Marcel was treated royally, as a man spending an exorbitant amount of money would be. The salesman practically ran to meet him at the door. "Mr. Mancy, how are you, sir?" He looked somewhat crazed, putting his arm on Marcel's back, gently leading him through the showroom and into his office. I'm sure he would have locked the door behind him to prevent him from changing his mind if he'd thought there might be the slightest possibility.

We sat in chairs across from him at his desk. He opened the top left drawer and retrieved an envelope, then reached it across to Marcel and beamed. "So, your big day is here. The car is just in the back, getting polished and ready for you. Here are some forms for you to keep."

He then looked over at me and said, "Hello. And you must be Mrs. Mancy." Oh, he was a sly one. Marcel looked delighted.

He extended his hand to me for a shake. I reluctantly gave him mine. I wasn't crazy about him or his big act. But obviously some people liked to be flattered, Marcel being one.

"Not yet, Andre, not yet," Marcel corrected him while giving me a wink.

"Well, she could do a lot worse than you, sir. A man who knows a great car when he sees one." He then addressed me: "The Tesla is the safest, quickest electric car on the road, and the savings on fuel add up the thousands per year. It can pay for itself over the years. Maybe he'll get you one of your own someday."

"Ha! Maybe one day. For now, Rachel will have to settle for an older Beemer."

"Nice."

I was sure he regarded me as nothing more than a sugar baby, a younger woman using and older guy for gifts and money, but neither his tone nor demeanor betrayed a thing. Then again, maybe it was I who felt like a sugar baby. *Oh God*, I thought, *what in the world am I doing?*

"There is your car now." He pointed to a gorgeous red Tesla being driven to the front doors. "You will find some gifts on the back seat for you and your sweetheart." He handed Marcel the automatic fob, shook our hands one more time, and we left the dealership. I looked back, and the salesman was grinning so widely, I swear I saw every tooth in his mouth. I'd imagined the commission from this sale alone would pay his next family vacation. I couldn't help but be happy for him.

In the back seat, we found Tesla-branded men's and women's hoodies in exactly the right sizes, small for me, medium for him. It was amazing that they provided that for me when they didn't even know I was coming. Their attention to detail was exceptional. I guess spending $100,000 would do that. Along with the hoodies, there were two logo baseball caps and two travel mugs. And just for Marcel, a pair of men's joggers. He looked quite pleased, as he should. It was a good day for him. Now to hand over my car. Would he remain as happy? I guessed I'd soon find out.

The vehicle transfer was smooth, except for the thirty-minute wait at the Ministry of Transportation office. Marcel was bored, and I was bored, and it took all the willpower I could muster not take out my phone and watch random stuff. I was just about to get it from my bag when Marcel took my hand, which surprised me. Why? We were going out again, I reminded myself. *Stop being surprised.* I had accepted a very expensive gift from, and yet I still wasn't connecting the dots. I didn't see of us as a couple. I looked at him, and he smiled at me reassuringly, and it worked. I smiled back and briefly placed my head on his shoulder.

I leaned up toward his ear and whispered, "Thank you."

And into my ear he whispered back, "No, thank you. I'm so glad you are back in my life."

When we left the Ministry of Transportation office, Marcel asked where I wanted to have lunch. I told him that I needed to get back for Daniel and that I had promised to take him swimming that afternoon. His disapproval was obvious.

"Where are you going swimming?" he asked abruptly.

Such a change. I didn't feel like answering him. I said, "I don't like your tone."

He immediately backed off. "I'm sorry." He sounded contrite. "I just thought that we would spend the day together. We could go for a drive in my new car. Test out the Tesla. I didn't mean to sound so angry. I'm just disappointed."

"I can't leave Daniel all day, Marcel. He's my responsibility. He was so sad when I left him this morning, I promised to take him swimming. And I am not going back on my word." I purposely did not tell him where we were swimming, and he wisely did not pursue it any further.

We said our goodbyes in the parking lot and made plans for later in the week to take the car for a drive in the country and then discover a new restaurant. He invited Daniel too, but I said Daniel would only get bored driving around in a car, even a Tesla, so Marcel would have to settle for only me. I studied his face when I said that, and it gave away nothing. Very smart. Very smart indeed.

Fourteen

Driving my BMW home was heaven. I opened the sunroof and blasted the radio. Even though the car was ten years old, the drive was phenomenal. I always loved BMWs from the time I was a little girl and my dad took me for drives in his own. Or maybe I loved drives with my dad, and that was why I loved BMWs. Well, whatever the case, it was a great car, plus it wasn't falling apart like my other crummy car, which I was going to donate to the Cars for Kids charity as soon as I got home.

My mother had lunch ready for me when I arrived, and after we ate, I called the charity car pickup for a next day pickup. *Goodbye old junker, and good riddance*, I thought. Daniel and I then made our way to Lara's for an afternoon in her pool.

The drive was ten minutes, being only four kilometers away. Pulling onto the street, Daniel watched for number fourteen, Lara's house. "There it is!" he said excitedly, pointing to the right, two houses ahead.

We pulled in the driveway then got out of the car and walked toward the porch. Lara, to my surprise, began jumping up and down in excitement, so spontaneous, childlike, and endearing. Nothing like the high-maintenance phony I had met the night we went out. The real Lara was lovable and genuine.

She ran to Daniel, scooped him up in her arms, and twirled him around. He was both startled and delighted. "You ready to have some fun? I have a big slide on my pool, it's the best!" She took him by the hand, and they started running to the side of the house toward the back.

"Wait, wait!" I yelled. "Daniel needs his lifejacket!" Life jacket secure, he jumped in before I had a chance to say boo. "Come in. Mommy! It's really nice," he yelled.

"I'm coming, I'm coming. Hold your horses," I replied, happy to watch him enjoying himself.

"You ready to go in, Rachel? You got your bathing suit on, or do you want to change first?"

"Under my sundress," I said happily.

"Then, let's swim," she said, stripping off her cover-up and diving into her pool, emerging at Daniel's side and throwing him into the air, much to his delight.

We spent the afternoon playing with Daniel, watching him jump off the side, attempt handstands, do summersaults, and go down the slide. Every time we turned our head for a second or decided to talk just to each other, he would scream out, "Watch me, watch me!" It was times like these that I thought of having a little brother or sister for him as a playmate.

After an hour or so of the Daniel Show, we finally got to enjoy some conversation while floating around on air mattresses. Daniel was tuckered out by then, happily drifting on his own floaty toy and not demanding all our attention.

"Do you always go out clubbing?" I asked.

"Usually at least one night of the weekend."

"I couldn't stand that place. Everyone there looked stuck-up. Or drunk."

"They are. Both. They're stuck-up drunks. But I would like to meet someone. I'm on the dating apps, and they're not really working for me, so once in a while, I try to meet a guy in person. Usually, I don't. But I have gone out on a couple of dates with guys I've met there. Believe it or not."

"I can't believe it. But then I think I stayed in the place for maybe thirty minutes. I don't know, I don't have the patience anymore for partiers. I was married to one for nine years. That'll give you your fill. But you haven't had that happen, so go for it. If it works for you, why not?"

"I'm just keeping my options open. I haven't met anyone yet. But I want to. I want to get married and have a baby. I *really* want a baby or maybe two. So much so that I'm thinking of freezing my eggs just in case I don't meet someone."

Somehow, I wasn't surprised that Lara wanted to have a baby. From the way she interacted with Daniel, it was plain she would make an amazing mother. But freeze her eggs? Now that surprised me. Puzzled, I asked, "Really? Isn't that a painful procedure? And why don't you think you'll meet someone?"

"I haven't so far, and I'm thirty."

"But you're very pretty and genuinely nice. I'm sure you'll meet a great guy soon. Maybe you should try a different club. One where people aren't throwing up on the floor."

"I meet lots of guys who want to sleep with me, but they don't want commitment. And right now, my eggs are still healthy, so it's the perfect time to freeze them, before they start going downhill, along with me. Oh, I don't know, Rachel, with these guys I'm meeting lately, I'm seriously contemplating it. And no, it's not a painful procedure when they take the eggs out. It's called egg retrieval because it's done under light sedation. The hormone treatment to stimulate the body to produce more eggs can cause bloating and be uncomfortable. But not unbearable."

"Have you given any thought as to who the father would be?"

She stared off into space momentarily, placing her hand under her chin and tapping it slowly with her index finger. "Sadly, that part I haven't figured out yet. I could try to find my own donor. Someone who is gorgeous, intelligent, grounded, good-natured, and funny. So let me know if you meet someone like that."

"I'm not sure that guy exists."

"I know, eh? I can use a sperm bank, where the father could be anonymous. Or I can choose one from photos. And they're all supposed to tested for genetic problems and STDs and all that good stuff." She stopped talking then gave her head a shake as if dislodging all the bad images from her mind, then continued, "Ugh, that all sounds wrong, doesn't it? Also scary is I could be lied to, like what happened in Ottawa when that psychotic, egomaniacal fertility doctor used his own sperm to impregnate his patients. So, basically, I haven't got that far in my planning. I'm just thinking of the egg part."

"You're really serious, aren't you? Well, I say go for it. That way if you don't meet someone, and I'm sure you will, you have a backup. And you know what? Probably as soon as you do it, you'll meet a great guy. Because don't things usually happen that way?"

She laughed. "I know, I was thinking that too. If only. But Rachel, I'm so sick of the guys I'm meeting. What about you? Have you met anyone nice lately?"

Because of the age difference, I didn't want to tell her about Marcel. And I couldn't tell her about Justin because that made me look like some dim-witted other woman. But it was Justin who entered my thoughts all the same. It was Justin who had a recurring role in my dreams. I wished things had been different, *he* had been different, and I could say it was him I had met. I hadn't ridded my mind of him yet. Marcel was helping. *Well*, I thought, *I better test the waters*. If I was to make a go of things with Marcel, I couldn't remain fearful of what others thought. And if Lara was going to be as good a friend as I thought she might be, then she wouldn't judge me.

So, here goes nothing. I said sheepishly, "Yeah, I'm sort of seeing this older guy." That sounded confident now, didn't it?

"What do you mean, sort of?"

"I am, I am seeing this older guy. I'm just getting used to it myself. I've never dated someone his age."

"Which is?"

"Fifty-two. But he looks really good, and he seems to adore me and Daniel." At least I hoped he adored or at least liked Daniel. I continued the buildup; I had to make him look good. "He's never been married, believe it or not, so I don't have to contend with an ex-wife."

"Or two, at his age," she interjected. Then laughed, which got me laughing too.

"Fine, you're right. But there are none, and that's the point. And he's successful and established, and I like that. More, I need that from a man. I'm close to thirty too. With a child! Being married to Alex was fun and exciting at first, but then he kept losing all our money gambling, and he'd go clubbing and chasing girls, and I couldn't keep up. I want older and settled. Someone who's able to supply me with some semblance of stability. In fact, he's a professor."

"Okay, I guess I get it, in a way, although I'm not sure I agree. So, how did you meet him?"

Then I remembered how I met him, and suddenly I was embarrassed. I could feel my cheeks getting hot. I'd met him at my father's funeral. He'd hit on me at my own father's funeral and then muddied the waters by sending the sympathy gifts so that while I was coping with everything that had happened, I wouldn't even think about where and how we met. He took the focus away from our meeting. Distracted me with presents. How could I tell Lara where we met? My head was spinning. Had he really used my own father's funeral as an opportunity to meet me? Surely not. No one could be that devious. I put it out of mind, but nevertheless, I answered that he worked with my dad at the university. She assumed I met him there.

"I hear those university professors can be quite the

philanderers. Maybe that was why he never married." Would she never let up?

"Lara, I don't really know. But anyway, I'm just getting to know him. I'll see where it goes. It's not serious." *I just let him give me a car.* That she didn't need to know, either.

I looked over at Daniel and said, "What's up, kiddo? You getting hungry?"

"Yeah, Mommy, can we get McDonalds?"

"Just because I ask you if you're hungry doesn't mean we are getting fast food," I answered, then to Lara I whispered, "I probably will go through the drive-thru at McDonalds or Wendy's. I don't feel like cooking. Unless my mother cooked. Which is highly unlikely."

Sensing that her questions about Marcel were the cause of my sudden wish to depart, Lara interjected, "Don't leave because of me and our conversation. I'm not judging you, Rachel. I'm really not. I like you, and I want to be good friends."

"Don't worry, I didn't think that." Not entirely, at least. I liked her too, and I knew I could really use a friend, so I wasn't going to let anything or anyone spoil that. I replied, "We're honestly getting hungry, so I think we should go. But I had a great time, and Lara, I feel like we're good friends already."

We all got out of the pool and dried off. As I was leaving, Lara's father pulled into the driveway, and I thought for a minute it was Marcel. They looked almost the same. My subconscious was working overtime. I thought maybe I was losing my mind, until Daniel said to me on the way home that Lara's dad looked just like Marcel. *Thanks, kid*, I thought. Because even if Marcel did look old, at least I wasn't losing my mind.

I phoned my mother on the way home to tell her I was thinking of going to "you know where," the code for McDonalds, in case she wanted me to pick her up something. She told me that supper was ready. I drove the roundabout way home so as not to pass McDonalds and cause a meltdown for Daniel, who was now picking up on code and expecting a stop at the drive-through.

When we pulled into the driveway, Marcel's new car was there. I entered the house to find him next to my mother, carrying plates outside to the patio table. They looked so good together, so natural, I was thrown for a loop. However, as much as my mother appeared to be calm, her underlying tension was obvious to me from the way she was chewing her bottom lip.

"Hey," I said to Marcel, "you didn't tell me you were coming over. Oh, and hi, Mom." I walked over and kissed her cheek. I was pissed but not sure why.

"I thought I would surprise you." *Yeah, no kidding*, I thought. *Or check up on me? Find out where I went swimming?* "And I called Deborah and asked her if I could bring supper over for all of you. I tried a new recipe, and it made enough for four, so I thought, why sit here by myself with all this great food when I knew you would be hungry after swimming, and you all could enjoy it with me."

I was starving. I looked over at the patio table and saw several Corning Ware containers. I walked over and opened each one. The smell was heavenly. Whoever said a way to a man's heart was through his stomach should have included women.

Watching me open lids, breath in the aromas, and look over each dish, Marcel said, "I made Mediterranean-style rice, grilled wild salmon, and organic chicken with Greek salad and French green beans with almonds. And I brought our wine." He gave me a wink and a smile, and I was too hungry to argue.

"Daniel, go wash up and I'll put my stuff away and be right back," I said without hesitation.

After a filling and delicious meal, I was clearing the table when a text came in from Lara.

Want to swim again tomorrow? That was fun, and I only

have two more days, then my holidays are over. Sad face emoji.

Not sure. I might have some school stuff to get for Daniel. But I will let you know in the morning. And thanks again, it was fun.

Marcel attempted to appear uninterested in who I was texting, but I could tell it was killing him not knowing, so I took some pity on him and said, "That was my friend Lara. I was swimming at her house today, and she wanted to know if I could come tomorrow."

"Thanks for letting me know," he answered sincerely.

In the garden, the three of us talked while Daniel played with his toy train. My mother asked Marcel if he was ready for the new school year. He answered that he was. She asked if all the same faculty were working; they were. He shared some stories about my dad and his art of teaching. He told my mom that he was always slightly jealous my father's ability to keep his class captivated and that he didn't come close to having his skill.

"But I do admit that although he made it look easy how he handled a classroom, I knew he prepared extensively for his classes and left nothing to chance. Every lunch and spare period he'd spend studying the material and preparing notes to share with the students. I'm much too lazy to do that. I know the stuff, so I teach what I know. I'm not as worried about delivery as he was. And it shows. His students always had a grade lead over mine. But he never bragged. Not once. What a guy. He's going to be missed. Wait till the returning students find out. They'll be mad it wasn't me instead of him." He smiled wryly at us and then said, "I guess I should be heading home now, but thank you so much for letting me share my extra food with you all. The company has been delightful."

My mother was without words at this point. Any reminders of my dad left her speechless, and I could tell she was swallowing back tears. She just said, "You're welcome, Marcel. I think Daniel and I will head upstairs to bed. I'll read to him tonight, Rachel. I need a diversion. You can see Marcel out."

I walked Marcel to the door, and when he opened it to leave, he turned back to me and leaned over and kissed me. I let him. And I didn't hate it. I even kissed him back.

"I really want this to work between us, Rachel."

"I know you do, Marcel. And that would be nice." And why not? I had experienced young, exciting, and poor. And look how that worked out. So why not try the opposite? It could work. I might be seeing him for the wrong reasons, but who has relationships for all the right reasons anyway? Does anyone? Some do, I'm sure, but lots don't. Most don't, I reassured myself. And right then, stability sounded good. And people trash talking didn't really bother me anyway. I was used to it.

He was about to walk away when his face changed. "By the way, and I hope you don't find this too presumptuous of me, but I've looked into getting you into some classes this September. From what I'm hearing, it sounds like a go. If you decide what you want to study."

"No, no, that's fantastic. I have been thinking about school. Thank you, Marcel, I'll go online and look at what is being offered. I don't know if I can decide that quickly, though. But I'll think about it."

"Well, you could always start part-time studies at night."

And that sounded good too, so I said I would look into it, and we made plans for supper the following evening at a restaurant.

"Just me and you this time, okay? Next time we'll take Daniel," Marcel added before saying his final goodbye and walking away. Nice way to ruin a perfect evening.

Fifteen

September is the best month of the year for every parent. They get to say goodbye to their darling child for a few hours a day while the child gets to learn and interact with other kids. Daniel started grade one effortlessly and with exuberance. Arriving at the school, while waiting in the yard he struck up an intense conversation with a little boy named James, who told Daniel about going to his cottage, swimming lessons, and a fight his dog got into. Not to be outdone, Daniel came back with his own exciting tales of his broken arm and going in a sailboat and a squirrel fight in our backyard. Fine, so Daniel was prone to exaggeration, I could see. I'd keep an eye on that. Plus, I'd talk to him later when he was away from his new friend to enforce the fact that a lie is a lie is a lie. We had lived through too many already, his father being a pathological liar. Lying came as easy to him as breathing. I'd have to make sure that I too didn't tell lies, even little white ones, especially around Daniel.

Walking home from school took about five minutes, since it was directly around the block from my mother's house. I heard my phone ring and answered.

"Hey, honey." Yes, Marcel was calling me honey.

"Hey, honey." And yes, I was too. It was official. He was my honey.

"Just wanted to remind you that you need to pick your courses by the end of the week, if you want to start in September."

"Marcel, don't be angry with me, but I can't decide what I want to study. I won't have a decision made by the end of the week."

"No problem, I don't want you to stress over this. Deciding what is right for you is something that can take time. Part-time courses and online courses are also an option. Just start by writing down your goal, your interests, and your strengths. And research the job market. That should help you narrow your search down a bit."

"Okay, that sounds good. You should have seen Daniel today when I dropped him off for his first day of school. He already has a best friend. He was so happy going into the school, his teacher had to remind him to turn around and say goodbye to me."

"That's wonderful. See how easy it is? You could be just like that."

"Ha, ha, ha. Last time I looked, I wasn't six years old."

"Thank goodness for that. Then you really would be a little too young for me." And he laughed.

"I'm not even touching that," I said, not laughing. I didn't appreciate the age difference reminders. I was trying my best to stay in denial.

"Okay, I have to go now. I have a class. I'll call you later. Bye," he said.

On arrival home, I found my mother in the back garden, crouched in a squat with her face buried into her hands, sobbing uncontrollably.

"What's wrong, Mom?" I ran to her side, crouched down, then fell backward onto my behind. Humiliated, though no one saw, I got up and brushed the dirt off my pants. Looking down at her, I couldn't help but admire how flexible she was, crouched, maintaining her balance like that. I guess her morning workouts paid off. Maybe I should start working out too.

My mother's muffled cries brought me back to the situation at hand. I rested my hand on her back. "Mom, what's wrong?"

She stood up, not losing balance or even stretching out stiffened muscles, wiped her eyes with the back of her hand, and said, "I'm just going to miss Tommy, that's all."

Startled, my heart pounded. Firmly but kindly, I answered, "You're going to miss Daniel, Mom, not Tommy. It's only for a few hours a day. He'll be back in no time. And come on, you've got me. I might be your second choice, but I'm not that bad." At that we heard Luna whimpering as if to say, "Me too, you've got me too."

Glancing at Luna, she exclaimed, "Oh, Luna, I haven't forgot about you. Yes, of course, I know I have you." She walked toward a confused Luna, knelt beside her, then wrapped her arms around Luna's neck and cried a little more into her fur. Suddenly, she stood up, brushing the fur from her slacks, and said, "You know what, I haven't had breakfast yet. Maybe that's what's wrong with me. Want to go to the Starving Artist for waffles? My treat."

"I would love to, and what's more, I'll take you up on that offer because I don't have a penny." Both literally and figuratively, seeing as the penny had been taken out of circulation years ago.

I was broke, Alex didn't pay any child support, I had no job, and the Canada Child Benefit I had been receiving left little after paying for the necessities of life. Treats like going to sit-down restaurants were out of the question. And I refused to ask my mother for money. I never had until now and was not about to start. She was graciously allowing Daniel and I live with her for nothing. Plus buying all the food, without complaints. However, I was expecting the complaints at any time. They were overdue, I figured. I needed a job so I could start contributing.

The Starving Artist's morning crowd had every table

occupied. There was a fifteen-minute wait just to be seated. The restaurant had only been open for six months, but it had already earned a reputation for being both delicious and nutritious. Everything served was made on the premises, and even the coffee beans were roasted fresh each day.

Sitting at our table, we watched as our server was run ragged. After about ten minutes more of waiting, we were about to stand up and leave when she approached and handed us our menus, apologizing profusely, explaining that the other server who normally worked the morning shift went into labor early, and they hadn't found her replacement, so she was single-handed. She added, "If you know anyone looking for a waitress job, we're desperate."

"I'm looking for a job," I offered. "And I can start tomorrow. And I have experience."

"Fantastic!" she exclaimed. "That's just fantastic. Would you talk to the owner, Steve, before you leave? He's at the cash. I'm sure he'll be thrilled. We didn't know what we were going to do."

Before leaving, I did talk to Steve, and he really was thrilled. His only requirement was that I wear black pants with a white shirt, if I had one, and if not I could work in pajamas, they were so desperate, he told me. Then he laughed, the relief in his voice palpable. I was to arrive for eight o'clock when the restaurant opened. He told me I would only be needed for three hours. The breakfast rush was over at eleven. That was perfect. Except for getting Daniel to school, which started at nine.

I glanced at Mom, who was standing at my side and not saying a word. Sheepishly, I asked, "Are you okay walking Daniel to school? I'll be done before lunchtime, so I can take care of him after that. I guess I should have checked with you."

Steve said, "Even if you can work until I find someone permanently, it would really help."

My mother pressed her lips together, displeased at being

put on the spot. Steve watched her. I watched her. Finally, she said, "Fine. You can give it a try. I can take care of Daniel in the morning. If it doesn't work out, then you can find a replacement for Rachel."

Marcel, on the other hand, was not as agreeable. After a lovely evening out, while sitting in his car in my driveway, he said, "Why would you want to wait on tables? What happened to going to school? Are you really that short of money?" Hm, which to answer first?

"Yes, I am short of money, and it's just three hours a day and close to home, and I'm not going back to school right now. I thought I told you that." I knew I had told him that. What was his problem?

"I'd rather give you some money to stay home with Daniel than take a job waiting tables. I find that work rather demeaning, Rachel," he said in a condescending tone, as if addressing a child. "What if someone saw you? Someone important, that is. What if they recognized your family and knowing your background thought that perhaps your parents mishandled their finances and now you're forced to work at anything you can find? Rumors could get started, and then think how embarrassed your mother would be."

"Rumors are lies, Marcel. And lies are not worth worrying over. If people are so petty and contrived so as to make up a lie about my family because they see me working as a waitress in a wonderful restaurant, by the way, then who cares? Should I care about people like that? I don't, and what's more, I don't think my mother would either. So maybe it's you who cares. Maybe it's you who thinks waitressing is beneath me because I'm dating you. And it reflects poorly on you. Is that what it really is, Marcel? Because that's what I'm starting to think."

When he didn't have anything to say in reply, I said, "We don't need to continue seeing each other, you know. You could find someone in your station. University-educated. With no children."

I knew that stung. I hadn't brought up Daniel till now, but lately it was becoming increasingly obvious that he would rather exclude Daniel from our plans. We needed to address that.

"No, Rachel, I don't want that. You're amazing. See? You're already teaching me life lessons. I have to stop caring so much what other people. Waitressing is good, honest work. That is as long as you claim your tips. Ha-ha. I think, too, I'm just a little possessive and maybe a little insecure. I would rather you be home than waiting on tables and chancing that you meet someone you like more than me. I don't want to lose you again. Because I love you."

"You don't mean that," I said, completely taken aback.

"I do. One thing that comes from age is self-awareness. And my feelings for you are genuine and powerful. But don't worry, I don't expect you to feel the same way at the moment. I'm going to earn your love."

"I don't know what to say." I sighed so loud, I surprised myself. Could he earn my love? No one had done that. Alex only lost my love, and Justin, oh well, what was there to say about Justin? I supposed I could come to love Marcel. If he loved my son. The big if. So, I confronted him. "What about Daniel? You don't seem to want to have him with us very often. He's fine with my mother, so that's not a problem, leaving him home, and I do think you know that. But if you are serious about us, really serious, and desire a future, Daniel has to be part of it. You need to get to know him."

Marcel nodded and bowed his head contritely then pulled me in for an embrace.

*

Waitressing was more exhausting than I had imagined, partly because I was having trouble falling asleep, even with my homeopathic remedies. And once I fell asleep, my dreams were disturbing and I often woke in a sweat. Repeatedly, I dreamed of being chased by a faceless man while trying to find Daniel. Or walking about in an unfamiliar building, unable to find the exit. So, after four or five hours of sleep I would drag myself out of bed at six to shower and drink some coffee before dressing and heading to the restaurant.

The actual work, however, while physically tiring, was surprisingly refreshing. I loved my customers, who ranged from retired couples playfully bickering and laughing to high school students oblivious to the problems of the world and simply enjoying life. They were my favorite, but I found myself having to hold back my tongue from dispensing sage advice such as "Don't marry young, wait to have kids, and love your mom and dad because you never know when they can disappear from your life." I knew it wouldn't be well received. Why should it? Who was I to them?

When my shift finished, Steve provided free food. Waffles were my usual choice. I avoided bacon and sausages, not for reasons as noble as vegetarianism, but more because I wanted to stay slim and avoid my mother's critical glare if she noted I'd gained a few pounds or increased a dress size. Plus, I was slightly vain. I liked being size six and intended to stay there.

After I ate, I drove over to the school to get my baby boy. I was finding, however, more often than not my mother had beaten me there and would be waiting with the other mothers and grandmothers, chatting away as if there was no tomorrow.

Once, I approached the women to join the conversation, and they all stopped talking. Had I been the topic of conversation? I looked at my mother, who was now turning a shade of purple, and guessed no longer. We stood in silence, waiting for the kids to be let out. A few minutes later they came bursting threw the double doors. Daniel came running out and straight into my mother's outstretched arms. Now it was me who changed color. He didn't even see me.

"Hey, kiddo," I said, and he looked my way. Immediately he ran to me, and I held him tight. I felt tears coming to my eyes and blinked hard to make them stop. I was being ridiculous, I knew, feeling jealous of my son's warm and loving relationship with my mother when I knew I should be grateful that he had someone beside me and Marguerita who loved him like that. After two weeks of arriving at the school to find my mother there ahead of me each day, I decided to let her be the one to get Daniel, as if she needed my permission. When I asked her if she wanted to make the arrangement permanent, she asked what I meant. It was already permanent in her mind.

I told Marcel what was going on. He was delighted. "Now we can have lunch through the week."

"I don't eat lunch. I'm stuffed from all the food I eat at the restaurant at eleven."

"No worries," he said, unfazed. "Just provide some coffee. I need to get away from the institution at lunch for a break. I'll bring my own lunch and just enjoy your exquisite company. Oh, and Daniel's too," he wisely added. I gave him the one raised eyebrow stare, to which he laughed heartily.

By mid-October, our family had fallen into a comfortable routine. I'd come home from work, get changed, make a sandwich for Daniel and a fresh pot of coffee for Marcel. Mom would come in with my baby, and sit by his side while he ate, then they'd play cards and she'd walk him back to school for his afternoon classes. And because Marcel was at our place most days, I couldn't really object, although I wanted to walk Daniel myself.

I felt as though I was shirking my duties toward Daniel.

Additionally, feelings of jealousy regarding Daniel's growing affection for my mother were emerging. I didn't know what to do about it other than insist I at least pick him up after school at the end of the day. I was torn. It was her house, she was letting us live here for nothing, and I had moved in with the intention of helping her work through her grief. Which was working. I just didn't foresee that her replacing me in Daniel's life would turn out to be her grief therapy.

While it was absolutely wonderful that she was getting back to her old self, even if it meant sacrificing my exclusivity to Daniel, there were some days she was what could only be called "off." On those days she possessed somewhat of a forced cheerfulness, quick to laugh and singing nonstop. Additionally, she was calling Daniel "Thomas" more frequently. In fact, it was happening so often, I had stopped correcting her. Daniel seemed oblivious to it, even answering to the name, knowing it meant him. I decided to let it slide but wondered if perhaps she was developing early-onset Alzheimer's or dementia and observed her for any other telltale signs. There were none, and I was grateful but decided to keep an eye on it.

Marguerita was becoming part of our lives as well. My mother visited her at least one evening per week, and she was dropping by our place regularly. At first there seemed to be a rivalry between the two grandmothers, but soon they adjusted to the role and enjoyed Daniel equally.

In addition, happily, Marcel was growing on me. He really was, and in a good way. Not in a smothering way a weed grows over a young seedling, choking its life. He was fitting into my life. When he arrived at lunch, he'd have a coffee while looking over students' work and preparing his own. And fifteen minutes before he'd head back, and we would sit in the garden and talk. He was interested in my life and wanted me to share what had happened at work or home. He shared what he thought interested me. Also, he was trying more with Daniel, asking him how his day was and what he did in school. He usually had us over on Saturdays. On good weather days, we went out in his boat, or sometimes we just hung out at his house, cooked together, then watched Disney movies in the evening.

Sunday evenings were kept for just the two of us, and we would go for a quiet, romantic dinner at a restaurant. Sometimes we tried new restaurants, but usually we went to his favorite, which was quite good.

On a cold and damp Sunday evening early November, we entered the restaurant, where the maître'd greeted us both, then turned to Marcel and said, "I have the chef's table reserved for you, as you requested, Mr. Mancy. Please follow me."

We walked back to a private area in the restaurant near the kitchen.

"This is different," I said. "What made you decide to reserve this table?"

"Oh, I had read about doing this. That way we have privacy, and we can watch as the head chef prepares our food. And he has promised to come out to answer any questions we may have about our meal."

"Well, you're the foodie. I'm just the eater. If it is cooked for me, that's enough to make me happy. No questions asked," I said, picking up my water for a sip.

"You're so funny. Well, you never know, you might just think of a question or two."

Our wine was placed on our table, and after Marcel approved it, the waiter poured us both a glass. As usual, it was excellent. As it should be, being one of the most expensive wines on the menu. Yes, I was getting a taste for fine red wine.

Next, the food arrived, our appetizers.

"Did you want to ask the chef a question about the food?" Marcel asked me.

I shook my head. I was busy eating, and I couldn't think of one question. All I knew was that it tasted pretty good. Marcel, on the other hand, waved the chef over.

He walked over, wiping his hands on his apron, smiling. "Yes, sir. How can I help you?"

"I just wanted to know if these prawns are the antibiotic-free ones that a grown right here in Ontario?" The chef assured him they were. "I thought they might be. They are excellent."

Then our entrees arrived, first Marcel's, and when my entree was about to be placed in front of me, Marcel said, "Before you chow down on this meal, Rachel, I want you to give particular attention to the presentation."

It was lovely, as always, and delicious. Marcel once more called over the chef to ask questions, this time about the lamb. Was it New Zealand or Ontario? And he wanted to know what herb he was tasting in the potato. And the carrot? Was it sautéed or baked? Did it really matter? But Marcel seemed to bask in the individual attention, although I was sensing a bit of annoyance on the part of the chef.

Before the dessert arrived, Marcel had me close my eyes.

"This dessert is going to blow you away. It is as gorgeous to behold as it is as tasty to eat. Okay, Rachel, you can open them now."

And on my plate was a tiny piece of cheesecake with a diamond ring on top. The words *Will You Marry Me* were written in chocolate sauce on the outside of the plate.

I looked at Marcel to see a huge smile, and from the kitchen the chef looked on curiously.

In shock, I waited a moment to answer, but then said, "I don't know what to say. I wasn't expecting this, and I'm really not sure what I want to do, Marcel."

He looked a little disappointed, his lower lip dropping into a pout. He said, "That is no problem. At all. Whatsoever. In fact, it's exactly what I expect from you and what I admire about you. I know you always are diligent and carefully plan for the future." Did I? That was news to me. But if I appeared that way, all the better.

He continued, "I understand if you want to wait to give me an answer, Rachel. I do. I just want you to know that I've never loved anybody like I love you."

I said nothing, but I did raise my eyebrows in concern. I had a hard time believing him, and as if reading my mind, he said in a hushed tone, "Rachel, I'm well aware of my reputation. I know I was a player. But I've finally found the one who completes me, as corny as that sounds. I mean, I found you, and now that you've come into my life, I see myself staying with you and only you for the rest of my life." A tear appeared in his right eye.

I could say I was completely taken by surprise by his proposal, but I would be lying. Lately, he had been hinting at making our relationship permanent, but I assumed he was going to ask me to move in with him. However, he had been very respectful of me up till now; we hadn't slept together, and he hadn't forced it. I wanted to wait, and although disappointed, Marcel was cool with it, telling me I mattered too much to him to mess things up by insisting on his own way. I was convinced his womanizing was a thing of the past. Making him wait was a great test. At this point in my life, what I wanted most for myself and Daniel was security, and I think Marcel knew it.

At home, an issue had arisen, causing me a new level of anxiety, making the idea of moving even more appealing. It was Daniel's growing dependence on my mother, together with her newfound strangeness. I needed to move out of her house and make a separate life for myself and my son. The sooner the better, both for her good and ours. What I needed at this point of my life was a good marriage, with no surprises. So I gave Marcel the answer he desired.

"I'd love to marry you, Marcel. I think you can give Daniel and me a wonderful life. And I will try to give you a wonderful life too."

He was elated, calling over the chef and anyone else who walked by for a high-five. It was very sweet. He told me he wanted to get married on New Year's Eve, and although it was close, I agreed. I knew it was for the tax credit. And I was fine with it. I was not deluded. Marcel was an intelligent, successful, and wealthy man. He became that way for a reason. Saving taxes included.

"Just one thing," I told him. "I'm not going to wear the ring right away. There are a few people I want to tell first so they can hear it from me before seeing the ring. In case you're wondering why I'm not putting it on. I think it's better that way." He was fine with that.

That evening, after I returned home and put Daniel to bed, I went downstairs to give my mother the news.

"Mom, I have something to tell you. Marcel and I are getting married New Year's Eve, and you're invited."

"You're joking, right?"

"Yes, I am joking that you're invited. You don't need an invitation. But no, I am not joking about getting married. He asked me to marry him, and I said yes."

"Why would you do that? He's so much older than you, Rachel. And I'll admit, he seems to have settled down a bit, but he's not the man for you. He is just not the man for you. I think you'll be making a mistake. Another mistake. Is that what you want?"

"Yes, that's exactly what I want, Mom. I want to make a mistake," I said sarcastically.

"I don't care if you don't want to hear what I have to say. I do not approve of this marriage."

"Mom, he's admitted to me that he was a womanizer but

has assured me that's in the past. I know he's older, but I am starting to love him too. We get along so well. And mostly I need someone for Daniel that won't uproot us like Alex did. You don't know what we lived through because I never told you. It was a nightmare. We never had any money. Alex couldn't keep a job for more than six months. And there were other things that I'd rather not talk about."

"Okay, I understand things were bad. And I'm sorry I wasn't there for you. I really am. Maybe if we had been talking, we could have helped your marriage. But I know that man you are planning to marry. Your dad told me enough about him. I find it hard to believe he will change. And what's more, he's getting what he always wanted anyway: someone much younger to control and make him look good."

"Mom, I need to make my own life. And I want to make it with him. You're so much better now than when Dad first died. I wasn't planning to stay here indefinitely with Daniel. It was temporary, to help you. And me too. And you helped a lot. But Daniel and I need to go."

"You think Daniel will want to go? He's been through so many changes in his short life. I think he is quite happy here. So don't speak for Daniel. It's what *you* want. And frankly, I'm not sure why."

"So that's it? You hate me now? Again? I just can't please you, can I? Mom, I need to make my own life. It's as simple as that. But I want you in my life this time. I need you. Okay? Will you do that? Will you stay in my life?"

"Well, I couldn't bear to let Daniel go," she answered coldly.

"But me? You could let me go?"

"Don't go there. This is not about you and me. I think you are making a terrible mistake. I can't approve of it. But I'm here for you. I won't abandon you again. Because you were here for me these last few months. I'm not sure I would have survived without you."

My mom took hold of the back of a kitchen chair and leaned forward. I thought she was going to fall, so I guided her to sit down. She placed her head on her arms folded on the table and started sobbing. I didn't try to stop her. I plugged the kettle in, got out two mugs, and put in herbal tea bags. The tea was made in a few minutes, and I placed her cup in front of her and sat in the opposite chair. Eventually she stopped crying and lifted her head to find a tea placed in front of her. She sniffed the air.

"Is this peppermint? I hate peppermint tea," she said, and we both started laughing.

When our laughing subsided and we had a few sips, I said, "Oh, and Mom, I'm not telling Daniel right away, okay? I think it's best to wait. I'm not sure how he'll handle the news, so I'd like to give it a bit of time."

My mother raised an eyebrow in a look that said so much. But she agreed. A little too exuberantly. In fact, she absolutely lit up and then suggested that Daniel not move with me at all. That I let him stay with her to finish his school year and then come in the summer.

"Absolutely not!" I told her. "That is six months, and I am not living without him for six months. And it's not as if he would have a setback changing schools. He's in grade one, for goodness' sake."

"Well, then, why wait to tell him? What are you scared of? That he will say he doesn't want to move? Again?" She was being quite smug.

"Of course he'll say that! I'm expecting that reaction. All children hate changes. But I am his mother. And I will do what is best for him."

"And that's what's best for Daniel, is it? Were you really thinking of what's best for him? Somehow, I don't think you were. In fact, I don't think it is best for either of you." Her tone softened, and she continued. "Rachel, I'm trying to let it go, I am, but truthfully, I just don't get it. Honestly, I'm gobsmacked. But I said I'll support you, and I won't go back on my word. I just hope and pray you change your mind."

"Don't count on it. And hoping and praying I change my mind isn't exactly the support I need. Can't you just try to be happy for me? Please? He's a good man. And I'll have stability. I need that." I reached across the table and took her hands, looked her in the eyes, and added, "I know what I am doing this time."

She didn't reply for a long moment. Her shoulders drooped, and suddenly she looked very tired. I felt ashamed of doing this to her. Then she said, "I sincerely hope you do. And don't worry, I won't tell Daniel. My lips are sealed." She made the hand zipping across her lip gesture, and I thanked her and we said our goodnights.

In my room, I was about to turn out my lamp when I received a text from Lara.

Can you come over tomorrow eve for a visit? I have something to show you.

I replied that I would see her at seven, then turned out my light, exhausted and ready to sleep. Of all things to do, arguing was my least favorite and always left me completely spent.

*

Breezing solo from my house at six forty-five the following evening, I suddenly and sadly realized my built-in babysitting service was soon going to come to an end. As much as Marcel enjoyed Daniel, he might resent being viewed as a babysitter. I bit my bottom lip and repeated over and over in my head, *I will not change my mind.*

Lara met me at the door, excited. She grasped my hand and pulled me up the stairs to her room.

What I could see of it looked beautiful, but mostly it was strewn with clothes. Clothes covered every surface, her bed, desk, armchair, and almost every square foot of space on the floor. However, they were not random. Clothes were sorted by color, item, and season. I stood at the door and crossed my arms at my chest.

"That is a lot of clothes. Having a purge, I see."

She raised her arms in a cheer. "Yes! I am finally doing it! Purging! I've been listening to decluttering podcasts, and I'm finally ready. *And* not only am I getting rid of excess clothes, I have also promised myself not to shop for a year. I'm feeling really guilty about my carbon footprint from all my consuming. I know it probably won't make more than a tiny dent on the environmental issue, but I need to do my part. Plus, it'll help me save money, which I'll need when and if I ever find a decent place to rent. Oh, by the way, I've saved you a spot over there to sit." She pointed to the only clothes-free spot on the floor, where there was barely enough room to sit with my legs pulled up and crossed.

Lara continued, "So here's what I have in mind. I have sorted my clothes by category. Winter, summer, sweaters, pants, dresses, etc. In that pile, for instance," she pointed to one on her bed, "I have five red sweaters. I want to pick one to keep. Just one. Or maybe two. No, no one! One, one, one."

I laughed. "Let me know when you finish arguing with yourself."

She placed her hands on the side of her head and screamed. "Argh! This is so hard. And that's why you are here. I need you to help me pick. One. Only one, okay? And anything I don't pick, if you like it, you can keep it. How does that sound?"

At this point, her mother peeked her head in the room and asked if everything was all right because she had heard Lara yelling. Lara assured her we were fine, and when her mom had left, we laughed till we almost cried.

"Okay, sounds good to me," I answered after our laughter died down.

"And be firm with me. Imagine you are dealing with Daniel. Even if I have a tantrum, stomp my feet, and throw myself on the floor, you can't give in and let me keep more than one from each category."

"Okay, deal. But, by the way, Daniel has never done that. Not once," I answered, slightly insulted that she would think that of him.

"Oh, I thought all kids had tantrums." I assured her they did not. "Thank God," she said. "I saw a kid have a major meltdown today at the drug store, and the mother was helpless. She couldn't stop him. Just had to drag him by his coat out the door. Made me have second thoughts about wanting a kid. Ever. I even thought that maybe I won't have to freeze those eggs after all."

"Nope, not all kids. You're good. But no promises. Yours might be the biggest brat of them all," I retorted.

"Probably would be. Let's get started. I have a feeling this is going to be a long process." She walked over to the pile of red sweaters and momentarily stood, head resting in hand, staring down at them.

Sorting through the clothes went much smoother than Lara had anticipated. Some of the clothes were so old, I swore I remembered seeing her wear them high school; they were dated, out of style, and very easy to say goodbye to. Others had fabric that was slightly shabby, worn, and pilling, and a few had stains. Those ones, too, were easy to discard. I found a few items I liked, including a turquoise cashmere sweater that was just too good to give away to charity. The rest she packed away in three green garbage bags and put them in her car to drop off the next day. Oh, and she did keep not two but three black sweaters, no tantrum necessary, because they were gorgeous and a girl can never have too many black sweaters.

We were sitting on the edge of her bed. Lara was looking around, satisfied with the accomplishment. Noticing the time, close to ten, I told her I would get going. Lara convinced me otherwise by offering a glass of wine.

"I would love one."

Lara poured us a red wine, made a platter of cheese and crackers, and we made our way to the living room sofa. The house was quiet. Her parents got up before 6:00 a.m., so they were already in bed, Lara said. She flicked the switch to the gas fireplace, and we sat in silence, watching the flames.

Lara broke the silence, declaring, "I love modern conveniences. Imagine the days when a fire would mean chopping a tree, hauling wood home, stacking it, and then having to start the fire and fuelling it all the time just to keep it going. Oh, and not to mention cleaning the fireplace afterward. To have the exact same thing that we have right here. Isn't this great?"

"I suppose." But truthfully, I love a real fire, complete with crackling, popping, and sparks. But I didn't want to tell her that, because I was working up the courage to talk about something else. To help, I took a deep breath then spoke. "I have some news to share."

"Good or bad?"

"Good. Really good," I answered enthusiastically. "I'm getting married."

"To whom?"

Was she serious? She had to be putting me on. But the look on her face said she was indeed serious and had no idea.

"To Marcel. On New Year's Eve. And I would like you to be my maid of honor. If you would do me that honor."

She didn't answer right away, just sat looking at me quizzically. Was she waiting for me to say I was joking? Or what?

Getting peeved at her hesitancy, I said, "You're keeping me

in suspense. What's the problem? I know it's New Year's Eve, and you might want to go to a party, but that's why I'm asking you now so you don't make other plans. And I promise you the reception is going to be a great party. We can dance, and I'll be having an open bar. But mostly it would mean so much to me if you would say yes. I'm only having one bridesmaid. And that is you, if you'll do it. Plus I'll pay for the dress, any one you want, or at least Marcel will, so you won't have to break your no shopping pledge."

She still didn't say a word, so, sighing audibly, I added, "Please, Lara, you're my best friend." She really was, and it felt good to say it. Not like I was going to go out and buy matching Best Friend Forever bracelets. But I loved acknowledging it to her and myself.

"You're my best friend too, Rachel. Wow, aren't we getting mushy?"

We both laughed. Lara picked up a piece of cheese, placed it on a cracker, and took a bite. After she finished eating it, she continued, "I just don't know what to say, Rachel. To tell you the truth, I'm kind of in shock. New Year's is so soon. I didn't even think you were still seeing him. You never talk about him."

"I know we're so comfortable together. He feels like someone I've been with forever, so I guess I haven't really been mentioning him much," I admitted. "But he's so generous. Did I tell you he gave me his old BMW?"

"Yes, Rachel, I saw your car. And you had told me. Is that why you are marrying him? Because he is generous and gave you a car?"

I felt myself getting hot with anger. I replied tartly, "Of course not. I love him."

"Really?" she asked as if in disbelief. "I don't get it. Why are you marrying him? He is so much older than you. Remember how you told me that I'll meet the right guy? I feel the same is true for you. And I don't think that guy is Marcel. I'm sorry, Rachel, I'm just a little shocked."

"Fine, forget I even asked you." Yes, I was getting my back up, but I was tired of being criticized for my decision, first by my mother and now my friend. I was marrying a man who loved me and would treat me the way I needed to be treated. He would be my security. And not just mine, but Daniel's as well. And I did love him. Maybe not the same way I loved Alex or even Justin, but I loved him enough to feel confident that I was making the right decision. And after that evening at the club and watching those guys my age, I wasn't so sure there were any perfect guys out there capable or mature enough to take on an instant family. Maybe for Lara, but for me? Not necessarily.

"I'm going to get going," I said and stood up, brought my glass to the kitchen, and made my way the front door.

"No, no wait," she pleaded. "I've hurt you. I can see that. Sometimes I can be so insensitive. Being an only child has made me that way. I'm kind of spoiled. At least, that's my excuse, and I'm sticking with it. But for you, I'll do it. I would love to be your maid of honor. It would be my privilege. But there is something I want from you."

I brightened a bit. "What's that?"

"I'd like to see how he is around family. My family, if he is going to become part of our lives. And Daniel. I want to see how he is with Daniel. So, can you all come for dinner next Saturday evening? I know my folks are around then, so it would work. And your mom is invited too."

"What if he doesn't pass your test? Are you going to change your mind?" I asked suspiciously.

"No. I give you my word. Unless you make me wear fluffy a pink dress."

We said goodnight, and I drove home happy.

*

Considering that I was becoming an expert in defending my decision to marry Marcel, I decided I would visit the last person I expected would give me a hard time and get it over with: Marguerita. I made arrangements for the following evening and told her I was coming over by myself.

I walked into her house through the only way I knew, the back door that opened into her kitchen. She was at her usual spot, the kitchen sink, washing dishes. I automatically picked up the tea towel and started drying. I had done this so many times in the years I was married to her son that it was second nature. Everything seemed familiar. It felt comforting and reassuring at the same time.

"So, what is so important that you made a trip to see me all by yourself?" she asked in her kind and inviting tone.

"I need your advice," I said. *I need your advice?* Had I really said that? I didn't want her advice. I wanted to let her know my news. Or did I? I opened that can of worms, had a Freudian slip, and decided to go with it. It might work. Maybe if I presented the news this way, as if asking her opinion, the outcome might be different. Maybe I wouldn't have to fight for what I wanted to do. Maybe she would tell me I was making a good decision and she was behind me 100 percent.

"Shoot," she told me. "I'm total ears." *All ears.* Well, she had the right idea, even if she got the wording wrong. I didn't correct her. I wasn't there for that.

"I had a marriage proposal."

"That's wonderful. I'm not surprised. And what is wrong? Are you not sure what to do?"

"No, I'm sure of what to do. I said yes, and the wedding is planned for New Year's Eve. The problem is that everyone thinks I'm making a mistake, because he's a lot older than me."

"And what about you? Do you think you might be making a mistake?"

"No, I don't, Marguerita. I'm confident in my decision. But how can I get everyone on my side? And you, especially, I need you on my side too. How can I get everyone to believe I am capable of making sound decisions?"

"I am not going to second-guess you, my love. You are the most mature, responsible young woman I know, and if you say that you are marrying a good man that will love you and my little grandson, then I believe you. And I am on your side."

"Really, just like that? You're not going to ask me to change my mind, wait for the right guy my age, or give it more time?"

"Not at all. In fact, I never told you, but my husband was twenty years older than me. And I loved him very much. Until he got a girlfriend in the house across the street from ours. Then I didn't love him so much. In fact, I tried to kill him one night."

"Really? You've never told me that. What happened?"

"I don't tell too many people that story. It is something that I try to forget. My sister remembers and tries to remind me all the time, though." She started laughing.

"Okay, this sounds too good. You have to let me know what you did."

"Okay, okay. Well, he came in the house after walking back across the street from her house and sat down at the kitchen table, plopped his feet on the chair in front of him and said, 'Where is my supper?' It was a nightmare back then. He felt no guilt at what he was doing and didn't care that I knew and that all the neighbors knew. He thought it was his right to sleep with whomever he wanted. Even our boys were aware of it. Although they were small, they knew all the same. We were always fighting, and he drank so much. Anyway, he was sitting there with his dirty boots up on the chair in front of him, drinking a beer, his back to me. I picked up the large cast iron frying pan and was about to hit him over the head with it when my little David walked into the room and saw what I was about to do and screamed. My husband turned around to see the frying pan held in my hands like I was holding a baseball bat, and he jumped up so fast, his beer went flying to the floor. He grabbed the frying pan out of my hands, threw it on the floor, called me *loca* and a few other words that I would rather not repeat, and then walked out the door and across the street back to his girlfriends. That very evening, I put my plans in motion to leave him, and two weeks later the boys and I were gone. Six months after that we came to Canada."

"Wow, that's quite the story."

"Yes, but not a nice one. So, you see, you married my young son, and he was a cheat, I married an older man, and he was a cheat. There are no guarantees. Age is not what makes a person who they are. However, an older man should know better. So, all in all, I am behind whatever you choose to do. What does Daniel think of him?" She pulled the plug from the sink, and we stood watching as the sudsy water drained away.

I answered, "He likes him. He took us sailing, which Daniel was crazy about. I know my mom already told you that he is a professor at the university, so he should be a good influence on Daniel. He's already teaching him chess." Well, they played once. Just a little stretch of the truth couldn't hurt. And besides, I knew they would play all the time once we were living together as a family.

"Well, then, he sounds wonderful, and I am very happy for you. And I will keep the date," she told me happily.

I threw my arms around her and hugged her tightly. I loved that woman!

Everyone that needed to know the news now knew, so when I went home that evening, I took the engagement ring from my jewelry box and put it on my finger. It was official.

Sixteen

Early Saturday evening rolled around. I was in the fourth outfit I had tried on; my makeup was perfect, and I was ready to go to Lara's for dinner with her family. I walked into Daniel's room to help him pick some clean clothes to change into plus have a little discussion with him. He wanted to wear his Spider-Man shirt with track pants, and I attempted to make him change his mind. We compromised by keeping the shirt but wearing nice corduroy trousers instead. I was applying product in his hair to make it curly when I said I had something to tell him.

"Daniel, we are going over to Lara's house tonight for supper because it's kind of a special occasion. They invited you and Grandma and me to come, *and* they invited Marcel. And that's because it's a celebration of something special that involves our family. But not Grandma. Just you and me and Marcel. We are going to be our own family soon and live at his house. He has asked me to marry him and wants us to live there. And I said yes."

"Is that why you are wearing that ring? Did he give you it?" How astute my little man was. He never failed to amaze me.

"Why, yes! You noticed. Do you like it?"

"It's nice. But Mommy, why didn't you ask me if I wanted to live at his house?" he asked. His big eyes staring at me filled with disappointment.

My heart ached for him. "I don't know, Daniel. I didn't think of asking you, honey. But don't worry, it will be wonderful. He loves you very much." I hoped. But I wasn't too concerned if he didn't, which I suspected was the case. He would come to love him in time. How could he not?

"Do we have to move? Won't Grandma be sad?" My angel had developed such empathy. I took him in my arms and squeezed him tight.

"We won't let her be sad. We'll visit all the time. And you can come and stay with her some weekends if you like. She will be fine. I wouldn't leave her if I didn't think so. And we can pick all new things for your new room. It will be exciting."

"Can I get a bed that looks like a car?" he asked, brightening a bit. And as easily as that, he was appeased. *Thank goodness*, I thought.

"I don't see why not. Now let's go downstairs and wait for Marcel. He should be here any minute."

*

We pulled into Lara's driveway, and Marcel jumped out to open the door for my mother first, then he opened mine. She smiled reluctantly at the chivalrous act. He'd win her over yet. We waited together at the front door, his arm on my waist while my hand rested on Daniel's shoulder and his hand held my mother's. What a picture of family bliss we must have made. Lara opened the door and gestured with her hand, imploring us to come on in. The house was surprisingly dark, but as soon as we entered, lights came on and we heard a thundering "Surprise!"

A banner hung from the two walls of the entrance to the dining room that said *Congratulations Marcel and Rachel*, and streamers and wedding ornaments were everywhere. I felt my face turning red, and Marcel looked equally as surprised and put on the spot. I turned to my mom and asked, "Did you know about this?" She just shook her head. Daniel was ecstatic, his eyes circling the room, taking it all in. And his joy increased even more when he saw Marguerita standing among our friends and relatives. He ran to her side and threw his arms around her waist.

I looked around the room and saw many familiar and some not so familiar faces. There was my Aunt Giselle and my former brothers-in-law. That was, indeed, a surprise. I never imagined they would support me moving on with anyone after Alex. I supposed they must have had a genuine affection for me after all. There were Candice and Sophie with one of the guys from the club. Many other people that I did not know at all were among the group, Marcel's friends and family. He was waving over at a few and laughing heartily. He took me by the hand and said, "C'mon, I need you to meet a few people.

"One minute, all right? I just want to thank Lara. I'll be right back."

I found Lara in the kitchen, arranging food on plates and opening bottles of wine. Her back was to me, so I snuck up from behind and wrapped my arms around her. She turned around and hugged me back. I'd never had a friend like her before.

"When did you decide to do this?" I asked. "I thought we were just coming for supper. You're quite the sneak, aren't you?"

"Right after you left the other night. I thought, who is going to throw my best friend an engagement party? Why, me, of course. So, I got busy and looked up names and got numbers and lots of people were on Facebook, and everyone was available. It being November helped because people generally don't have that much going on, so everyone said they could come. And your Aunt Giselle and Marguerita insisted on helping me with food, so, along with my mother, we managed to pull it together."

"Your mother helped you too?" I could feel tears coming to

my eyes. "She hardly knows me." I was overwhelmed.

"Oh, stop it! She knows that I love you, and that's enough for her. You'd do the same for me."

"I would and I will when you are engaged. No matter what. Even if you moved to Australia, I would go there just to make an engagement party for you. And I love you too. I know it sounds cliché, but you're the best!" I threw my arms around her again, and tears were flowing now. I heard her sniffling close to my ear.

She held me at arm's length and said, "Go out there! Everyone is here for you. Oh, you and Marcel too." She gave me a wink.

I walked up to Marcel, who was engaged in conversation with a woman who, it turned out, was his sister, Nadine. She wore a very low-cut blouse and extremely tight jeans. I was surprised someone her age dressed that way. However, she was warm and friendly and hugged me while welcoming me to the family. She excused herself to get a glass of wine, and Marcel whispered in my ear that she was on the prowl. "She's been like that since she was fourteen. Getting worse lately. I think she's having a midlife crisis. Wants to be fourteen again."

"That's mean," I said. He shrugged.

"Look," he said, pointing to a table in the corner that was covered in gifts. In the middle of the table was a box that contained envelopes.

"Oh, my goodness," I exclaimed. "Gifts! How lovely. Now, I'm truly blown away. I really wasn't expecting gifts."

We made the rounds, and Marcel introduced me to his friends and family, and I did the same for him. He was very gracious to Lara's friends and charmed them with his wit. Even Marguerita and her sons laughed at everything he said. And he was equally as interested in them. Giselle and my mom were by a wall, talking about their trip and discussing where they would go the following year but stopped to engage in conversation with Marcel and me. I couldn't help but think he looked like the perfect match for my aunt and wondered if anyone else was thinking the same thing, watching them side-by-side, laughing away.

"Marcel, I think I'll go find Daniel and get some food. Is that okay?"

"Of course. I'll get something in a bit." He kissed my cheek and as I walked away patted my behind, much to my chagrin. I turned around, and he gave me his devilish grin and a wink, and I smiled back. Reluctantly. My fiancé! *Oh dear,* I thought.

In the kitchen beside the food table were some chairs. On two of them were Daniel and Marguerita, eating and chatting away in animated conversation. I grabbed some food and sat beside them.

"Wow, this is quite the discussion you're having. What's so exciting?"

"I was just telling Daniel about growing up in Ecuador and all the interesting things I did as a child."

"Lita played hopscotch. And I told her we have a hopscotch at school too. And they played a game with marbles. One kid would have to shoot another kid's marble out of the way. Can we get marbles, Mommy?" He was very excited.

"You betcha. I can look on Amazon and find some. Or, better still, I'll try to find a local store that sells them. Should we bring them over next time we visit Lita so you and she can play? How does that sound, Lita?"

"Sounds perfect." She turned to Daniel. "But be prepared to be beaten. I never let anyone win. I don't care how little or cute they are or even how much I love them." With that she gave his cheek a playful pinch and said, "You will only beat me when you get good enough."

"Oh, I'll be better than you, fast. I'm going to practice lots and lots at home," he said, deadpan. She laughed so hard, I thought she might choke on her food. She drank some water and laughed some more.

"Okay, you two, I better get out there and socialize. After all, it is my party."

"And Marcel's," Daniel reminded me. I stood, kissed him on the top of his head, and re-entered the party.

I stopped to talk with Candice and Sophie and her boyfriend, who I found out was Tavi. "Hey, Candice and Sophie, I never got a chance to apologize for leaving like I did that night, so I want to do that now, okay?"

Candice spoke first. "You don't have to do that. We were a little bit worried at first, but then Lara saw the text that you had left, so we were good. That was a long time ago. Congratulations, by the way." She leaned over and gave me a hug and a brush on my cheek with her lips.

"Yes, congratulations. You found a marrying type. One in a million. Even if he is an older guy." Sophie looked at Tavi and asked, "Am I going to have to wait that long for you to want to get married? I'll be an old woman by then."

"Twenty years? Should be about right. Unless I've dumped your ass before then," he answered.

The conversation was going in a direction I didn't care for, so I scanned the room, looking for Marcel. I spotted him across the room, closer to the front hallway, and was about to make my way toward him when I realized it wasn't Marcel I was looking at. It was Lara's father, my fiancé's twin. I was marrying my best friend's father's twin. Suddenly, my mistake threw me so much that I got lightheaded. I found the couch and sat beside a couple of people I didn't know but assumed were Marcel's friends.

It was a man and his wife who were indeed Marcel's oldest friends and had known him since high school, thirty years ago. The man started telling me some of their antics and how Marcel had dated his wife's cousin until she moved to the States. He named some of the concerts they attended together, and none of the bands or the songs were familiar. It was another generation.

Soon, they excused themselves, stating that they weren't used to staying up late and were going to head home. It was only 10:00 p.m. I thanked them for coming. I didn't get up to see them out. I was numb and began to feel slightly nauseous. What was I getting myself into? Was ten o'clock going to be a late night out once we were married and settled in?

Suddenly, Marcel was beside me, plopping himself down so fast, his feet flew up in the air. He was wearing a grin from cheek to cheek and was obviously having the time of his life. I wished I could have said the same. Oblivious to my somewhat subdued and sullen mood, he asked, "Having a good time?" If he had looked at my face before asking, he would have had his answer.

I turned my head to look at him directly. "Do you think it's late, Marcel? Do you want to get going?" I was not smiling.

The smile left his face and was replaced by a look of concern. "No, of course not. Unless you want to go. Are you not feeling well? We can go if you like, but I think we are expected to look at gifts."

A wave of relief came over me. Sometimes I really could get ahead of myself. "Well, let's do it," I answered.

*

As a rule, Sunday mornings I designated as time for Daniel and me. We customarily took Luna for a nice long walk and then played a game when we got home. He was especially chatty the morning after my engagement party.

"I had a good time at your party, Mommy. I ate so many of the little sausages, and I had three pieces of cake. And Lara gave me all the pieces with the flowers on them when I asked for them. But they didn't really taste that good. I thought they would be the best part, but they were kind of yucky. I didn't spit them out, though. Because you told me not to do that, remember? You said it was rude to spit out food when we're eating out. So, I ate them, but they weren't very good."

"I'm very proud of you for remembering not to spit out food and for eating something you didn't really like. And now you know not to ask for the flower pieces, don't you? And you were very good last night, even though there were no kids for you to play with. You are becoming very mature."

He screwed up his face as if I had just insulted him. "No, I am not."

I laughed and answered, "That's a good thing, Daniel. It means you're growing up."

"Oh! Yeah, I am!" he exclaimed and then took a branch from the ground and smacked Luna on the backside.

"Hey! Don't do that to the dog! Now, *that* was not mature!" I said, and we both laughed. Believing it was the smack to Luna that had drawn a laugh, he attempted another one before I grabbed the stick and threw it away. He had just turned all of six years old, after all. What did I expect? Then he spat on the ground. Fast and direct, rather impressive, although still gross, like I have seen many men do so many times before. And I've hated it each time.

"Who taught you that?"

"No one. I just like doing it," he answered sincerely.

"Well, stop it. It's disgusting," I answered bluntly. He pouted but didn't spit again.

Marcel and I were going to send our thank-you cards that afternoon, and I stopped at a stationery store to pick some up to bring to his house. Lara had recorded the names of each person and the gift they gave us, so I was good to go. I was not going to be one of those people who send out thank-you cards six months after the event. I thought that rather gauche. Why bother sending a thank-you at all? The following week was perfect.

Marcel had all the gifts and money on his dining room table, and I gave each a thoughtful and careful examination. I wanted every note to be personal and from the heart. I looked to see what the gift told me about the person who bought it and the message it spoke. I remembered times I bought gifts for people and the thought that would go into each one, and even though they may not have been exactly what the person wanted, I had hoped they would love or at least like it. On the table before me were high-quality bedding sets and one matching cotton bathrobe set. A few people had given us artwork, and many had gifted us of bottles of expensive wine, Marcel's love and hobby. On top of that were gift cards and, of course, cash in envelopes. I had my work cut out.

I was about to start writing and had decided to practice a few on scrap paper before using the actual cards first. I wrote:

Marcel and I would like to thank you very much for attending our engagement party, especially on such short notice. The wine looks delicious, and we can't wait to try it with our first dinner we eat together as a married couple. We are looking forward to seeing you at the wedding.

Something like that, I thought. I read it over and decided to ask Marcel if he had something to add.

"Yes, honey, I have something I've been thinking about that I'd like to discuss with you." He had been sitting on his couch and glanced up from his tablet.

"In the thank-you cards, I mean. Do you have something to add to the thank-you cards? Something coming just from you?" I swore he could be so daft sometimes.

"No, you go ahead. I'm sure they will be perfect. We can talk later. I have to do some papers. We can talk over dinner."

The cards took all afternoon, and thankfully I had bought enough. On our way to the restaurant, we stopped at a mailbox to make the drop. Our favorite restaurant was very quiet, and we were seated immediately. I wasn't particularly hungry, so I just ordered an appetizer and a salad, and we both had wine.

Marcel had a coffee in front of him and was nervously tapping his fingers on the table. Whatever he wanted to discuss was causing him some discomfort, so I decided to make it easier for him. "Okay, honey, what was it you wanted to talk about?"

"Firstly, Rachel, I want to tell you that I love you very much and have never been happier in my life."

"Okay? That's good to hear, but I'm sure that's not what you wanted to talk about. Spit it out. I'm all ears." I hated stalling tactics. Daniel used them all the time. I didn't appreciate them from a grown man.

"Next summer after the school year ends, there are two consulting positions I'm interested in pursuing. Problem is, they require a great deal of preparation before I will even be considered to be put in the running. And that is in addition to my other obligations. So, after the wedding I will be putting my nose to the grindstone, so to speak, and will be working long hours with a lot of concentration required."

"That's okay, I guess, Daniel will keep me busy. I don't need constant company." I smiled at him.

"That's what I wanted to talk to you about. I will need to have complete silence around me when I am working. So, here is what I am proposing. And hear me out before you answer. I think Daniel should stay at your mother's house and finish the school year before moving in with us. By then, I'll have all my work done, and then I won't require quiet around the house. I know what boys are like, Rachel; I was one myself. They have lots of energy and need to burn it off. Winter months being stuck in the house and my need for absolute quiet are not good combinations for a little boy with high energy. And I talked to your mother. She loves the idea. Plus, he doesn't have to change schools halfway through the year." He crossed his arms and smiled as if he was the most brilliant man alive. I, on the other hand, was livid.

"When would I see him? And you already talked to my mother about it? What else have you done behind my back?" I stopped talking and took a couple of deep breaths to regain my composure before continuing. "Marcel, I need my son. I need to be with my son. Why are you springing this on me now? If you had told me that before I said I would marry you, it would have changed everything." I spoke as calmly as I could, although my anger was accelerating quickly. However, I tried to stay quiet to avoid a scene.

"Because I just found out about them last week. Thursday, to be exact. Both on the same day. They will mean a lot of money for us if I land even one of the positions. And after this, I won't apply for any more consulting positions till Daniel is grown and moved out. You have my word."

I was speechless, so he continued. "And you won't need to work once we are married, so you can take him to school in the morning if you like, and that way you can see him every day. And Friday after school, he can come back to our place and stay till Monday morning. So, it's just a few days through the week he will be with your mother, and for just a few months. I promise, Rachel."

I felt myself starting to cry, so Marcel took my hands. I snatched them away from him. I took some tissue from my purse and wiped the tears away. I didn't even want to look at him. I turned my head to the side and was about to get up and go somewhere. Anywhere, the bathroom, the lobby, anywhere but at this table with him. I turned from the table when I felt his hand on me, pulling me back.

"Don't go." I looked at him, and his eyes, too, were filled with tears.

I sat back down and handed him a tissue. After a long moment, he spoke again. "I know this is a crummy thing to spring on you, and I would say I'm sorry I didn't tell you before you said yes to me, but I'm glad you said yes and that this was not a deal-breaker. I promise you with all my heart it will just be a few months, and the weekends will be for all of us. I will not do any preparation work for the consulting positions on the weekend. Please, sweetheart, please."

"This is a lot to ask of me, Marcel. I can't answer you now. I'll tell you tomorrow. Right now, I need to go home."

My mother was playing euchre on her iPad when I got home. She looked up and announced that she was through with that game for the day. Then she added, "How was your day?"

"Why didn't you tell me that Marcel had talked to you about Daniel staying here? Don't you think that is something I would have liked to have been warned about?" I answered angrily.

"Because it wasn't my place to tell you. It was all his idea, so he was the one who needed to tell you. I did tell Marcel that it was unfair to spring this on you and that he shouldn't be surprised if you called the whole thing off. I also told him I was good with whatever you decided, because I am. And you know that. You don't have to marry him at all. You can both stay here as long as you want."

"Wouldn't you like that? To be right again," I retorted.

"No, I would not. Look, Rachel, it's up to you. But I love having Daniel around, I'm not going to deny that. A few more months probably won't destroy him either. It might even be good. Not as disruptive as changing schools and all. But if you can't do it, you can't do it. Only you can decide."

I sat on the living room chair, buried my head in my hands, and rocked back and forth. I felt a headache coming on. "I know that, Mom. Tomorrow, I'll decide tomorrow." I walked over to her on the couch, wrapped my arms around her, and rested my head on her shoulder. We sat together in silence. After a little while I kissed her on the cheek and said goodnight.

That night I looked at the ceiling for a good two hours before finally falling asleep, and when I did the bad dreams were consistent and unrelenting. The first dream was sometime after my wedding, and I had left Daniel with my mother. I arrived to pick him up for school, but he wasn't there. My mother said that he had walked by himself because he didn't want to wait for me, so after yelling at her for letting a little boy walk by himself, I drove off, frantically looking for him, to no avail. I was screaming his name when I woke up. It took a while to fall back asleep, and then the second bad dream started. I was telling Lara about Marcel's plan, and she said, "I told you so. I hated him from the moment I saw him. He's evil." And then she just kept repeating, "He's evil." I started shaking her and pleading with her to stop saying that, but she only laughed maniacally. That dream left me breathless.

The last dream of the night was of Marcel. A good and kindhearted Marcel. And a much younger version. He appeared as I had seen him in earlier photos. He reassured me that we were in it for life, and I felt a wave of love wash over me such as I had never felt before. He told me how much he loved Daniel and was sorry he had to ask this of me. We were in his living room, and he had the fireplace going. He knelt down in front of me, took my hands in his, and said, "We'll all be together after this. We'll be the happiest darn family you have ever seen. I give you my word, my love."

And Daniel was there too. And he was saying, "It's fine, Mommy. Don't be sad. I'll keep Grandma company, and then in the summer we'll be together."

I looked at him and asked, "Are you sure?" And he was nodding when I woke up.

And that last dream helped me decide. I would ask Daniel how he felt about the idea. I would know immediately if he was being truthful. If he showed any hesitation toward the idea, any at all, I would quash it. And Marcel could take us both or not at all.

The following evening, after we ate dinner and had cleared the table, we worked on Daniel's homework. He finished coloring the pictures that accompanied his spelling words and was putting his stuff in his backpack when I told him I had something important I wished to discuss with him. He told me he wanted to hang up his backpack in the hallway first so he wouldn't forget and not know where it was in the morning. I said that was a good idea.

Daniel pulled out the kitchen chair across from mine and sitting, hands clasped at his lap, said, "Yes, Mommy?" So grown-up. So serious. I just loved that sweet little boy. I could eat him up. I walked to his chair, crouched down to be at his level, and wrapped my arms around his tiny frame. After a good squeeze, I released him, and looking him in the eye, I laid it all out for him.

When I had finished, he waited a moment before asking, "You're going to come with me to school every morning?"

I nodded and said, "Absolutely."

"And every weekend we'll be at Marcel's?"

"Yes, but it won't be just Marcel's house; it will our house too."

"I don't mind, Mommy," he answered cheerily.

"Are you sure?"

"Yes, Mommy, I'm sure. But I have a question."

"Okay, anything. What, sweetie?"

"Grandma made chocolate chip cookies today and said I could have two after supper if it was okay with you. Is that okay, Mommy?"

"Only if I can give you another giant squeeze."

The following morning, I gave my notice at the café and was taken slightly aback when instead of looking disappointed at my announcement, Steve looked relieved. He even let out an audible sigh.

"Good news, is it? My notice?" I asked, miffed.

"No, no, no!" He laughed. "I'm so sorry. This is not what it seems. Cheyenne called me this morning and asked if she can come back early. Her husband was laid off and can stay with the baby, so she asked if I had a position for her. And stupid me, said yes. But I didn't! Until now. I was racking my brain trying to figure out what I could get her to do. And how I would pay her."

"Oh, well, I guess that's better. I thought you were happy I was leaving."

"Never! You have been ideal. The customers love you. We all love you. I wish I had a position for you both. I'm really going to miss you. So, *now* I can digest that you are quitting. Can I ask you why? Did you get another job? Are you moving? Why would you ever want to leave the best job in the world?"

"I'm getting married. New Year's Eve. In fact, I want to give you an invitation." And I pulled it out of my purse and handed it to him. He beamed then pulled me into an enormous bear hug.

Releasing me, he exclaimed, "To tell you the truth, I did notice that ring but didn't want to stick my nose where it didn't belong and ask you. Well, that is wonderful news. And I wouldn't miss it for the world."

Marcel was at the house at lunch, but this time instead of going into the house to wait with my mother, he was sitting in his car, waiting for me to come home first. I pulled in the driveway, and as soon as I stopped the car he hopped out of his and sprinted over to open my car door. I stepped out and didn't say a word. I could tell he was nervous. As he should be. I was enjoying watching him squirm. He followed me to the front door, but before I could put the key in the lock, he put his hand on my shoulder and asked me to wait. I turned around to face him.

"I need to know your decision, Rachel. If you don't want to

see me again, I want to say my goodbye to you now. I'm afraid of how I might react if that is the case, and I'll just leave quietly if this is goodbye. But I hope it is not."

I hesitated a moment before answering. There was a lump in my throat, and I had a hard time speaking. I took a couple of deep breaths and said, "It's not, Marcel. We'll make it work. I'm in this for good. And Daniel said he doesn't mind staying with my mother. That was the deciding factor — how he felt about it. But you're really killing me making me stay away from my baby for half the week." And I felt defeated. My shoulders literally slumped.

"You've made me the happiest man in the world. It will work, and watch and see how fast these few months fly by." He pulled me into a warm embrace and kissed me so intensely, it made me forget what we had been talking about. Until we pulled apart.

I looked him in the eye while poking him in the shoulder with my index finger. "You're going to owe me. Big-time."

Seventeen

The last day at work was depressing. I had become close to many of my customers and coworkers, and I really didn't want to say goodbye. So, my intention was to avoid the drama and tears, which would be coming mostly from me, and not to say a word about leaving. However, when I entered the café, on the wall behind the cash register where the food pickup window was located a sign hung that said *Goodbye Rachel – We Will Miss You*. I cried the moment I saw it.

I punched Steve on the arm and said, "Why did you do that? You big softie. Now you know all the customers will ask me about leaving, and I'll be crying all morning."

"Oh, don't get emotional around me. I did it because it makes me look good. And it will be good for business if people think I really care."

"Oh, right, because you don't care, of course." I hugged him tightly and then went to the hooks in the back to find my apron and put it on for the last time. It I hugged too before putting it on. *Oh, my goodness, I thought, this has to stop or I'll be hugging the cups of coffee before I bring them to the table.*

The first couple I served were Ralph and Nadine, who came in every morning at eight thirty after they completed their five-kilometer walk. Rain or shine, sleet or snow, they walked. They were in their late seventies and looked ten years younger. They told me that it was the walking that did it. From the day they both retired at age sixty-five, they never missed a day of walking.

"We intend to enjoy our retirement. And if our health is bad, that won't be possible." Ralph and Nadine explained that they kept healthy by "eating clean," lots of grains and fruits and vegetables, no refined sugars, and very little meat or dairy. Except their coffee with real cream, the one treat they allowed themselves each day.

Ralph gestured toward the empty chair at their table for me to sit down, and since they were the only customers in the restaurant, and I wasn't needed elsewhere, I did indeed take a seat.

"So, little lady," he said. "I hear you are going off and getting married and leaving us. You never asked my permission."

"Or mine," echoed Nadine.

"Oh dear, didn't I? I distinctly remember asking your permission to get married. Okay, I'm asking now then. Do I have your permission?"

"Yes, you do. But only if the guy is good enough for you. Is he good enough for you? Tell me honestly." Ralph stared at me intently. In jest, I believed.

"He is, Ralph." I looked over at Nadine and said, "He is, Nadine. I promise you both. He teaches at the university. He's a wonderful man."

"Okay, then, that sounds fine. But most importantly, does he cook?" Nadine asked jokingly.

"Believe it or not, he does! Which I am so happy about. He loves cooking, and that is perfect because I hate it. But I don't mind helping in the preparation part, chopping veggies or the tidying-up part. So we really are a match in that department."

"Well, that sounds good," said Ralph. "As long as he treats you well, because if he doesn't, you just come and find me. I might be in my seventies, but I'm fit for my age, and I could give him a good working over if he needs one. And Steve over there would help me."

I was laughing now and put my hand on his arm. "I don't think that will be needed, but thanks for the offer anyway. Tell me one thing, though, and while you are having your coffee you can think it over. What would you say makes a strong marriage? You two certainly have one, and I want to have what you both have. Maybe you could write it out for me, and then I could keep it and read it when I need to. I'll go get you a paper."

"We will do that," said Nadine. I brought a paper and then got busy serving the new customers that entered the café.

The rest of the regulars said the usual congratulations, and a few asked for my address because they wished to send me a wedding card. Some asked for email address so they could email me their best wishes.

The high-school students who came about 10:20 were for the most part indifferent, exactly as I would have been at their age. One group that entered was made up of three girls and one boy. He had an acoustic guitar and played it softly while the three girls looked at their phones. As he played, he often glanced across at a girl with medium-length sandy brown hair and high cheekbones. Across the bridge of her delicate nose were tiny freckles, and when she looked back, she flashed a perfunctory smile. He played for her, and she played on her phone. I felt like snatching that stupid phone from her and screaming, "Listen to him, you idiot. He's playing for you. This may never happen again. Possibly ever!"

Instead, I told him his playing was wonderful and to keep it up. "Maybe you will be famous one day, Canada's next Shawn Mendes, and I'll see you at the Grammys," I said sincerely. Even if the girl with the freckles on her nose didn't appreciate his talent, I certainly did, along with all the other customers.

At 11:00 a.m. I hung up my apron and gave Steve a big hug, then Sandy the cashier and Mo, our cook. I cried all the way home.

*

Two weeks before the wedding, Lara arranged for my girls' night out or stagette or whatever they call that thing that is supposed to happen before a woman gets married. She ordered a massive oversized limousine to hold me and six other girls. Of course, Candice and Sophie came along, as well as a few other girls I knew from high school. Not that well, but well enough to help fill a limousine and round out the party number.

I was the last person to be picked up and stepped into the limousine to see six very pretty and well-dressed young women waiting for me to enter. They cheered when I walked in, and my face reddened. I sat in the chosen seat while Lara walked over to me and cloaked me with mauve sash that read *Bride to Be*. She put on her sash *Maid of Honor* and handed the others sashes that read P*arty Animal, The Flirt, Selfie Addict, Hot Mess*, and *Miss Behaving*. Each of us sashed up, and Lara opened a cooler and took out a bottle of Champagne. The first drink of many was poured, and Lara knocked on the glass to give instructions to our driver to depart for our first destination, A Cocktail Class. I knew this would be a night to remember, or not remember, more than likely. Three cocktails in, Lara tipped our very funny instructor, and we exited a little unsteadily into the limousine and to our final destination, The Club Saturn.

We jumped the queue for the very popular nightclub after Lara explained to the extremely large and muscular bouncer who we were and that we had reserved a table with bottle service. The club had its usual lineup mostly of guys looking slightly impatient and anxious. Some made perfunctory catcalls as we walked by. One yelled out, "Hey, Miss Behaving, want to misbehave with me?" She waved her finger at him in a tch-tch gesture, and my three drinks and one glass of Champagne had me thinking that was the funniest thing I had ever seen. I too waved my finger at him.

Lara looked over at me and said, "I think I'll be keeping a close eye on you tonight."

"And me, you!" I practically yelled at her while pointing my finger into her forehead and laughing hysterically.

We made our way through the dancing and swaying crowd to our table, and the first bottle of vodka arrived with little shot glasses. I had two shots and then threw my arms around Lara and kissed her sloppily on the cheek, exclaiming enthusiastically that she was the best friend I ever had. That was the last thing I remembered from that evening.

The next morning, I awoke on my bed fully clothed with my head pounding. Daniel was standing above me, just staring. I sat up slowly and looked around. The clock beside my bed read 11:37. I hadn't slept that late since high school.

"Hey, honey," I said.

"Hi. Mommy. Are you okay? I was worried about you, so I watched to make sure you would wake up and that you wouldn't die."

"Oh, sweetie, I'm not going to die." Although I kind of wished I would. Or at least sleep another ten hours until I didn't feel like death. "Okay," I said as I swung my legs over the bed. "Daniel, I'm going to go in the shower, so go downstairs and see Grandma now, please. Tell her I'm up and will be down shortly. Would you do that, please?"

I stayed in the shower, alternating the hot and cold water until I thought I would be able to put on a brave face that said all was good and that I was myself and hadn't been totally drunk out of my mind the night before. I wondered how Alex operated hung over so often and for so many years. I had never felt so rotten in my life and vowed I would never let that happen again. It just wasn't worth it. I didn't even remember the evening. Was it good? Did I have fun? I was dying to talk to Lara and ask her how it was. I hoped they all had a good time. After all, it was my celebration. Some host I was.

I walked into the kitchen, unnoticed, to find my mother doting on Daniel, the two of them lost in their own little world, planning their next trip to the zoo. I sensed that I was already invisible, as if already gone. I was miserable. On top of a first-class hangover, this was the last thing I needed, to be inconsequential to my own son. I went back to bed.

An hour or so later, my mother called me, announcing I had a visitor at the door. I sent her a text to come upstairs, since I was not going to yell back and forth with her, but I did wish to know who it was.

"Would you like to have a seat in the living room, and I'm sure Rachel will be right down. She needs my help with something for a moment," I heard my mother say.

A woman's voice said, "Thank you very much." At least I knew my visitor was female.

I was sitting at the edge of my bed, my head bent over and resting on my outstretched legs, trying to get rid of my headache, when my mother came in.

She coughed to get my attention. "You look like death," she said when I looked up.

"Thanks, and I feel like it too. Who is down there? I'm not in any shape for visitors today. Why did you ask her in?"

"She told she met you once before and has some important information for you. She said her name is Angeline. I told her no at first and asked her to give me her number so you could call her, but she insisted and promised she wouldn't stay long."

"Okay, thanks, at least you tried. I have no idea who this person is. I have never met anyone named Angeline. But if she came here personally to tell me something, I guess I better go see what it is." I sighed deeply and asked my mom to tell her I would be right down. I stood very slowly.

The moment I saw her sitting on our sofa, I recognized her. The Angeline from the restaurant who was so distraught talking to Marcel. This time she didn't look distraught, or disturbed, or anything else. She looked poised and in control.

"Hello, Angeline, what can I do for you?" I did not exchange any pleasantries with her, although I attempted not to sound too annoyed. I knew exactly why she had come: to warn me not to marry Marcel. What else could it be? To give me her best wishes?

"Hello, Rachel. Thank you for seeing me. I know you weren't expecting me, and this won't take long." She stood from the couch and walked over, reaching out to shake hands. After I shook her hand, I gestured back to the couch. She sat down while I sat across from her on the chair. Daniel walked into the room and bashfully said hello. He was always shy around pretty women. And she was, indeed, more than pretty; she was beautiful, with her long black hair and almond-shaped eyes. Most striking was her perfectly shaped lips painted in the boldest red I had ever seen. She pulled it off marvelously. She looked like a supermodel or a movie star. Even I was starting to feel a bit shy, sitting there in track pants and an old t-shirt, no makeup. I knew that I looked my worst. All I could think was, *Marcel dumped her?*

"Daniel, this is Angeline. She has come here to talk with me for a few minutes. Would you please go see Grandma in the kitchen and leave us alone? It's important."

"Okay, Mommy. Bye, Angeline." He left the room, and I called to him not to try to listen, knowing how much he loved eavesdropping. Then I sent my mother a text asking her to make sure both of them allowed me some privacy and did not listen in. She responded with an emoji of a sassy tongue-protruding funny face. I giggled.

"He's sweet," said Angeline. "Marcel is good with him?" she asked, sounding incredulous.

"Of course." I wasn't going to disclose anything to her. "What did you come to tell me, Angeline?" I wanted her to get to the point and then leave.

"I found out about your upcoming marriage to Marcel. Someone posted it on Facebook. I wasn't going to come and see you, but I felt compelled to. I know you probably won't believe me, but regardless, I want to warn you about him."

"I don't want to hear anything from you. I have no way of knowing if what you say is truthful or out of jealousy. So, you're right, I am not going to believe anything you say. You might as well save your breath. I'm getting married in two weeks, and nothing is going to change that."

Then, as if she hadn't heard me, she said, "I quit university after he was done with me. I couldn't bear to go back in that building again and see him. He did a number on me. After he discarded me like a dirty old tissue, I stayed in bed for three weeks and only got up to drink water or eat a piece of toast. He gave me no explanation for any of it. No one deserves to be treated the way he treated me."

"I don't want to hear this, Angeline. I'm sorry it didn't work out for you, but that's not my problem. I'm good. People break up all the time. Listen to all the sad love songs. You just went through your own breakup, and it was hard on you. I understand."

"No, I don't think you do. I think you *will*, unfortunately. Then you'll remember that I came to warn you. But it will be too late."

"Well, thank you anyway for your concern."

"Let me just tell you one more thing. Rachel, I am not a man-hater or anything like that. I love men and everything to do with romance. I don't like to go very long without being in a relationship, but I would never, ever, get involved with Marcel again, even if he was the last man on Earth. That may sound clichéd, but whoever coined that said it for a reason, and I am saying it now because I mean it. I would rather go down to my deathbed a celibate nun than ever let that man near me again."

"Great, that's nice. Thanks for coming. I think you should go now." I stayed sitting as she walked out the door. After she left, I was unable to move as if I was glued to my seat. I squeezed my eyes shut because my headache had morphed into something fierce. And now I was pissed off to boot. Daniel peeked around the corner at me.

"Mommy, she's gone now. Can I come and sit with you?"

"Sure, baby, sure." I held my arms out, and he climbed on my lap and we sat together, rocking back and forth. Why did that stupid woman come to see me? I wished to rock away all my foreboding. I had told her I was good, but in reality I was not. I feared I was rushing headlong into a category five hurricane with nothing more than a cheap umbrella. I was counting on the hurricane to veer off course. And yet I did not change my mind. I told myself everything would work out. I convinced myself that I just getting cold feet, prewedding jitters, and that Angeline was nothing more than jealous. In less than two weeks I was getting married, no matter what.

Everything would be fine.

Eighteen

New Year's Eve Day was extremely cold but sunny and dry. Considering many of our guests had made a lengthy drive to attend, it was a relief that driving conditions remained good. We may have had half the guests for our wedding had it snowed. The makeup artist and hairstylist arrived at my house at 8:00 a.m. My mother was scheduled to be first, followed by me, then Lara. All the while, the photographer was snapping away. I was sitting on a kitchen chair having my makeup applied when my mother walked by me. I did a double-take. She had never looked so beautiful. She was exquisite. Her eye makeup made her green eyes stand out like never before, and her hair was in a perfect French roll. Lara attempted a whistled catcall. Daniel mimicked her. Mom blushed.

Sitting as still as I possibly could in order not to be burned by a hot curling iron, I said, "Mom, you look beautiful. Dad would be so proud of you if he were here."

"He never liked makeup, but I agree, Rachel, I think he would have been proud of me. Want to hear something funny? When I saw how lovely I turned out, I actually thought wait till your dad sees me. Sometimes I forget he's not here."

She looked like she was about to cry until, thankfully, Daniel took her hand and said, "You look really nice, Grandma."

Then she hugged him tight and said, "Okay, little man, are you ready to put on your new suit?"

That was close, I thought. We really didn't have time to fix her makeup all over again if she messed it up by crying.

When each of us were finished our makeup and hair and had our wedding clothes on, we called the limousine to be picked up. Lara kept repeating how nervous she was and asking me why I was so cool and collected.

"Well, this isn't the first time for me, you know," I answered jokingly and gave her a wink.

"C'mon. Be serious! You must be nervous. You're getting married. Your life is about to change. You'll be somebody's wife. I'll probably hardly ever see you."

"Lara, having Daniel was the biggest change in my life. I don't think my life is going to be so different now. Marcel is so easygoing. We can still hang out all the time. He has so much to keep him busy, he'll be glad I have other things to do. Just you wait and see."

The photographer captured one last picture of us all together in my mother's living room, then we left the house.

Our wedding ceremony, conducted by a nondenominational minister, was held in the same venue as the reception. The hall looked spectacular. Marcel had hired a wedding planning company that had overseen many exceptional weddings of the who's who in our city, including the son of the mayor of Toronto and the granddaughter of the original principal ballerina of the Toronto International Ballet. He didn't go wrong.

The evening was flawless. Marcel had found a band that was adept at playing any song requested of it, and because I told him that my former mother-in-law was Latin American, he also made sure they were able to play salsa, merengue, and cumbia. When at around 11:00 p.m. the band started playing the Latin rhythms, Marguerita's date, a man I did not know but who seemed quite pleasant, took Marguerita by the hand to the dance floor, where they expertly executed the moves and steps that make Latin dance so exciting. No one dared to step onto the dance floor until they had finished and the music reverted back to the songs everyone had grown up with and knew like the backs of their hands.

At midnight, my mother approached me with my tired Daniel by her side and told me she was going to take him home. He was rubbing his eyes. I felt a lump form in my throat as I pulled him in for an embrace. I didn't want to let go but finally lowered my hands. I felt as if I was losing him forever. Tears were stinging my eyes.

"Marcel and I will be away for a week, but as soon as I get back, I'm going to come and see you. And I'll send you an email every day when I'm away. So make sure you ask Grandma to check her emails for you. And the first weekend you are over at our new house, you're going to be so happy when you see all the toys Marcel bought for you. You won't have to bring any. We have new LEGO sets and so much more. We can play all day. We'll have so much fun." I embraced him again and didn't let go until my mother said they needed to leave.

I didn't talk to Marcel on the way home; the lump in my throat kept getting in my way. He didn't seem to mind. We walked into the dark and quiet house in silence. No Luna to greet us and no Daniel chattering away. I thought of him at my mother's without me, and my anger at Marcel flared.

"I don't understand why Daniel can't live with us!" I erupted like a volcano. I was distraught. I had never spent one night away from my little boy before.

Unfazed, Marcel simply answered, "Rachel, we discussed it all before. Maybe when you mature, you'll be able to see reason." Did he just say what I thought he said? He did, indeed, and was now at his Scotch, pouring himself a drink.

"Well, that was certainly unkind and uncalled for. So, you think I am immature?"

"Not exactly, but I do think there is a level of maturity that comes with age. And you are just not there yet. I am not finding fault with you; it is only normal to think as a twenty-nine-year-old when one is that age. I was no different at your age, and one day you will realize that and come to the same conclusion. And, Rachel, you agreed to the arrangement, so I don't know why we are even discussing it. At all. Tonight, especially."

He walked over and wrapped his arms around me, and I tried to put our conversation out of my mind. But I couldn't, and once again found myself on the brink of tears. He kissed me passionately, oblivious to the fact it was not being reciprocated. We walked upstairs to our bedroom and made love, after which I cried myself to sleep.

So, to say our marriage got off to rocky start would be an understatement. Our honeymoon did have its high points; we stayed at a five-plus-star resort in Cancun, and Marcel was waited on hand and foot, as he wished. Witnessing how quickly he adapted to being treated like royalty was certainly an eye-opener. However, he was gracious, pleasant, and kidded around with the staff, especially the pretty girls, and he tipped generously, so he was well liked. He was in his element.

On the last day of our honeymoon, a group of guys in their twenties checked in. Sitting with Marcel under an umbrella by the pool in our lounge chairs, I noticed one of them kept glancing at me. Marcel had his face buried in the last of the four novels he'd brought and didn't even notice. And the guy was good-looking. Very good-looking. I tried not to look back. I mean, I was on my honeymoon! With the man I loved and was married to, for better or worse till death do us part. How could another guy even attract my attention? Never in all the years I was married to Alex had I found another man the least bit attractive. I became rattled and decided to go somewhere else.

"Marcel, I'm going to go to the gift shops to see if I can find something to bring to everyone at home. Do you want to come with me?"

"No, I'm going to stay down here. But you go ahead. Take my credit card." He pulled out the card from his phone cover and handed it to me. "Actually, I think I'll lie out in the sun for a bit and enjoy these rays before we have to go back to the cold. Could you put some more sunscreen on me please, Rachel?" He dragged his chair from beneath the umbrella into the direct sun and lay on his stomach, arms stretched overhead.

After he was sufficiently covered with sunscreen and had ordered another beer from the waiter, I put on my bathing suit cover and headed over to the shops. I was standing in front of the postcard stand, reading the captions, when someone behind me said hello. I jumped.

"Sorry, I didn't mean to scare you. I'm always doing that to people." It was the guy from the pool. The guy I had been trying to get away from. And he looked even better up close. I sensed my face turning red.

"Yeah, you shouldn't sneak up on people like that. But it's okay, I think my heart has returned to normal now."

He laughed, held out his hand, and introduced himself as Anthony from Texas.

"So, how is this place? We just got in this morning. How's the disco?"

"It's pretty dead, but the food is great and the beach is fantastic, and I understand the bars downtown are where everyone goes to party."

"Yeah, I think my friends have that planned for tomorrow night. Tonight, we're just hanging around. What about you?" I knew where this conversation was heading, so I lifted my left hand to his eye level and reached for a postcard so he could see my wedding ring. I achieved the desired result. He got the point.

"That man at the beach your husband?"

"That he is. Six days now."

"I was hoping he was your father. So, do you fool around?"

"Ha, ha, ha, I don't think so. Enjoy the rest of your vacation." I beelined out of the shop, even more rattled than before, and went back to our room, where I stayed for an hour. When I got back to the pool, I was relieved to find the guy was gone. I picked up one of the poorly written novels I had brought but hadn't finished and didn't look up until we left the pool. The next day we flew home, and, thankfully, I never saw Anthony from Texas again.

*

Just four weeks into our marriage, Marcel began to show his true colors. I discovered he possessed a very bad temper that flared up easily and with no warning.

"Rachel!" he yelled upon entering the house. I was in the kitchen and heard him perfectly. Yelling was completely unnecessary. Unless it was. Had something horrible occurred? I hurried to the front hall.

"What? Did something happen?" I asked him with concern.

"Yes, this world has become filled with imbeciles. What month are we in?"

"Don't you know? February. Why?"

"Is February fall?" he demanded.

"Of course not. Where are you going with this? What's wrong?" Now I was getting annoyed.

"Everyday on my drive back from work I see a sign on the side of the highway that says *Fall Sale*. Every damn day! And every day I think, don't they know it isn't fall anymore? In fact, it's almost spring. And nobody has the brains enough to go out to the sign and take some of those changeable letters and correct them. It's not rocket science. The stupidity of people!" And with that, he walked into his office, slamming the door on the way. I shook my head. What kind of childish tantrum was that?

At supper, Marcel remained sulky and silent. Finally, I spoke up. It was ridiculous. "Are you still angry about the sign on the road?"

"Yes, that and other things, Rachel, including the new department head and my new schedule. Oh, and to top it off, the Tesla got a recall notice today. So, I guess you could say I'm peeved about a few things. That was just the topper."

"Well, at least it's Thursday, and you only have one more day till the weekend. And Daniel will be here to brighten things up. You have to admit, his cheerfulness is contagious."

"If you say so," he replied while cutting his chicken cutlet.

"You don't say so? He's a joy. The happiest little boy I have every known, despite the fact that he doesn't live with his own mother for more than half the week. How do you think you would have felt if you hadn't seen your mother for half of every week when you were little? Or how your own mother would have felt being separated from you."

With that, he placed his knife and fork on his plate, stood up, and walked out of the room into his office and closed the door behind him. When he came to bed that night, he never spoke a word to me. His silence lasted through the weekend. Daniel, sensing the tension, attempted to lighten the mood. He built LEGO cars and houses and presented them to Marcel as an appeasement. Marcel took them from him dutifully without so much as a thank-you. The third time it happened, I told Daniel to put on his coat because we were going out.

Sitting in the car, I got out my phone and texted Lara. *Are you around? Care for a visit from Daniel and me?*

She responded immediately to come right over. It had snowed throughout the day, and I found myself driving on unplowed roads. It took twice as long as it normally would have, and on our way we passed one car accident, then a car that had driven into a ditch. It was a bit of a nail-biter, but Daniel, oblivious to the road conditions, kept me from panicking by chattering away about his new friend at school. Finally, we pulled into the driveway and then made our way to the front door in what was now a full-blown blizzard. No sooner had we rung the bell than Lara opened it as if she had been standing there waiting for us the whole time.

"Get in here. What a day. I can't believe you drove in this, but I'm glad you did, I'm so bored. If I have to look at Instagram or Facebook one more time, I'll slit my wrists," Lara exclaimed.

"Well then, it was worth the drive, if I saved your life."

We took off our snowy coats and boots, walking past the living room where Lara's parents were watching TV. Daniel and I said hello and then we went to the basement to hang out. When we got comfortable, I asked Lara if she could give Daniel her iPad with headphones so that we could talk in privacy without him listening in. She raised an eyebrow at me in concern but agreed and went off to get her iPad. When I had set Daniel up with his favorite movie, *Dumbo*, and I made sure he couldn't hear me by calling his name a couple of times, I turned to Lara, grabbed her forearm, and said, "Help."

"What's wrong?"

"Oh God, Lara, I think I've made a huge mistake marrying Marcel." And then I was crying.

I stole a quick glance in Daniel's direction, but he was engrossed in his movie and didn't notice. However, I wiped away the tears and pulled myself together. I couldn't have him see me like that. He already sensed problems, but I didn't want him to worry. He had been through so much already in his short life.

"It's a new marriage, Rachel. Maybe you two are just having difficulty adjusting. I've heard that's quite common. You just need to work out the bugs," she said reassuringly.

"I thought so at first, but now I don't know. He's changed so much. He's so different now. But I guess I didn't really know him. I don't know what I was thinking. But the Marcel when we were dating is not the same Marcel I have now. He gets angry so easily, and about the most trivial things, and then he just stops talking to me for days. I feel so lonely living with him. And I don't dare tell my mom, because she tried to talk me out of it. I'm really stuck."

"Have you told him how you feel?"

"He knows how he makes me feel. He can see me crying, but it doesn't seem to affect him in the least. It's like I'm not even there. Like I'm invisible to him."

"You need to have a talk, whether you think he knows or not. Let him know how his giving you the silent treatment makes you feel. Maybe you can get him to go to counseling with you. If he won't tell you why he's acting so badly, maybe he would tell a professional what's at the root of this. Like you said, you don't really know him. You thought he would be a great husband, but he obviously has issues that make him act the way he does, and if he talked to someone it could help."

"I have to do something. It might help. Lara, I didn't tell you, but a woman he used to be involved with came over to my house to try to warn me about him. And of course, I didn't listen. The day after our night out."

"And I didn't tell you that night, you were so drunk, and you started crying and asking me if I thought you were making a mistake."

I buried my face in my hands and groaned. "And here I thought I was going to make my life easier, and now it's a huge mess."

"Just try suggesting to him that you both attend counseling; that way he won't take it as a personal attack. It's worth a try."

I felt a little unburdened and encouraged by our conversation. "Yeah, maybe you're right. But do you want to hear the worst thing of all? He doesn't even do any cooking. He said he loves cooking but lets me do it all. And I hate cooking!"

"Oh, you didn't tell me that! Well, I would divorce him for sure." We both laughed. Which felt great.

"Can we go over and try out that pool table over there?" I asked. We spent the next few hours playing pool, and Daniel ditched his movie as soon as he saw us there. We explained the basics, and next thing I knew he was beating both of us. It didn't take much to beat me, since I was terrible, but Lara was quite good. Well, needless to say, Lara was amazed, as was I, but mostly I was proud and made a mental note to myself to get him a pool table.

We made our way out of the basement around nine, and as soon as I looked out the window, I knew that driving anywhere was going to be impossible. Another foot of snow had fallen, and my car was buried. The road was not even visible. But did it look beautiful! Absolutely breathtaking. Lara offered to make up the guest room, and I gladly accepted.

I was debating whether or not to let Marcel know my plans. I wasn't sure he cared. He didn't ask where I was going when I left and in fact had not said more than two words to me the entire day. My phone sounded a text.

Where are you? I'm worried.

That's a turn, I thought. **Well, good.** He should be worried about me. If he wasn't worried, I would be really concerned. In spite of my anger, I found myself smiling.

I'm at Lara's. We are going to stay the night because the roads aren't drivable, I answered.

Good thinking. The roads should be cleared by the morning, so you will be able to come back safe. I love you and I miss you. And I'm sorry. No sad-face emoji. Thank goodness. This was not emoji territory. There was nothing emoji-like happening between us. We were way past that.

Yes, I'll see you in the morning. Goodnight.

When Daniel and I returned to the house the following day, Marcel was in his office working but came out as soon as he saw us. I didn't say anything, just removed my coat and helped Daniel with his. We stood looking at each other for a long moment, then he approached me almost timidly. He took me into his arms and held me close. Then he pulled Daniel into our embrace.

"You okay?" he asked nervously.

"No, not really," I answered calmly. I was not going to discuss this around Daniel. "We can talk about things later when Daniel is at my mother's."

I dropped Daniel off after dinner, and when I got back Marcel had made a fire and opened a bottle of wine and poured a glass for each of us. He was sitting on the couch, waiting. I sat down beside him but at a distance so as not to be touching. I took a sip of my wine, which was excellent. So I took another.

"What do you think? Good?" he asked, enjoying watching the pleasure on my face with each sip.

"Amazing. Wonderful. I've never had a red wine this good."

"It should be. It is a very expensive wine that I've had aging downstairs in my wine cellar for ten years. I was keeping it to open on a special occasion."

"And this is a special occasion?" I asked warily.

"Yes, it is, for the simple reason I didn't scare you away for good." He dropped his head and looked at his lap in what appeared to be remorse.

"Well, frankly, I considered it. You can't do this to me, Marcel. Be so angry for really nothing. And then not talk to me for days. And Daniel feels it too. It's not fair. We don't deserve that kind of treatment," I said.

"You're right. I know I've been a real ass. And I don't even know why. I could tell you that it's because of work and that I think they are trying to get some senior people out, including me, but that would be just a poor excuse for bad behavior. What I will tell you is that I'll make a determined effort to get control over my emotions and actions and treat you better from now on. Like you deserve to be treated."

"What about talking to a professional? We could attend marriage counseling together. I'm sure it could only help. After all, you've never been married before, and maybe you just weren't prepared for the change."

"Let me try on my own first, and if you don't see a change in me, I promise I will attend marriage counseling with you."

"I'm going to hold you to that," I said sternly at first, but then I couldn't help but smile when he held his hands in a mock prayer and looking upward mouthed, "Thank you, God."

Nineteen

True to his word, Marcel started to act better. The problem was I had a sneaking suspicion that it truly was just that: an act. He also became like the man he was before we married. He'd run to my car door to open it up, he'd cook gourmet meals and laugh at all my lame jokes, and he'd make a few of his own. Trouble was, experiencing him turn so sullen and withdrawn for no good reason had made me wary of the new and improved Marcel. Maybe the Marcel I had come to know and love in the short time before our marriage was an act too. However, I had agreed that if he made a change, I would accept that. Now, I needed to live up to my part of the bargain and stop being suspicious and purge the doubts from my mind. And heart.

To help do that, I decided to keep myself occupied. My days, when Marcel was at work, were spent renovating. First on the agenda was the spare room, stripping off the old wallpaper that had been there for decades, then turning it into a permanent bedroom for my little boy for when he moved in after the school year. It was a huge job, since the house was an older one built in the 1920s, and it seemed that the wallpaper was just as old. Once removed, the repair to the walls was another huge project. Then I intended to rent out a floor sander and redo the hardwood. When I had that room redone and completely furnished, I would take on a few more projects. It seemed that living all his years as a bachelor, he had neglected much of the house. It was quite dated and in need of a facelift, along with some new and modern accessories and accents. HomeSense became my new favorite haunt.

Unfortunately, his renewed love of cooking was waning somewhat, so I decided to pick up the slack. And why not? He never scrimped when it came to buying quality food and didn't even flinch if I told him I had bought a new and expensive flavored passion fruit vinegar or an artisanal cheese at five times the price of the grocery store brand. He had piles of *Gourmet* magazine that were calling my name. Urging the inner chef to "come on out," I was getting to be quite a good cook, and Marcel was an appreciative recipient. He never failed to compliment me, even when the meal wasn't quite up to par. Then I knew, absolutely, that he was acting.

Time was marching on toward the end of March, and my doubts, like the tide, were slowly ebbing away. But sometimes, like the waves of the sea, they would wash back in. He was good to Daniel on the weekends, but not great, and cracks were starting to appear. Many times, I found that Marcel wouldn't really be listening when Daniel talked. One Saturday morning after we had finished our breakfast and were sitting around the kitchen table, Daniel called his name four times, with no response from Marcel.

Finally, I snapped, "Marcel! Daniel is talking to you."

Marcel made eye contact with Daniel, then sighed deeply, as if annoyed, before asking, "Yes, what is it, Daniel?" Rather coolly, I thought. Hmm, was the irritable and angry Marcel making a comeback? I surely hoped not.

So, while Daniel and I had experienced a brief respite from Marcel's constant surliness, it hadn't been a true reversal. Again, he was losing his temper a little too often, and the silent treatment had returned. It didn't last as long, however. He seemed more aware and never let it go more than a few hours and always apologized before the night was over.

"I heard it said, never let the sun set in a provoked state," Marcel would joke to try to get on my good side, especially since he didn't want to miss out on an opportunity to have sex, which sometimes worked for him and sometimes didn't. Surliness is not exactly a turn-on, and many a night we went to sleep without touching each other at all.

His other bad habit made an unwelcome reappearance. He had taken to retreating to his office immediately after supper. Our small talk was slowly but surely disappearing.

This time I didn't turn to Lara. This was my problem, and I needed to figure for myself how best to handle the situation. I read a lot of books about marriage and relationships. I listened to many podcasts. I was starting to feel like something of an expert myself, and some of the suggestions actually worked; I was able to draw him out without making him feel as if I was putting him on the spot. I was hopeful, because what other choice did I have? Just despair.

It was a Tuesday morning in the middle of April when my mother asked me to come to her place after I dropped Daniel at school because she had received a letter for me. I was feeling rather upbeat and positive about life in general. Okay, maybe things weren't the absolute best with Marcel and me, but they weren't the worst either. However, a new situation had arisen: he was staying out late on Thursdays after playing squash and giving me no plausible explanation. I had planned to resolve that next. It was on my to-do list. But putting Marcel troubles aside, what thrilled me was springtime! The weather was delightful, the trees had sprouted their leaves, and the days were long. I was even thinking of suggesting to Marcel that we should take up tennis. Not that I could play, but I was willing to learn. Couldn't be that hard, smacking a ball back and forth.

I walked into my mother's house to be greeted by a wagging

Luna. I crouched down to give her a hug and found a huge dog tongue right in my mouth. I did not miss that!

"Hey, Mom, I'm here," I yelled. "Where are you?"

"Upstairs in my room. I'm just putting away some laundry. The letter is on the kitchen table. I'll be down shortly; I'm almost finished."

We were really good at yelling back and forth.

I looked at the envelope on the table, and the writing of the handwritten name and address looked familiar. Where had I seen that writing before? Then I remembered: Alex, my ex-husband. Why had he sent me a letter? I opened it with some trepidation. I read it through once, and not believing what I was reading, I read it a second time. Then I placed it on the table and got myself a glass of cold water because I thought I might faint.

When my mother entered the room, she took one look at me and asked, "Bad news?"

I pointed to the letter. "Read it for yourself."

She held it up and started reading aloud.

"Dear Rachel, I hope you are well. Firstly, I want to tell you that I know it's been a long time since we have spoken and that I left you in a terrible spot when I walked out, and for that I'm sorry. I'm really sorry. I guess we were just too young when we started seeing each other (high school!) and then got married too fast, and we didn't get a chance to mature before it was all over.

"Anyway, since our divorce, I've done some maturing. I met a great woman, Cierra, and she helped me get my act together. She is a dental hygienist, and she insisted that I make something of myself, so I took a trade and now am working as an apprentice electrician at her father's electrical company. I'm doing well, and when I become a journeyman, I'll be making the big bucks.

"I intend to pay my debts to the credit cards too.

"Anyway, Cierra and I were talking about Daniel. And we

want him to be part of our lives. We have a nice house that we bought when we were just living together, and recently, we got married so that he can feel he has a secure family with me and because we are expecting a baby girl in four months.

"I've also been visiting my mother regularly, and she doesn't hate me so much these days. And she told me what is happening with you. That you got married to an older, established guy (good for you) and that you only have Daniel with you on the weekends and he lives at your mom's during the week. So, in view of that, Cierra and I think that I should apply for custody of him. He can live with me, his father, full-time, and you can keep the same arrangement and have him on weekends. Or every other weekend. Plus, I am a little concerned with him at your mom's, considering he broke his arm in her custody because she was drinking.

"I will be hiring a lawyer soon to proceed with my plan but wanted to give you the heads-up first so we can maybe work things out and save some money. If you want to talk to me, my phone number is 416-998-7766.

Sincerely,

Alex."

My mother's face lost all color. She clutched the back of the chair and sat down slowly. We sat together in silence, both of us gobsmacked. I feverishly started combing my fingers over my scalp and through my hair. Maybe I could scratch an idea into my head. I looked at my mother, who was starting to cry.

"Stop it!" I ordered. "This is not going to happen. If he thinks he can just come back and demand to have him like that, he has another think coming. And I can't believe Marguerita! What a traitor. As soon as I leave here, I'm going straight there to scream at her. How could she do that to me? And to you! You're supposed to be friends now."

My mother just sat there sobbing. I took a few deep breaths

to calm myself down. This certainly wasn't doing either of us any good.

"Mom," I said calmly, "I'm going to have to bring Daniel to live with me full-time. To hell with Marcel's proposition or whatever it is he is doing. Anyway, he works in the quiet of his office, and that won't change with Daniel around. Besides, this is more important. I'm sure he'll understand and agree, given the circumstances." I sighed deeply then continued. "Who would have seen this coming? That Alex would meet a *mature* woman. Help him become mature. She's controlling and conniving and horrible. I know just the type. They don't like seeing other people they consider a rival in any way, shape, or form do well. Argh, Alex doesn't even know the arrangement. That it wasn't permanent!" I was now back into a full-blown rant. "And he never gave me a penny for child support. That will not look good on him. What's more, he was never even around when we lived together and Daniel was a baby! He didn't care about seeing him then when we were in the same home! Oh, but he wants him now. He wants to be a *family*. Yeah, right. I'm fighting this, Mom. But in the meantime, Daniel will have to come over to my place now. Today."

Through her tears and sniffles, she replied, "Yes, of course. I never should have gone along with keeping him in the first place, and then this wouldn't have happened. You would have had to bring him with you, and Marcel would have had to learn to live with it. Or should I say, him."

"Oh, well, we can't change the past. I'm going over to see Marguerita."

I grabbed my purse off the counter and turned toward the front door when my mother said, "Not without me. I want some answers too. Give me two minutes to splash my face and I'll be right out."

I sat in my car, thumping my thumb on the steering wheel,

my heart beating wildly, waiting for her. I noticed my phone sitting in my purse. I was tempted to phone Alex and tell him where to go and then thought I could just text him. *Dear Alex, Go to hell, you will never get Daniel. Ever!*

I stopped myself; I knew better. If he intended to get a lawyer, I had better be overly careful and not do anything that could be used against me. And that included what I said to that Judas, Marguerita.

My mother got into the car, buckled her seatbelt, then put her hand on mine, and as if reading my mind, she said, "Rachel, I was thinking. We better be careful what we say to Marguerita. We don't want anything used against us."

A short twenty-minute drive had us standing on Marguerita's porch and knocking on her front door. When she opened it to find us standing there, her face immediately became guilt-ridden.

She just stared at us, not speaking and not inviting us in.

"Marguerita, we need to talk. May we come in, please?" I asked calmly, trying to eliminate any trace of animosity from my tone. But she knew. How could she not?

She waved us in, and we walked past her to the living room on the right and took a seat. Mom and I sat on the couch, and Marguerita sat opposite us in an armchair.

"What's going on with Alex?" I asked.

"Oh, I don't know what's got into him. I think his new wife would do anything to make him happy. And I think that Alex must have said he misses Daniel, and now she thinks he should have Daniel. That's how it feels to me. And her father owns a big electrical company that hired Alex, so he feels important working there, plus he wants to please her. I didn't encourage it, Rachel." She looked at my mom. "Honestly, I didn't, Deborah."

"From the sound of the letter, Marguerita, it certainly sounds as if you did. How could you tell Alex that Daniel broke his arm because I was drinking? I thought you were my friend!" my mother proclaimed sadly. She was soon tearing up.

"I *am* your friend! And Rachel, I love you like a daughter. And I know you're a wonderful mother. But I didn't tell Alex you had a glass of wine when Daniel broke his arm. He asked to see some pictures of Daniel, and in one of them he had his arm in a sling, so Alex asked what happened. I just told him that Daniel fell, and my big-mouth sister Rosa was here, and it was her who offered the information that you had a glass of wine when it happened and that they questioned you at the hospital. She thought it was funny. And actually, he did too. And Cierra was laughing too. I never thought that he would try to take Daniel and then use that information against you. Not in a million years. I'm not talking to him now. I'm so mad at him. I know it's Cierra's idea. He may have had bad habits, but he never would have been malicious toward you, Rachel, and Daniel. He has told me so many times that even though he didn't stay married to you, he knew you were a responsible mother and that all the times he was out running around, he always knew his little boy was taken care of."

Was her explanation true, or was she trying to cover her tracks? I wasn't sure, but regardless, the damage was done, and now I had to fix it. I looked her in the eye and said angrily, "Yeah, well, all that time he was running around and not paying rent and gambling our money away is going to come back to haunt him, because if he thinks one glass of wine that my mother drank is going to make me look bad, I've got a lot more on him than that. And next time you see him, you can tell him that Daniel no longer lives at my mother's. He's coming to live with me. Today. Permanently."

Next thing I knew, she was crying too, along with my mother. I was too angry to cry. But she did soften me. Slightly.

"I'm so sorry, Rachel. I don't know what I can do. I still love

Alex too, you know. He's my son. And I do believe he's sincere and wants to see Daniel. But taking him from you I am 99.9 percent sure was his wife's idea when she heard Daniel doesn't live with you. Honestly, I think she would do anything for Alex. She seems to worship the ground he walks on. But, truthfully, from what Alex said, I get the idea he is really missing Daniel. But I am not going to support him in what he is doing by trying to get him permanently. And you have my word I would never go to court and say that Deborah was drinking when Daniel broke his arm."

Try as she might to convince me Alex's wife was doing this to assure Alex of her love and devotion, it was not flying with me. What Cierra was doing was far more manipulative, in my opinion. First, she got him the good job with Daddy, then became pregnant with their baby, and had them purchase a house Alex would never be able to afford. Last, but not least, she would help him get custody of his son. Soon she would have him so indebted to her, he could never walk out. And just try to cheat on that woman and see what happened to your life.

And that was fine, if it was the way she rolled. It was fine to get him a great job, have a baby, and buy him a house, but taking my baby from me crossed the line. She was not sweet and loving; she was strong and determined and would get what she wanted any way she needed to. That's the way I saw her, even if she showed a different side to Alex, her mother-in-law, and the world.

"Marguerita, it's not going to come to that now that Daniel is living with me. And if Alex truly wants to see Daniel, we can come to some kind of arrangement. Daniel has a right to see his father too. Occasionally." I was spent and couldn't even think about when or how we would arrange that. "Marguerita, please just tell Alex that Daniel lives with me now, everyday. He has no reason think Daniel should live with him. Would you do that for me, please?"

"Of course, my darling. Don't worry. Alex will change his mind. I'll make sure."

I could see how visibly shaken she was by all this and how unfair it was for her to be caught in the middle. I gave her a warm hug and said, "I know, I know you will. I love you, Marguerita, and I don't blame you. I'm just really upset." She and my mom hugged and cried and didn't let go until I cleared my throat, and they laughed and we left.

When I picked Daniel up from school later that day and told him he was coming to live with me, he was so excited, he stood by the car and jumped up and down, yelling, "Yay, yay, yay!" I was relieved; I'd been unsure of his reaction. Maybe he had grown too attached to my mother and would tell me he loved her more and didn't want to come. Or maybe he would tell me he hated Marcel and didn't want to live with him. But neither of those was the case. He was happy. I hadn't lost him! I was ecstatic. Marcel's reaction to the news, on the other hand, would not be one of joy, of that I was sure. Just how adversely he reacted would be the question — mild irritation or extreme anger. Probably somewhere in the middle. That was the best I could wish for, I figured.

When Marcel walked in at dinnertime, he found Daniel and me in the kitchen preparing vegetables and stirring pots. Well, I was stirring pots and Daniel tearing apart lettuce and placing it in a bowl. It was lovely to have the company of my chatterbox little boy. Marcel stood in the doorway, and we both turned simultaneously and said, "Hello." He walked over, gave me a kiss, and then whispered, "What's going on?"

"Well, honey, we have a new addition to our family. Daniel is coming to live with us." I noticed his face redden, so I added hastily, "Which we can have a nice long talk about later tonight, if that's all right."

"Oh, yeah, that we will. That we will." He went into his office and slammed the door.

"Is Marcel mad, Mommy?" Daniel asked.

"No, no, he just has lots of work to do, and that door slams sometimes. We need to fix it. He's not mad. He loves us very much," I said reassuringly, to myself as much as to him.

After Daniel had gone to bed, I went back down stairs to the kitchen to clean the supper mess. I was loading the dishwasher with my headphones on listening to salsa music when I felt a hand on my arm as I grabbed for another dirty plate on the counter. I almost hit the ceiling, I jumped so high.

It was Marcel, of course. Standing there, deadpan. I took out my headphones and said, "You can't go around startling people like that. I almost had a heart attack." I smiled at him, attempting to coax one from him in return. No such luck.

"Is that so? Well, Rachel, I'd love to care about you and what affects you and what doesn't. I really would. But I think from now on, it might be a little difficult considering you have stopped caring about me."

"What are you talking about? I have not stopped caring about you. Let me put the dishwasher on, and we can talk. Five minutes at most. Sit at the table, and I'll be right there."

He sat, arms crossed with a scowl, and watched my every movement. Dishes loaded and soap in the dispenser, I turned the machine on and sat at the table with him.

"Would you like a decaf coffee or tea?"

He just shook his head. I felt defeated already, and we hadn't even begun our conversation.

"Well?" he asked. "What's going on? And this better be good, Rachel."

"I got a letter sent to my mother's from Alex saying he intended to see a lawyer and take full custody of Daniel. He found out Daniel was staying at my mother's during the week and that my mother had drank a glass of wine the night Daniel broke his arm, so he thought taking him away from me would be a piece of cake. I had no choice but to bring Daniel here. I couldn't give Alex any reason at all to start proceedings."

"And you didn't think to ask me? It is my house, after all, plus we had an arrangement."

"I know, but *had* is the word. Had an arrangement. This predicament changed things. I was threatened with the loss of my child. You must see how that would change things. I had no choice. I needed to put a stop to this before it went any further and lawyers got involved."

"What exactly did the letter say?"

"He said he knew the living arrangements, and that now he was married — by the way, he got married — he thought he could offer Daniel more stable living conditions. And that I could get him on the weekends. Or every other weekend. Like other divorced people."

"Rachel, that would have been perfect. At least you wouldn't have gone back on your arrangement with me. You should have taken some time to consider it, but mostly you should have talked it over with me before you moved him into my house," he said in all seriousness.

I was incredulous. "*Your* house? This is *your* house?"

"Of course it's my house. Don't be daft. You moved into *my* house. We didn't buy it together. I owned it long before I even met you."

"Oh, I kind of thought it was *our* house. Now that we are married." Incredibly, I didn't raise my voice, sound sarcastic, or even slightly annoyed. I needed his true thoughts, not to put him on the defensive.

"No, it's not. It's still all my house. And you should not have brought him here. June would have been soon enough."

"You would have been good with June then? Are you sure? Or would you have tried to make him stay at my mother's even then?" He didn't answer. He didn't need to. I knew the answer.

We sat in silence for a long while. Finally, he spoke. "Just make sure he is dead quiet in the evenings when I am working in my office. If I am not bothered, he can stay."

"Marcel, he is staying. It's not a question of if. He is staying as much as I am staying, and if you don't want him here you can say goodbye to us both."

"I'm going to bed."

I stayed downstairs and watched my taped episodes of Conan O'Brien. I needed something, anything, to make me laugh. Conan always delivered.

Twenty

The following week, a second letter from Alex arrived at Marcel's. It read:

Dear Rachel,

I'm glad you have worked things out and have decided to give Daniel some stability and let him live with you permanently. I truly had concerns with the arrangements you had made. From what I remember you telling me about your mother, she was kind of psychotic. It surprised me very much that you went ahead and left him with her, considering what kind of woman she is.

I want to let you know that although I am not going to try to take Daniel, I still could have hired a lawyer and proceeded with my plan, regardless of this decision you made to bring him to live with you. It seems that you just made a knee-jerk reaction based on my letter to you, and I now question if Daniel is getting the best care. It is possible you have changed and are now getting used to living the high life, married to a university professor, and consider yourself above everyone. Maybe having a little boy around will stifle your high-rolling style. I don't know. I don't like to think that, but people change. I know I did. For the better. Thanks to Cierra.

Anyway, my mother said that you are willing to work out some visiting arrangements so we can avoid costly lawyers, and I think that would be preferable. My wife has already put so much money and time into trying to help me improve my life (and she has!), I really don't want to burden her any more than I need to. And our baby will be here soon, so she has to take care of herself.

I look forward to talking to you soon. The sooner we can make arrangements, the better for all of us. Especially Daniel, who has missed so much time with his father already.

Sincerely,

Alex

I took a few deep breaths to relax after reading that nonsense, which I was pretty sure Cierra had penned. Before replying, I mulled over a few things. I wished I could reply that whatever I had told him about my mother in the past had no bearing on the present and that he should have given me a warning when I shared my feelings with him that they might be used against me in the future. Something like, *Don't divulge anything about anyone with me because I will use it against you later.* Or maybe I could say that if he was capable of such miraculous changes, as he professed, then why not others? Could not my mother be a changed person as well? And what was more, she was.

But since he was handing out an olive branch, sort of, I decided to text him something more conciliatory and leave my thoughts to myself.

Hi Alex, I just got your letter. I'm happy that your life has taken a turn for the better. We all deserve to be happy. And I think Daniel would enjoy spending time with you and finally getting to know his father. Would you like him, not this weekend, but the following? Let's talk on the phone to make arrangements. I think it would be easier than texting. If you like, you can call me tonight anytime after 7. Rachel

That was the best I could do, and I thought it was good, plus I got in one dig. After all, he deserved it. He wanted to take my baby away, insulted my mother and me, and turned his mother against me, or at least tried to. If that was harsh, saying he was *finally* going to get to know his son, so be it. It was the truth. And I hoped it stung. But knowing how thick he was, I was pretty sure he wouldn't even get it.

That evening, Marcel didn't come home from work till close to ten, and Daniel was already in bed when he walked in the door. I guessed he had planned it that way. He hadn't phoned or even texted me to tell me he would be late. And I had made his favorite supper, spaghetti with meatballs made from scratch and freshly made tomato sauce. I guessed this was the beginning of the turmoil. He did not intend to make things easy for me. I was sitting on the couch watching *The Crown* when he entered the house. He removed his shoes and then sat beside me on the couch. He stretched his legs out in front of him and folded his hands behind his head. He didn't say a word.

He smelled different. I smelled alcohol, but it was something more than that. There was a perfumy smell. And he looked different. Like nothing really bothered him, and whatever Daniel and I were doing was not important. The expression on his face said he didn't stay out because of anger; he stayed out because he had something better to do. A text came in on his phone, but he didn't look at it.

"Aren't you going to see who that is from?"

"I know who it is from. I went to the bar after work today, and having had a couple of drinks the guys said to let them know I got home safely."

"So don't you think you should do that?"

"No, I'm not a baby. I don't answer to them. Why should they care anyway? I don't care if they get home okay." He stretched his arms over his head and yawned loudly. I was annoyed.

"Fine," I said. *Don't let me see your phone.* "But why didn't you let me know where you were tonight? I had made supper and was expecting you by five. Daniel and I waited to eat with you."

"Rachel, you don't need me to eat supper with you. You have your baby. That was what you intended to do all along, so now you got your way. Don't pretend you want me here to have supper with you," he said, never once looking at me but staring at the television screen.

"Marcel, you're my husband. I want to be with you. Isn't that why we got married? To be together? Don't you see that I had to bring him here or lose him? Surely, you don't want that for me."

"It's all about you, isn't it, Rachel? Not my work or our future. Poor Rachel having to share her baby with his father. You must have been used to getting your way and just couldn't take it having to compromise for once."

"I can't believe what you are saying. Why don't you go to bed? I'm going to stay up for a while anyway."

He rose from the couch, stumbling slightly before regaining his footing. I guessed he was more drunk than I had realized. Boozing it up with his workmates and who knew who else? And then driving home! I wished he had tripped and beaned his head off the marble mantel. I was so angry, it took all I had to stop myself from throwing something at him. I clenched my hands and felt my fingernails digging into my flesh. When I went to bed around midnight, he was snoring away and didn't even hear me get into bed. I cried myself to sleep.

The next day, after dropping Daniel off, I went by the café. I missed everyone and needed a pick-me-up. Steve shouted a greeting as I walked in, and the cook looked out from the window and waved the spatula in the air to say hello. When I approached the counter, Steve took me into his arms and gave me his famous bear hug. I wished it would never end.

I sat on a counter stool and smiled at him.

"What's wrong?"

"It's that obvious?" I replied. "I haven't even said anything yet."

"It's written all over your face. What's going on? Tell me. I'm all ears."

"I don't know, Steve. I didn't come in here to tell you my problems. I just wanted to see everyone. But if you really want to hear, I'll tell you. And maybe a man's opinion might help. Couldn't hurt at this point."

After I told him the whole story, I waited for his reply. A couple of moments passed, and then he sucked in his cheeks before he let out a slow whistle. He looked at his hands and folded his fingers. The suspense was killing me.

"Steve. Tell me. What should I do?"

He sighed before speaking. "Rachel, I don't know the man. But I know from some of my friends who have never married or even lived with someone that they can become somewhat selfish and a little out of touch. He just doesn't get how strong the bond is between a mother and her child. Maybe he never had that growing up. You don't know anything about his family, do you? His parents alive?"

"No, his mom died when he was in his twenties, and then his dad died a few years after he lost his mom."

"What does he say about his mother? What kind of woman was she?"

"Nothing, really. He doesn't talk about her. It's been over twenty years that she has been gone."

"I don't know, Rachel. Maybe his childhood has a bearing on how he reacts to you and Daniel. Maybe he's jealous. Or maybe he's just a dick. Like I said, I don't know the man."

"I don't think I know him either, Steve. This is really a different side to him. He never acted like this when we were dating."

"Well then, you need to talk to him. Communication is the key. Because if he's acting out because you changed the arrangement, you need to nip it in the bud. If you don't talk about things, nothing will get solved. My marriage had a few bumps too. But we worked them out. And you can too. I know you. You're a great girl. Just shower him with affection and praise. Let him know how much you need him. Men love that. Think of all the great things he has accomplished and remind him of them and how much you admire him for them. Pile it on. It can't hurt. Even if it isn't entirely true. Maybe you'll soften him a bit."

"Seriously?" I asked doubtfully.

He shrugged. "Sure, why not? Might be just the thing that will work. You'll get through this. It's a new marriage. That's when things can seem the worst, but they're not. You just have to iron out the wrinkles. I'm positive. And if not, you can always come back and work here. Dishes always need washing."

"Hahaha. Well, if you only have dishwashing available for me, I better make my marriage work." I felt lighter and happier for having unburdened to Steve, and what was more, I was planning to implement his suggestions — to a degree. I turned around and saw my favorite couple in the world drinking coffee, so I stayed and talked to them for a few more moments, and we shared pictures, me of the wedding and my new house and them of their lovely four grandchildren and one great grandchild. I hugged them and walked back to Steve for one more bear hug before I left.

I sat in the car, and before I drove away took out my phone and texted Marcel.

Please try to come home early today. I really missed your smile yesterday and hearing all about your day. I'll send Daniel to my mom's tonight to we can have some us time. xoxoxo

Ten minutes later, my phone alerted me to a text. *Be home by five. We'll go out for a romantic dinner.*

I texted my mom next to get the okay from her, and when she answered immediately, *Of course!!!* I could only smile.

Marcel and I did have a remarkable evening. And I didn't even have to broach the subject of his behavior. He arrived home with a beautiful bouquet, placing it in my arms at the door and saying, "I've been a real jackass to you. And you don't deserve it. I'm going to try my best to adjust to everything, but you're going to have to be patient with me. Just remind me of my promise to you when I screw up, and I'll readjust. Can you do that? Please?"

I told him I would hold him to that, and then we didn't mention it again. We went to dinner at the Old Mill. Following dinner, a jazz band played and Marcel and I danced. He was an extraordinary dancer and so easy to follow. He buried his face in my hair, and I nuzzled my face into his neck, drinking in his scent. Once home, we made love. It was exquisite, and I was absolutely convinced our marriage would succeed.

When I picked up Daniel the following morning for school, my mother looked anxious standing at the door and wringing her hands. I promised to return after dropping him off.

I entered her house, and she was crying at the kitchen table, her head rested on folded arms. I sat across from her and waited till she stopped. When her sobbing subsided, she took a tissue and blew her nose then apologized.

"For what?"

"For losing it. Rachel, I've been a bit of a basket case since Daniel has left. I think I've finally been grieving your dad, now that I'm alone. This is the first time I've lived alone in thirty years. It's just so, so hard." And then, as if on cue, Luna walked over to my mother and rested her big furry head on her lap. My mother gave a little laugh and said, "Okay, sorry, Luna. I forgot about you. I'm not totally alone." She patted the dog.

"This is an enormous change for you. I can't imagine what you're going through."

"I'm not trying to make you feel guilty for taking Daniel. I know that he needs to be with you. And I suppose my unhinged emotions are normal. I've been reading up on the stages of grief. Some people grieve at different points. Mine is coming now. All of it. I feel like I've opened the floodgates. I didn't even know a person could have so many tears." And then she was crying again. And I was too.

A few moments later, I suggested we look through old family albums, and she loved the idea. The books came out, the coffee was put on, and the morning was spent laughing and crying in a repeated cycle that anyone, were they to observe us, would surely think we had lost our minds. It did us the world of good.

When it was time for me to pick up Daniel, my mother agreed that she would look into joining a support group for widows and widowers. I made her promise to call me when she was feeling despair. Not that I would necessarily know the perfect thing to say, but at least she wouldn't have to feel so all alone. She promised she would.

"And you know what is so darn maddening about everything? I thought I had a real friend in Marguerita. And now I just don't feel the same about her. I believe her. I don't think she meant to harm us, but she did. And I don't know if I can get past it. I haven't called her."

"Has she called you?"

"She has sent a few texts saying good morning, but I haven't been too responsive, so I think she has figured it out. We've lost what we had."

"Yeah, I know what you mean. I haven't contacted her either. And now I don't have to feel guilty about Daniel not seeing her, because when Alex has him for some weekends, he can bring him by to her. Now that they are buddies again. It really sucks, though. Maybe in time, we'll get over this." She agreed, and I kissed her cheek and left.

On my way to the school, I called Giselle on my Bluetooth. She picked up on the second ring.

"Hello, angel. To what do I owe this pleasure?"

"Hello, Aunt Giselle, I'm just giving you a call to ask a little favor. And to see how you are. How are you?"

"Wonderful, but busy. One of my bands I represent was asked to perform at the Junos, so we're busy arranging everything to make that happen. Meaning rescheduling concert dates, which is a lot harder than it sounds. I'm just on my way to an appointment now. I'm not complaining, though, I love it. The busier, the better. And how about you? How's married life treating you?"

"Really good. We are both going through a little adjustment period, but I think we'll get there." In actuality, I wasn't as enthusiastic about my life as she was about hers, so I quickly changed the subject and got to the point. "Anyway, Aunt Giselle, I'm calling because I'm worried about Mom. Since I've been gone, she's been having a tough time. She could use some support now that she's all alone. I know you're busy, but even if you could call her maybe a couple of times a week, it would probably really help."

"Oh my, of course! I've been meaning to call her anyway. I'll call her tonight, sweetie. Promise." Then she yelled, "Hey, you, jackass, there is such a thing as a signal light. Sorry about that, Rachel, the idiot just cut me off, and I almost hit him. Thank goodness I have a dashcam for all these idiot drivers out here."

I just laughed. "I know, okay, I'll let you go because driving really does require all our attention, and guess what, I'm driving too. So, thanks for doing that, and I'm planning to have you over to my new place for dinner one day soon, so expect a call."

"I'm counting on it. Take care, Rachel, and give that darling little boy of yours a big squeeze for me."

"I'll give him two. Bye for now, Aunt Giselle." I disconnected and sighed deeply, satisfied that she would be a huge help to my mom, knowing she was good to her word. Because it was true that if you wanted something done, you gave it to somebody busy, knowing the busy person is one who is not only not lazy but conscientious as well. I made a mental note to ask Marcel about a dinner date for my lovely auntie.

Twenty-One

Daniel and I walked into the house, arms loaded down with groceries. Well, at least, my arms were, while his were holding his new toy he had managed to cajole me into buying. Since when did food stores carry toys? And I thought refusing chocolate bars was hard enough. But in reality, it was a really cool toy, a remote-control car that didn't require batteries, so I was sold on it. And it wasn't too expensive. Daniel took it out to the back patio while I unloaded the groceries and put out what I intended to cook that evening: homemade gnocchi made from scratch with creamy ricotta and Parmesan, paired with pancetta-studded tomato-garlic sauce. I had looked at this recipe earlier in one of Marcel's *Gourmet* magazines and decided to give it a try. I was excited and especially anxious to see the look of approval from Marcel when his plate was put in front of him. Also, he had the perfect wine to pair with it. I was aware of that from spotting it in his collection.

Marcel told me he was working a little later in order to complete a project, and I could expect him at six. Six o'clock on the dot, supper was ready. At six thirty, he was still not home. And he had not texted or called. I paced the kitchen; it was now seven. I glanced at Daniel playing quietly on his iPad to see if he noticed how agitated I was becoming. His game was keeping him completely occupied, thankfully, but when I heard his stomach rumble, followed by my own, I said, "Okay, little man, we aren't waiting any longer to eat. Finish up your game and put the iPad away. I'm going to put supper on the table."

As delicious as supper was, it was wasted on me. I was furious. Not only had I planned and executed the perfect family dinner, but that evening I was going to talk to Marcel and Daniel about upping their status from Marcel and Daniel to father and son. I had talked to Daniel, and he liked the idea of calling him Dad, and I was sure, or at least hopeful Marcel would warm to the idea as well. I thought it would help draw them closer. So much for that idea. Marcel wasn't even concerned about his closeness with me at this point. Imagining the three of us as one big happy family was starting to look like wishful thinking at best. Sadly, the idea of leaving him was playing ever more frequently in my thoughts again. Frustrated and disappointed, I could hear my fork hitting the plate while I noisily stabbed at the gnocchi.

Daniel, as if reading my mind, said, "Mommy, don't be mad at Marcel. I love the gnocchi. This is the best food you have ever made. I can eat it all so it won't be wasted." He even made a circle on his tummy with his hand to indicate how delicious it was. I had to laugh.

"Oh, sweetheart, you don't have to do that. You'll be too full. But you can certainly have more if you like. And it won't get wasted. I'll put it in the fridge, and we can have it for leftovers. But thank you for thinking about my feelings. Don't ever stop being thoughtful, my love. Don't ever stop." And then my anger dissipated and was replaced by profound sadness. I thought of the thoughtless men in my life and wondered at what point they became like that and changed from sweet, thoughtful, loving boys into self-serving and inconsiderate men. Was it destined to happen to Daniel too? Not if I could help it. But how could I? How would I even know if it was? I felt tears forming and got up, taking my plate to the counter so I could turn my face away from him.

I was soon slumped over the counter, crying into my folded arms to muffle the sobs. I felt little arms around my waist and gentle pats on my side, which made me smile and straighten up. I grabbed a tissue, blew my nose, and said, "That's enough of that. May I give your new car a try?"

Marcel came home shortly after ten, this time completely sober. I didn't say a word to him; in fact, I found it hard even to look at him. Once again, he sat beside me and proceeded to spew out his excuses. He said the guys in the department wanted to take him out for dinner to celebrate competing the project. I said, "Whatever."

"I guess I should have warned you. I need my space, Rachel. I still need you, but you have to let me have independent time without having to check in with you every time I want to do something. I'm good any time you want to go hang out at your mom's or Lara's. We are both adults. We can still love each other and have a good marriage and have time on our own."

"We will have a marriage. Not a good marriage. At least, that is not my idea of a good marriage. And it is not what I thought we would have."

He sighed and said, "Oh well. Sorry." He did not sound the least bit sorry. He sounded rather jovial. He walked over to the fridge and opened it wide. Noticing the leftovers, he said, "This looks good. I'm starved. The restaurant was we went to was superb, but sizes were made for small children. I've seen bigger portions in a Happy Meal." He got it out of the fridge, whistling while he put it on a plate and heated it up in the microwave. Then he sat at the table, out of my sight, thank goodness, and ate every last morsel of all my hard work intended to knock his socks off. A meal to make him feel he was the luckiest man alive to have a wife like me. When he finished, he rinsed his plate, placed it in the dishwasher, and called out to me before walking upstairs to bed. "That was great, Rachel. Hit the spot." I grabbed a blanket and pillow and slept on the couch that night, making sure I awoke before Daniel so he would be none the wiser.

The next few days, Marcel came home after work followed by an evening where he stayed out. It seemed after three or four evenings coming straight home would be followed by one where he didn't. I never again made such an intricate meal from scratch, and it made no difference to him. He didn't notice and would eat whatever I served. Sometimes he sat around to chat after supper, and other times he headed straight to his office, which I was given orders to stay out of. I was not to "mess it up." He had "important papers" in there. I was addressed as if I was a child. If he received a call or text, he never took them in front of me but would find a private spot. I was quickly developing a mistrust that I hated. My stomach felt tight most of the time, and I was getting tension headaches. But to Daniel I appeared fine. And that was how I intended to keep it. Little children find it hard to be discreet, so to Daniel our home life needed to appear happy, because he would soon be visiting his father. And if Daniel let it be known there were problems, Alex would think it reason enough to get custody of my baby. And his visit was fast approaching — the next day.

*

Daniel sat on the edge of his bed while I packed his weekend bag with his favorite *Paw Patrol* pajamas and *Paw Patrol* sweatshirts. He wore his *Paw Patrol* sneakers. Looking at him, one might get the idea he liked *Paw Patrol*. To leave no room for criticism from his new stepmother, the night before I bathed him, scrubbing all his dirty nails, both fingers and toes clean. His beautiful golden locks were shampooed with an all-natural shampoo that smelled of coconut and vanilla. Amazing.

Bag packed, sitting next to him on his bed, I couldn't stop

myself burying my nose in his hair, sniffing in the scent. I didn't want him to go in the first place and wished the smell would implant itself in the scent memory area of my brain, so that when I was missing him, I could open the shampoo bottle and smell away. I told him to take along his security blanket, a ratty yellow thing, just in case, but I think he wanted to impress his dad and said he wouldn't need it. Seven o'clock on the dot, we heard the doorbell ring.

It was one of the nights that Marcel happened to come home after work, thankfully, if just for appearance's sake. When he answered the door to Alex, I was surprised to hear Marcel chatting away and singing the praises of how intelligent Daniel was and how well behaved. Of course, he didn't really feel that way, but he said those things for my benefit to let Alex believe we were a well adjusted, happy family, and for that I was grateful.

I should have been over the moon at his attempts to help, but reality made me realize it was just another manifestation of his natural ability to lie. It only confirmed what I now suspected was true. He had lied while dating me, put on a front to make me think he was something he was not, and it worked. What I couldn't figure out was why he did that. Did he think marriage was a good idea then but had now changed his mind? Why did he not just stay single if he was bound to end up in a marriage that wasn't genuine?

Daniel and I walked down the stairs to see Alex standing at the door, looking uncomfortable, shifting his weight from foot to foot. Their small talk had all but dried up, and Marcel was starting to look annoyed at having to be there, making conversation with someone he believed was so far beneath his station. Of that, I was positive. I looked at the two men that were my husbands, one present and one past, and felt profound disappointment. One husband that had come to take my baby away and the other that didn't really love me.

When I got to the door with Daniel, Marcel kissed my cheek and excused himself. "It was nice to meet you, Alex. Take care of our little boy. And Daniel, be a good boy and listen to your daddy and new stepmom. I'll see you in a couple of days." He leaned down and squeezed him tight then gave him a kiss on the cheek. Thankfully, nobody saw my eyes roll.

I crouched down beside Daniel, looked him in the eyes, and said, "Bye, baby, I'll miss you. But you can call me anytime. Daddy has my number, so just ask him if you want to talk to me, okay? And you'll be back in two days, so it'll go fast."

"Don't worry, Mommy, I'll be fine. Daddy will take care of me." He looked up at his dad, who smiled down at him, warm and sincere, and I knew Daniel was in good hands. As much as Alex had messed up in the past, he *was* his father, and I believed he genuinely loved him. Or at least wanted this chance to try to show his love and make up for lost time.

I stood up, smiled at Alex, and said, "Would you please update me and let me know how things are going? And have Daniel give me a call?" Turning to Daniel, I said, "If you are not having too much fun, that is, will you give me a call?"

"Well, we do have a lot of fun things planned. But I'll make sure he calls," Alex said, taking him by the hand.

"I'll call you, Mommy. I promise."

I stood at the door, waving, till the car left the driveway, and then I sighed deeply before turning back into the house. To the left of me was Marcel's office, where I saw him seated, feet up on his desk and laughing at something on his phone. Something or someone was amusing him very much, and it wasn't me. I grabbed my car keys and my purse and left.

I drove around for a while, heading north at every other turn. Before I knew it, I was on a two-lane highway in the country. It was mid May, and the signs of summer were in abundance. The farmers' fields were planted, and every now and then I got that old familiar smell of manure through the window that reminded me why I wasn't a country girl. I drove pass cows grazing in the fields, horses prancing, and groups of sheep doing what, baaing. I guess. They were just standing around waiting to be sheered, I supposed. The idyllic scenes had a calming effect on me, but after a forty-five-minute drive directly north, I supposed I should head back.

At a country corner, three old churches on three of the corners and a general store on the fourth, I decided to turn around. I pulled into the parking lot of the general store, suddenly craving chocolate. I went inside and bought a Mars bar and was about to leave when the old guy behind the counter, obviously bored to tears, asked, "You new around here?"

"Oh, no, no. I'm just out for a drive. I'm from Toronto. I'm heading back now; I've driven far enough for one day. But you have a lovely spot here." My mistake; I had started a conversation, and the lonely store clerk was not going to let me go easily.

"You any relation to the Spencers that live on 4th Street?" he asked. "You look just like Mrs. Spencer's sister that used to come up to stay with her for the summers to watch her kids."

"No, 'fraid not," I answered, backing slowly toward the exit.

"Hmmm." He held his hand on his chin and patted his nose. "You look so familiar to me. You on TV? One of those decorating shows in the city."

"Nope, not there either." I had to smile. That was flattering.

"You must be on TV. I've seen you on TV before. I'm sure." He was adamant. I wanted to answer that I thought I would remember being on TV. But I couldn't be rude, and besides, I wanted to leave, so I decided to end the conversation as smoothly and politely as possible.

"I swear, I've never been on TV before, and I am not Mrs. Spencer's sister. But if you like, I could give you my autograph before I leave. I've never done that before either, so it would be quite the honor."

"Oh, you're a hoot," he replied, laughing. "Well, all I can say is that if you are not on TV, you should be so yeah, I'll take your autograph, and I can tell everyone I knew her before she was famous."

"No, *you're* a hoot. Okay, I'll buy one of those greeting cards just for you and sign it. That way, you'll sell something too. How does that sound?"

"Pick the one with the owl. My favorite bird. They're all blank, so you can write what you like."

From among the cards with drawings of various animals, I grabbed the owl card from the revolving rack. After my sticker shock from seeing the price on the back, ten dollars, I said, "That's kind of a steep price for a greeting card, wouldn't you say?" Maybe he was smarter than he made himself out to be.

"Oh, that's because they are prints from a local artist who lives on Third Concession. Marilyn Carmichael. You might have heard of her. She used to live in Toronto and had shows in some of the galleries in Yorkville before she moved up here. Anyway, all the proceeds go toward a women's shelter she set up in Alliston after her daughter was killed by her abusive common-law husband."

Talk about making me feel like a stupid cheapskate. Of course, the cards were for a noble cause. This was small-town Ontario. One look at them and you could see they were prints of drawings. My heart felt like it would break at this artist's story. I picked four more to bring home and frame.

"Such a worthy cause. I'm buying five, so now I do hope I am famous one day and can make this money back. Okay, what's your name?" He told me it was Kent. I opened the card and wrote, *To Kent, wishing you a lovely summer and a wonderful life. Rachel Armstrong.*

And as soon as I signed it, I realized my Freudian slip. I had signed my maiden name. But I wasn't sorry or mad at myself or anything. I was coming to the sad conclusion that I wasn't really married to Marcel. Maybe in name, but that wouldn't be enough to hold us together. We had an extremely weak and tenuous union. It seemed to be at a tipping point.

"Nice meeting you, Kent, you made my day." I turned to leave.

"Likewise. It's not everyday we get famous folk in these parts," he said, going along with the ruse right to the end.

We both laughed, and I went back to my car. Before driving, I texted Lara and asked her if she wanted company. She answered that she would love that but was on a date. *Good for you, I hope he is good enough for you*, I answered.

I think so, first date. I'll talk to you tomorrow.

I thought about visiting my mother, but I really didn't want her to know that things were not going well for Marcel and me. I just couldn't bear to hear her "I told you so," or worse, her look of pity. I decided to go the movies.

Eight movies were playing at the megaplex in my area, and there was not one that I truly wished to watch. However, I picked one that I thought I would dislike the least, a family-rated movie from Pixar, and bought my ticket. I went to the Tim Hortons counter, purchased a decaf coffee, and walked toward cinema eight. I had fifteen minutes till the movie and entered a theater with about twenty people. I watched the trailers and the ads, then the movie started. Twenty minutes in, I fell asleep and woke up to the closing credits. Till then, I hadn't been aware of how exhausted I was. I had been averaging about six hours of sleep a night, and my dreams lately were filled with disturbing and upsetting images. But waking suddenly in an unfamiliar setting, I felt silly and out of sorts as I exited through glass doors and found my car in the sprawling parking lot.

I pulled into my driveway about eleven and went inside to an empty house. I was still exhausted and headed directly to bed. Alone in that big, empty house only served to convince me that I didn't belong there. Once again, I cried myself to sleep. Marcel sauntered in the house Saturday afternoon all showered and refreshed. Wherever he has staying, he was well taken care of.

"Hi Rachel, how are you? Hear anything from Daniel?" he asked nonchalantly.

"Seriously? You're asking me about Daniel? Why bother? You don't care about him. Or me, obviously. You don't need to pretend you do. It's really not necessary."

"Okay." He walked upstairs toward our bedroom. I followed, furious. He was not going to walk away like that and not give me any answers. No Daniel in the house meant I could yell and scream at him if I wanted to, and at this moment that was exactly what I wanted to do. We needed to have it out. Or we were done.

I stood at the doorway and watched him take off his watch and place it on his dresser. He unbuttoned his shirt took it off and threw it in the hamper. He looked my direction and said, "Did you want something?" I clenched my teeth in anger and restrained myself from charging him.

Calmly, I said, "Yes, in fact, I do. I want to know what the hell is going on with you? Where have you been?"

"I don't like your tone," he said offhandedly.

"Marcel, where have you been?" I asked him again, a little louder this time.

"You don't need to know. It won't help anything. It won't make you feel better. If I told you that I'm not sleeping around, you wouldn't believe me anyway."

"Yeah, I doubt I would. I just don't get it. Why did you marry me? You obviously don't want to be married. Do you want to separate? Is that it?"

"I want you to grow the hell up, Rachel. Stop acting like a

spoiled child that can get what she wants every time she asks for it. I didn't want this living arrangement, and you forced me to live with your child, and now I'm not. When I don't feel like it, I don't come home."

"Where are you staying? I deserve to know that."

"You don't deserve to know anything. I'm going to have a nap now, so could you please leave me alone?"

"Do you want me to leave for good? Just say the word, I'll pack my bags, and Daniel and I will be out of your hair for good."

"I already told you that you need to give me my space, and we will be fine. I am not sleeping around; I just stay at a friend's now and then because I feel hemmed in by what you've done to me. I don't want to separate, Rachel. Right now, I would like to have a nap. When I get up, we can go for dinner if you like."

I figured we'd talk more then, plus he closed his eyes as he put his head on the pillow, so I agreed and left him alone. Three hours later, we were at a restaurant, still fighting. The more I tried to get to the bottom of things and come up with solutions, the more he would refuse to speak. Finally, I said that I was going to arrange some counseling for us both.

"Rachel, if we can stop talking about this now, I'll agree to go." And from that point on we had a pleasant evening. Sort of. My distrust and disappointment were simmering under the surface, and I found it difficult to dispel my negative thoughts. I kept looking at him and wondering if I had married a sociopath. He made jokes and charmed all the waitstaff, but every now and then he received texts that try as he might to avoid looking at, he was compelled, and soon his phone would slip out of his pocket and he would glance to his side.

*

Daniel was dropped off by Alex and Cierra Sunday evening at six.

He jumped out of the back seat and ran to me, standing at the front door. He practically sprang into my open arms. That felt so good. Heavenly. I was afraid he'd come home sulking and asking to stay longer with his dad. I had to get over this unnecessary and unfounded jealousy, especially since these visits were about to become a regular thing, every other weekend. Nevertheless, I squeezed Daniel tight and swung him around a few times before putting him down. We stood holding hands, watching until his dad's car drove away, my smile stretching my cheeks.

Marcel was in his office, and Daniel peeked his head in and said, "Hello, Marcel, I'm back."

"Great, kid, did you have fun?" he asked, looking away from his computer briefly, then turning back before he got his answer.

My very perceptive little boy knew quite well that Marcel was not expecting an answer, so he turned himself away from the office and followed me to the kitchen, where I was tidying up after supper.

"You hungry? Because I made blueberry muffins this morning, and they're really yummy. I ate two myself, and even Marcel ate two, and he doesn't even like muffins. That's how good they are." I took the container from the fridge and placed it in front of him.

"I'm really full, Mommy. We had a lot of food at Lita's today. She had a party for me. We had lots of pizza and chicken wings. And she made a big cake with chocolate icing, and we had a piñata."

"Well, isn't that nice," I said, trying to hide the sarcasm. A party to welcome him back into her family again. And out of mine. The sting of betrayal was like a stab to my heart, and I was now convincing myself, perhaps wrongly because of hurt, that Marguerita was the one who had told Alex what happened the night Daniel broke his arm, not her sister Rosa. After all, what was I to her? Just the woman who married her son and then divorced him. Alex was blood, the fruitage of her womb. Not me. I understood to a degree this familial loyalty, but a new disdain for Marguerita was forming in my mind all the same. I hated myself for it, but couldn't help it.

We sat across from each other, me eating a muffin and Daniel drinking a glass of milk, and we shared our experiences from the weekend. I told him about my drive in the country and the old man at the store and would have told him about the movie if I had only been awake for it, and he told me about his dad's house, which was big and very clean, and that Cierra waited for you to finish with a dish and then took it right away to put in the dishwasher.

"Daddy says she is anal, and then he gives me a wink when he says it. I asked him what it meant, and he said sort of too fussy. But he says he likes it, because she knows where everything is all the time. And he said to tell you that she is great at doing laundry."

"Ha!" I said, then laughed remembering my laundry days as a newly married young woman. My mother had always done all our family's laundry at home. Nobody had told me you couldn't put dark items with light. I just threw them all together, and when a load came out a weird shade of blue from a new dark blue t-shirt, I learned the hard way. But Alex and I had so many laughs from all our mishaps, it almost made them worth it. And he gave Daniel that message to let me know laundry isn't everything.

Later that evening, when Daniel was lying in bed, tucked under his blankets, I picked some bedtime stories. I started reading the first one but felt an involuntary lump form in my throat and tears come to my eyes. I quickly swallowed and tilted my head back to stop myself from crying, but it was too late. Daniel had seen the tears.

"Why are you crying, Mommy?" he asked in his sweet little boy voice.

"I'm just so happy you are home. And I missed you so much. That's all. I'm happy."

The truth, that I was overly emotional from the stress of an unhappy marriage, was something I couldn't tell him. Plus, I hadn't honestly admitted to myself that our marriage was a complete sham. I still had some hopes riding on counseling. If only the tiniest hope. And, what was more, I truly was overjoyed that Daniel was home and here with me.

"I'm happy too, Mommy. If you want to cry, that's okay. I can read the book to you if you like."

I told him that I would like that very much, and he read all three stories to me in record time, because in fact he didn't read a word. He knew them all by memory, and the words raced from his lips faster than he could turn the pages. And the delight that gave me sent tingles down to my very soul, and I wanted to cry once again.

Twenty-Two

After dropping Daniel at school the following day, I decided to pay my mother a long overdue visit. I walked into the house to be greeted by a wagging Luna. No mother in view; I was momentarily relieved. My marriage was exhausting me, I looked noticeably stressed and unhappy, and so I'd been avoiding her. Not the good daughter. But I just wasn't up to her third degree, which she was so proficient at applying. But now that Marcel had agreed to marriage counseling, we seemed in a sort of lull. The calm before the next storm, I knew, but being in better place, even if only temporarily, I was ready to face my mother.

I walked through the house, with by Luna at my side, to find her in the garden, talking to a guy. As I approached, I recognized him: Justin. My heart jumped, which made me mad at myself. I would have turned around and left, but they both saw me.

Justin looked a little shy and asked how I was. I felt my face turning red. How did he do this to me all these months later? I thought I had buried any feelings I had for him long ago.

"I'm good. Thank you. How are you?"

"Fine, and thank you for asking." His eyes bore through me before he turned to my mother and said, "I'll email you a quote for all the work you need, and then you can let me know if you want to go ahead. How does that sound?"

"Perfect, but I don't need a quote. I trust you completely and would like you to start as soon as possible."

"All the same, I'm sending one. And now I'll get out of your hair. And congratulations on your marriage, Rachel. I'm happy for you."

I was speechless. I didn't want him to be happy for me, although I was sure the words were only platitudes. He turned away quickly, so, thankfully, my failure to respond went unnoticed by my mother. Had he given me one more minute, I too would have congratulated him — insincerely.

Inside the house, my mother made me us cappuccinos with her new and very expensive coffee machine. Then, from the cupboard she took out biscotti she had made the day before. It was perfect. I looked at her over the coffee cup, and she looked wonderful. She appeared well rested and in good health. Better than I did, I was sure. Marcel's erratic behavior had taken a toll, and I was sure my lack of sleep showed on my face by way of dark circles under my eyes. But if it did, my mother did not say so. God love her. Sometimes.

"You look great, Mom. What's happening? You getting out more or something?"

"Yes, Giselle has been dragging me out with her to different venues when she has gigs, and then we've been doing restaurants and lots of stuff. And I've enrolled in some part-time evening photography classes at Humber College. I just love it. Before you go, I'll show you some of my pictures. They're quite good, I think, if I do say so myself."

"Because who will if you don't?" I finished for her, and we both laughed. "Oh, dear, I hope I don't hand that cliché on to Daniel. I think it has really worn itself out, don't you?"

"No, I don't. I love clichés. They're fascinating, especially if you look at their origin. For example," she interrupted herself, raised her finger as if to say *wait*, and said, "Hey Google, what is the origin of 'the whole nine yards'?"

And then ever accommodating Google proceeded to tell us.

"According to an article in NPR, there are many theories. Some people say it dates back to when square-riggers had three masts, each with three yards supporting the sails, so the whole nine yards meant the sails were fully set. Would you like to know more?"

"No, thank you, Google. See, I told you that clichés are interesting."

"I guess," I said, but the reference to sailing reminded me of Marcel before we were married, and suddenly I had a bad taste in my mouth. I continued, "But Mom, you really do look great. What else are you doing? Did you get some work done on your face or something? You look younger."

"No, no, no. What I am doing is taking care of myself. Really taking care of myself, for the first time in my life. I changed my diet, and I'm not exactly a vegan, but I have practically removed animal products. I eat mostly vegetables, fruits, and grains and drink plenty of water. And alcohol is only for special occasions. And I am sleeping better too. And that's it. Giselle has guided me through it all. She is so knowledgeable about everything. I only wish I had known all this before your dad died, because he wouldn't have had his heart attack if we had had proper diets."

"You don't know that for a fact."

"I'm pretty sure. But anyway, I can't change the past, only the future. And one thing I know for certain is that your dad would not have wanted me to let my life turn to crap. He loved me very much, as I loved him, and I am doing all this for him. I want to live my life in a way that would have made him very happy if he was alive."

"Well, I think that's great. We want you to stick around longer too, both Daniel and I. So, keep it up. You're doing something right. And tell Giselle that I noticed the amazing results from her gentle but effective prodding."

"Gentle? Giselle? Whatever gave you that idea?" She laughed.

"Your aunt is anything but gentle. She'd practically scream at me if I told her that I bought a bag of potato chips. But it was what I needed. I don't know whatever gave you the idea Giselle was gentle. She's a sergeant major. She manages groups of rock musicians. Mostly guys. And they respect her."

"Okay, I stand corrected." I laughed too.

When our laughter had subsided, my mom asked, "How are things with you and Marcel?" Observing my expression change, she interjected, "We don't have to talk about it if you don't want to."

"No, that's fine. They're not great. He's really unhappy Daniel came to live with us before our agreed-upon time. He's been kind of a jerk. Anyway, we are going to go see a marriage counselor, so that's a plus. He didn't want to for the longest time. Actually, our appointment is Wednesday evening. Could you watch Daniel?"

She agreed, and we sat a little longer in the garden, talking mostly about Daniel and school, and before I knew it, it was time to pick him up.

*

The marriage counselor kept us waiting fifteen minutes for the appointment, putting Marcel on edge right from the start. She apologized sincerely, but Marcel was having no part of it. It didn't help that our counselor was a woman. Marcel, I had come to realize, had difficulty with women. Including me. But he had asked me to pick a counselor, and this one had come highly recommended, so she was it. And he was fine with it, until now. She had kept him waiting, so he stubbornly refused to talk.

Our counselor very wisely did not attempt to get him to engage. She spoke in broad terms to us both. She explained that couples who attend counseling or couples therapy have had improvements to their marriages, and these have lasted well beyond the sessions. As long as twenty-four months later. She said it was wise we started early in our marriage, because waiting too long can make treatment harder, if not impossible to get back on track. Then, looking directly at Marcel, she said therapy can only work if both partners show up to session equally invested in the work. Our goal, she told us before leaving, was to repair our emotional connection and improve vital communication — the lifeline of marriage.

I walked out of her office feeling renewed and hopeful. Marcel, on the other hand, was sullen and withdrawn.

On the drive home, neither of us said a word, until finally I felt I was going insane and blurted out, "So, what did you think of her? I know you didn't like that she made us wait, but aside from that, didn't she make great points? Don't you think it will help our marriage?"

He put his hand on my hand on my lap and said, "If you say so, Rachel, but I didn't hear anything new. I've heard everything she said before. Frankly, I think it will be a waste of time and money. Which is something I've noticed you've been going through a lot of lately."

"What are you talking about? I haven't gone shopping in ages. Everything I have bought is either groceries or for the house."

"Yes, but can't you show a little constraint with the groceries? I noticed you went into the Metro twice this week and spent over one hundred dollars each time."

"You know inflation has been driving prices up. Plus, we ran out of quite a few of the basics this week. I had to buy things like toilet paper and paper towels and dishwasher soap, and they're expensive. But I also bought that artisanal cheese you love and some amazing fruits and vegetables. I know they can be a little more costly at that store, but I thought you want the best quality. I was thinking of you, Marcel. I didn't know you had a problem with me spending on food."

"Can you just try to be a little more conservative with my money? It doesn't grow on trees, you know."

"I think I've heard that before, but I never thought I would hear it from you. Would you like to do the grocery shopping?" I was really getting angry.

"No, no, I don't have time for that, but maybe I'll set a budget for you so you can keep the spending within limits."

"I'm having a bit of a problem here, Marcel. Firstly, I would like to know what you did with the old Marcel. The one that gave me a car. That I didn't even ask for, by the way. The generous, kind-hearted Marcel seems to have vanished. Where did he go?" I asked, deflated.

"Nowhere. It's just that now we are a family, we need to act like one and keep our spending in check. Working for the benefit of the whole family." He leaned over and turned on the radio to a classical music station, which was fine with me, because I was done talking. Any hopefulness I had from our session with the marriage counselor disappeared like a morning mist.

For the next few days, Marcel came home directly from work, but it seemed as if it was only to find fault with either Daniel or me. And Daniel had a new attitude too since his visits to his dad. From the looks of things, someone, and Daniel would not tell me who, had told him that since Marcel was not his real father, he didn't have to listen to him. I couldn't imagine it would have been Cierra, because then the same logic would apply to listening to her, or rather, not listening to her. It sounded like something Alex would say, foolishly, because he too had a little problem with authority. He hated it. It was one of the main reasons he never held a job for more than six months when we were together. He would become resentful when given commands from someone he thought he was smarter than, which was pretty well everyone, and then would end up being fired due to insubordination. And Alex was probably a little jealous of Marcel, afraid he would replace him as a father figure in Daniel's life. If only he knew there was no worry of that happening. Ever.

An example of the new Daniel happened the first Friday following his visit to his dad's. He was going to bed and walked to Marcel, who was sitting on the couch, to say goodnight. They gave each other an awkward hug, but then Marcel told Daniel that before he went upstairs to bed he needed to place his shoes neatly at the door.

"You've left them too much toward the middle of the hall, and someone could trip over them. Please place them by the wall," Marcel said. Not harshly, but not kindly either.

"I don't want to," Daniel said. I thought my eyeballs would pop out of my head. I couldn't believe my ears.

Marcel stood immediately and crossed his arms at his chest. "What did you say to me?"

"I don't want to. I think they are fine. And I don't have to listen to you. You are not my father." Daniel sidled up to me and grabbed my hand. "C'mon, Mommy, let's go upstairs for our stories."

I looked over at Marcel and just shrugged as if to say *I have no idea where this is all coming from.* It was kind of funny. He was six years old and standing up to a man much bigger than himself. I was shocked but not too worried. It was probably just a phase. Testing us out to see our limits. He needed a little discipline and correction. But Marcel was having no part of it and did not see it like that.

He walked over to Daniel, picked him up by the front of his shirt, and held him up till they were face to face. Then he brought his forehead up to Daniel's to the point they were touching. "Never say no to me again, Daniel. Do you hear? Or you will be sorry." Then he let go, dropping him down to the floor, and Daniel didn't land on his feet but fell flat on his behind on the hardwood. And it hurt him. However, it infuriated me, my heart started pounding and I clenched my hands.

"Marcel!" I yelled. "You didn't have to hurt him! What is wrong with you? He's just a little boy testing you out. He just needed to have things explained to him. You didn't win by doing that. You'll just make him scared of you, if that's what you want." All the while, Daniel was sitting on the floor where he had fallen, wailing at the top of his lungs.

"That's exactly what I want. A little fear is what he needs. He needs to know his place."

"And what is that, Marcel? Or is there a place for him? Or me?"

"This is not about us, Rachel. This is about Daniel learning to respect adults. Enough with the drama. Stop blowing it out of proportion. He's not even hurt. Now he's just playing it for what it's worth because he has you completely on his side, and I'm, well, I'm the big bad wolf."

I was done talking to Marcel. Really done. Exasperated, I lifted Daniel off the floor and said, "Okay, sweetie, let's get you upstairs for our stories. You'll be okay. Marcel didn't mean to drop you. Let's go. I'll read you an extra story tonight if you like." He sniffled and wiped his eyes with the back of his hands, and we went upstairs.

*

That evening, Marcel climbed into bed beside me and placed his arm around my waist, attempting to pull me close. Without a word, I hopped out of bed, grabbed my pillow, and left the room to go sleep on the couch. As I walked down the hall, I heard him laughing. I lay awake half the night, crying. The following morning, I awoke to the smell of coffee and bacon and the sound of Marcel and Daniel chatting away in the kitchen. I walked in, and had I not known different, I would have thought I was seeing a picture of family bliss.

"Morning, my lovely. Daniel and I made you breakfast," Marcel said cheerfully.

"I cracked the eggs and mixed them, Mommy. And Marcel let me butter the toast," Daniel chirped happily. Such a forgiving little boy who had been through so much in so few years. I stared at him in amazement. Marcel, on the other hand, I had difficulty even looking at. But he was oblivious.

"So, today, after we eat, I thought we could go sailing. I checked the weather, and we have the perfect day for it. Just a few clouds, and there are five to twelve knots of breeze on the broad beam. It's champagne sailing ahead," Marcel said enthusiastically. I was not sharing it. However, Daniel was.

"Can we, Mommy? Please? Please?" He held his hands up in a prayer position, and his begging eyes made it impossible to say no. My determination to stay angry was softening.

"Fine. Would you put my breakfast on warm in the oven, please, and I'll shower and get ready first before I eat, and then we can leave right after."

"And Daniel and I can pack some drinks and snacks for the boat. How does that sound, kiddo?"

Daniel jumped up and down, practically shouting, "Yay, yay, yay!"

I smiled reluctantly and left to shower. Walking back down the stairs, I heard Daniel crying.

Then I heard Marcel, "Sorry, kiddo, but this is an emergency. I forgot about my important meeting today. I promise we'll make up for it next week."

I walked into the kitchen to see Daniel very red-eyed and teary, his runny nose dripping into his mouth. I grabbed a tissue and handed it to him. "Wipe your nose, Daniel," I said, and turning to Marcel, I asked, "What's going on?"

"Something has come up, and I have to go out. We'll sail next week, okay?" He wasn't asking my approval. He ran out of the kitchen, upstairs to our room to grab God knows what, and then practically ran from the house.

I turned on *Paw Patrol* for Daniel on the TV and grabbed my phone and texted Lara.

Feel like company today? Daniel and me?

The response was immediate. *Yes!!!! And bring your bathing suits. Pool's open!*

I sat beside my still crying little boy, placed my arms around his shoulders, and asked, "How does swimming at Lara's house sound?" He wiped his tears with the back of his hands and reluctantly smiled.

When Lara opened the door to us, we were greeted with hugs from her and enthusiastic jumps from her adorable new Golden Retriever puppy. Daniel was ecstatic. Sailing had all but disappeared from his mind.

"Want to play with the puppy for a while before we swim, Daniel? I don't mind. I just made fresh coffee and I'm ready for cup number two with your mom anyway."

"Is that okay, Mommy?" he asked. I nodded, and Lara showed him the basket of toys. Daniel and Pluto played tug-of-war and joyfully chased each other around the house.

We brought toys, Daniel, and the dog along with our coffees to the back deck, stretched our legs out on her loungers, and started to catch up.

"How are things with you and Marcel?" she asked, and I immediately put out my stop-sign hand, signaling I didn't want to talk about him at the moment. "That bad, eh?"

"Yup. That bad. But who is the guy you were out with? Is it still going on?"

"Oh." She held her hand to her heart and smiled. "I'm afraid if I talk about him, I'll jinx it. That's why I haven't even posted pictures of us on Instagram or Facebook. I know, I know, stop rolling your eyes." I guess I had unknowingly done that. She continued, "Jinxing is just a superstition, but I'm so darn happy. I don't want anything to spoil it. His name is Jayden. We see each other every weekend, and through the week we have been meeting for supper at least one or two nights. He has a great job in Internet marketing, and he has no baggage. Good family. Whom I have met, by the way, so I know he isn't hiding anything from me. I really hit the jackpot with him, Rachel. That's all, I think. And he feels the same. It's wonderful. It really is. Here, let me show you a picture. I'm sure that won't jinx us."

"I feel privileged." I looked over at the selfie of Lara and Jayden, both smiling wide for the camera. Looking at them together, one could only describe them as, clichéd as it sounds, madly in love. Their smiles made me smile too. I turned to Lara and said, "Well, well, well, very good-looking. And him too. Hahaha. But don't you two look happy. So, I take it you're not still thinking about freezing your eggs then?"

"Oh." She laughed. "Well, not at the moment. It may not have to be an option after all."

"Does he want kids? Have you talked about that? I'm not sure how much you guys have talked about your future."

"We have, and he does. But we're still in the early stages, so we try not to get too serious. But I think we both feel the same. How about you? Are you going to have another baby?"

She looked at my face and my downward turned lips and knew the answer. "Oh, Rachel, what happened? Why is everything so bad between you?"

"I don't know. I really don't know what I did, but he has changed so much. He's become so mean and indifferent toward me. And he has been staying out. Today he made plans with us and then all of a sudden said he was going out. He never tells me where and in fact said I shouldn't ask him, just give him his freedom. I feel like I'm in a prison. And I can't tell my mom how bad it is because she warned me, and now I have nowhere to go. Plus, the joke is we went for a couples therapy session and he refused to talk. It's a nightmare, Lara. I'm living a nightmare but trying to pretend I'm happy for Daniel's sake."

"Where do you think he's going? Is he seeing someone?"

"Probably. And you want to know the worst part? I don't really care. I mean, I care in that I wanted our marriage to work, but now I'm not sure how I feel about him. I've grown a little numb. He said he goes out because he feels smothered by the instant family, but I don't believe him. And he was in the past a major womanizer his whole life, according to what my dad told my mother. The worst part was that he used to get involved with the students, and my mom said it brought a lot of disgrace on the faculty. He seemed so sincere before we were married. He wanted to settle down, he said. Was tired of the playing around, he said. Such a crock. Such a liar. You would have thought I would be able to identify a liar after living with Alex for eight years. I guess he's a more experienced liar and has it down to a fine art. And I just saw what I wanted to see."

"I think you owe it to yourself to find out if he's cheating. Not just to know; you need to protect your health. What if he gives you a sexually transmitted disease? Not to mention your self-esteem. This is not good for you. I care about you. Rachel, you look tired. Are you not sleeping well?"

"No, I haven't been for weeks. It's taking a toll. And I've lost weight. I know everyone wishes they had that problem, but it's not good. I haven't even had a period in three months from the stress my body is under."

"Are you sure it's the stress causing you not to have periods and not that you are pregnant?"

"No, I can't be pregnant. He hardly even touches me these days. That's another reason I suspect he has someone else he sees when he goes out. I'm sure I'm not pregnant. This happened when Alex put me through the same thing; I lost weight and my periods stopped. It's stress-related. I've lost over ten pounds."

"Has a doctor told you that? Have you done a pregnancy test?"

"Lara, I'm not pregnant. I know that. I knew how I felt when I was pregnant, and this is not the same. I'm not even thinking that. Hey, I don't want to talk about him anymore. It's too depressing. He just brings me down. Let's swim."

Twenty-Three

Lara had put a bug in my ear, so I decided to stop at a pharmacy on the way home and pick up a pregnancy test, because in all honestly, I wasn't a hundred percent sure, and I wanted to find out. I *needed* to find out. To throw Daniel off the scent, not let him know what I was doing or what I was buying in the store, I picked up a buggy and threw a variety of items in as we walked the isles. Bandages, Aspirin, toilet paper, a toy for him, pads, tampons, a pregnancy test, and a gossip magazine. After Daniel saw the toy, he no longer asked about anything else. The total amount was close to $100, and Marcel hadn't taken away my credit card yet, so as far as I was concerned he could take a flying leap off a short cliff if he didn't like me using it.

We walked into a quiet and dark house. Marcel had not come back. I felt like I was living in a stranger's house. I wondered what I was doing there. The many changes and touches I had made to make his house our own now looked pointless. They had not turned Marcel into a loving and stable family man and now only served the purpose of making me feel foolish.

Daniel was exhausted from the hours of swimming and playing with Lara's pup, and he fell asleep the moment his head hit the pillow, three paragraphs into his first storybook. I placed it back on the shelf and leaned over to kiss his forehead before I turned out his light and left his room.

I found the pregnancy test in the bag and took it to the

bathroom. I sat on the closed lid of the toilet and opened the box. The instructions explained that the test was 99 percent accurate and I would have the results in two minutes. Two minutes to find out if my life was ruined. Only two minutes. How cruel. Then I read that the best time to find the results are in the morning, and that settled it. Ten hours and two minutes. I would wait till the morning. I sighed in relief.

It was now after ten, and still no Marcel. No texts or calls either. He had stopped informing me of his whereabouts a long time ago, and why I thought tonight would be any different, I had no idea. My thoughts kept wandering back to the picture of Lara and Jayden, and I had simultaneous feelings of jealousy and happiness. I went over to the wine shelf and browsed the selection. Having heard an aged wine is best, I found the oldest bottle and opened it. It was a 2008 Cabernet Franc, and it was yummy. And this from a girl who doesn't usually like red wine. I wanted to stop at the second glass but finished it off, tout de suite, as they would say in jolly old France, where my lovely wine originated, all the while listening to Sad Songs from the CBC radio app. I stumbled up to bed around midnight and had my best sleep in ages.

I awoke the next morning to Daniel sitting beside me, iPad in hand, quietly watching *Paw Patrol*. The clock read 11:00 a.m. I rubbed my eyes and sat up feeling slightly nauseous and headachy. Then I remembered the wine. I swung my legs over the side of our very large, very high bed and made the small jump to the floor.

"Hey, kiddo, you must be starving. Have you been in here all morning beside me, watching videos?"

He nodded at me and said, "I am a little hungry."

"Of course, you are. You should have woken me up. Fine, let me just go to the bathroom, and then I'll make up waffles."

I walked into the bathroom, and sitting on the counter,

staring me in the face, was the pregnancy test. I had completely forgotten about it. It could wait till after breakfast. I knew I was putting it off, scared to be wrong. Scared to be pregnant. But another half hour wouldn't make any difference.

We finished eating and tidying up by noon, and Daniel got out his LEGO while I trudged slowly up the dreaded stairs to the bathroom and took the test.

I sat on the toilet seat put my head in my hands and cried. Even though I was 99.9 percent positive I was not pregnant, that .1 percent was the scary part. What would I do if I was pregnant? Inform my wonderful husband, only to hear his response, which I guessed would be to get rid of it, I was sure. Or maybe that was what I would hear in my own head. Something I would not even have imagined in my worst nightmare. I would never have chosen to end my child's life. Before. But now? Things were different. Things were abysmal. So, I thought, maybe I should just end my own life. That's what I had come to. I was pathetic. My choices were pathetic and not improving. They were getting worse. Maybe, I thought, I shouldn't even live. But then I remembered Daniel, gave my head a shake, and turned to the counter.

I bravely did the test, and as I had suspected, I was not pregnant. I made a fist-pump and sighed deeply. I threw the urine into the toilet and the rest of the refuse into the bin and skipped down the stairs to my baby, where I hugged him tightly and sent a text to Lara. *Not preggers!!!!!* Followed by Champagne bottle and fireworks emojis.

You still need to find out what he is doing! she replied.

Yes, Mother, thanks for that, I texted back.

I was so relieved, ecstatic, and nothing was going to spoil it. I decided Daniel and I would have a visit with my mother. Even if she was at her worst, she would not dampen my spirits. Maybe I could spread a little joy her way. Maybe it would be contagious.

It wasn't necessary. My mother was great, and we had a wonderful afternoon listening to music from my childhood, playing cards, and then looking through old photos. Daniel especially loved seeing pictures of Thomas. Everything about Thomas fascinated Daniel. But mostly, he was morbidly intrigued with the concept of him dying. After all, they were about the same age when Thomas was suddenly gone.

Daniel looked at one photo of Thomas with a football in hand and said in all seriousness, "I have the same football. Am I going to die like Thomas?"

I was about to grab him and hold him tight when my mother beat me to it. "Never. It was just a terrible accident, but we would never let one happen to you!"

"But why did it happen to Thomas?" Completely serious, he wanted an answer. My mother was about to start crying, so I interjected, "Because bad things happen sometimes. But not to everyone. And especially not to you. Okay? So, stop worrying." And just then we heard the doorbell and Luna's loud bark. Saved by the bell. The food we had ordered from our local Chinese restaurant had arrived. My mother, in keeping with the spontaneous and enjoyable atmosphere of our visit, had ditched her strict diet and dived into all the yummy, greasy food, even licking her fingers.

When Daniel and I pulled into our driveway shortly before eight, I saw Marcel's car in his usual spot. It took me by surprise; he was gone so often, both physically and mentally. I felt anger rise in my chest but resolved not to start a fight with him. At least not until Daniel was in bed and sound asleep. I could see I would have no problem keeping that resolution, since he did not so much as glance my way when we walked in. Things were deteriorating, it seemed, at breakneck speed. And I had no idea why. But would soon find out.

Daniel and I went through the usual routine, stories, songs, and goodnight kisses. I waited at his side till I saw him drift off, then shut off his lamp and went down the stairs to see Marcel. I wanted answers. I wanted truth.

He was sitting at the kitchen island, and when I entered, he pointed to the empty wine bottle. "You drank my $300 bottle of wine I was keeping for a special occasion."

"Yeah, so?" What gall. He stayed out all night for the umpteenth time and complained that I drank his wine. I stared at him in disbelief.

"Meh, nothing." He shrugged. "I guess I can't blame you. Just a waste, that's all," he added offhandedly.

"I'm a waste. I get it. You must regret giving me that car. That's a waste too then, isn't it?"

"No, I didn't want that car, but I did want that wine. It was given to me by someone very important."

"Much more important than me, I take it. Which probably isn't very difficult to be, is it? Am I on your list as the least important person to you? Tell me, I'd love to know. I deserve to know."

"Oh, stop being so melodramatic. You are important."

"Just not to you, right? So, what's up, Marcel? Do you want me to leave? Are you trying to drive me out?"

"No, I don't want you to leave. I'm enjoying seeing you when I come home, and sometimes I even like your little tyke. He's not that bad."

"But you're seeing someone else, so I find that hard to believe."

"I'm not. I just need a break from this family you've thrust on me. I can take it in measured increments, just not constantly." He looked at his phone, attempting to ignore me. I was having no part of it.

"That's just bull, I know it and you know it. Yesterday morning, you made plans with this family I thrust upon you, and then you walked out. I guess your girlfriend made herself available. Marcel, I know you're cheating. I lived with a cheat for nine years. I deserve the truth. We don't have to keep doing this, you know. You can have your freedom again. You gave it a try, and it didn't work for you. I gave it a try too. We need to stop wasting our time."

He waved his hand as if brushing away a fly. "We're fine. You're making a big to-do out of nothing. Rachel, I can't talk about this now. I have work to do for tomorrow's class." He walked out, and I went to bed but didn't sleep. I was far too infuriated. My adrenalin was racing.

*

Monday, after dropping Daniel at school, I walked back into our house determined to find something that would help me come closer to knowing what Marcel was up to. I had up till now stayed out of his precious office, as he had requested, but I no longer felt obligated to keep my word. Exactly twenty-four hours before, I had considered ending my life because of this man. I was past the point of respecting boundaries.

First place I looked was his computer. And, as I knew it would be, the screen was locked and I did not know the password. I tried a couple I thought might work, the name of his university, his birthdate, our street address, but none of them worked. I gave up on the idea of getting into it and decided just to look through papers and journals. He had a filing cabinet filled with journals going back five years. I started reading.

He had daily entries of curriculum policies and strategies, assessments of students with remarks that ranged from academic potential to attractiveness. Always female attractiveness. The creepy side of Marcel was becoming evident. None of the entries documented any of the relationships he had formed. But his intentions were obvious from the notes. He would comment on the provocative clothing of whatever female student was his target and his intention to arrange a one-on-one interview with her. After that, he never wrote a single word about her. Whether she spurned his advances or he got his way, I had no way of knowing from the journals. But from my mother, I knew in many cases he had.

I was wasting time reading five-year-old journals and went straight to the present ones. Sure enough, a female student was catching his eye, and sure enough he had arranged a meeting. About one month ago, the same time he began staying out all night. Going back from there, he wrote about a different girl that caught his eye who "always wore the tight red sweater." I went back a few more pages but started to feel nauseous. More of the same. I'd had enough.

I opened the top drawer of his desk and found a stack of letters. Going through them, I found the usual bills, utility notices, and letters from his alma mater. Then I saw a hand-addressed letter to him from his university department. It was dated last October, just before our engagement. I read through it once then got myself a glass of water because upon reading the contents, the room started spinning, and I was sure I would faint. Slowly and carefully sitting in Marcel's leather office chair, I began reading it again.

It came from the department head, Tom Solomon, and every part of it was handwritten in ink. Surely to avoid any record. But, foolishly, Marcel had kept it. For what? A souvenir? Proof of his abilities as a player? The gist of it was this: Marcel had entered into far too many sexual relationships with students, and the university's reputation was being tarnished. Although he had been spoken to on numerous occasions, he had failed to stop sleeping with students and was not discreet. The university was fielding many lawsuit threats, and Marcel was at the root of a good portion of those. The last incident reported to Tom was of a more serious nature. It involved a female student who said she was sexually assaulted by Marcel on numerous occasions and felt she had a moral and social duty to report these, first to Tom as the department head, and then if nothing was done about it, she would go to the police. She stated that Marcel had used his position of power to cause fear in her and to make her depend on him.

Tom went on to state that he believed her and therefore assured her of his full cooperation into investigating her allegations and subsequently addressing them. He advised Marcel from this point on to keep his "nose clean" and to stop initiating any sexual relationships with any students. The other piece of advice to Marcel was where I became involved. He told him that in view of the situation, it would be prudent find a suitable partner.

He wrote, *Find yourself a suitable partner and get married. Stop indulging in promiscuous relationships and thus ruining the reputation of our fine institution. In addition, should a lawsuit arise, being a married man will no doubt give you an advantage. These things I write you both as your colleague and friend.*

Twenty-Four

I held the letter in front of me and stared at it. I knew I should feel anger, outrage, and humiliation, but strangely, on second reading my equilibrium was restored, and all I felt was a deep sense of relief. I had questioned myself over and over again, wondering what I did to Marcel to make his love grow cold, and now I had the answer. He had no love to begin with. He married me because of a very persuasive suggestion.

But why had I married him? For one, I was approaching thirty, which is scary. Plus I thought, mistakenly, that he loved me and would provide security that both Daniel and I needed. And I had loved him. A little. I thought that given time our love could be cultivated and would indeed flourish. I had heard of some arranged marriages that did just that. And thought ours would too.

Now, I knew better. Not only was our marriage not going to become stronger, but he had also already shown he was more interested in cultivating love with other women. I pondered the situation and now understood why he had put no effort into the marriage counseling. He had no intention of making our marriage strong. It was nothing more than a façade, doomed from the beginning. And I put Daniel through it all. That evening, I would tell Marcel I was leaving. Perhaps I would tell him why. Did I care if he was angry with me for going through his office? Not in the least. If I had the energy, I would tell him about the letter. By now I was truly indifferent. As I knew he was. Telling everyone else was going to be the problem. *Egads,* I thought, *how many people will be calling me a gullible fool, if not to my face, at least in their minds?*

I looked at the time on my phone and gasped. I had to leave the house in ten minutes if I didn't want to be late to pick up Daniel. I stood up and immediately felt myself get weak at the knees, and my head started spinning again. I guess I wasn't fine. I was in shock. I sat back down and messaged my mother, asking her to pick up Daniel at school. She told me she would and then asked me how long I would be leaving him with her. I thought for a few minutes and texted, Would you be able to keep him for the night? Some things have come up with Marcel, and it would be better if Daniel was not home.

I got a thumbs-up emoji for an answer. I went into the basement, found two large suitcases, and then went upstairs to Daniel's bedroom and started packing his clothes. Again, I felt lightheaded and realized I hadn't eaten since 8:00 a.m. I made myself a cheese sandwich with the artisanal cheese that I thought Marcel loved so much and ate it along with couple of dill pickles. Eating my sandwich, I watched out the window as the squirrels chased each other around a large maple. I envied them and their carefree existence, nothing to make them upset. Unless, of course, a hungry hawk was nearby and thought they would make a delicious meal. I made my way back to Daniel's room, and within three hours all his clothes and toys were packed. I went into my room and began organizing my things. When I looked at the clock, I saw it was six o'clock. Marcel had not come home. I wanted to start packing my things but realized I had no suitcases. I hopped into my car and went to the Bay to buy myself a few on Marcel's account, with absolutely no guilt whatsoever, and if I hadn't been in such a hurry, I would have headed to the jewelry counter to see what else caught my eye.

When I got back home, there was still no sign of Marcel, and it was close to eight. I went to my room and started packing but was suddenly exhausted and needed to sit down. Emotionally, I was spent. Going back downstairs, I poured a glass of white wine and sat down to put my feet up and fritter away time on Facebook and Instagram. I could pack the rest of my things in the morning.

My phone alerted me to a text from Lara. *Jayden and I are close by. Can we stop by and say hello? So I can show him off?*

Tonight is not good. Sorry, I replied.

I attempted to distract myself with useless information, but as I sat there, the ludicrousness of my situation finally dawned on me, and I couldn't concentrate on anything. It was as if I had just now digested the news, and the outcome was leaving me with severe heartburn. Marcel had used and uprooted not only me, but also my little boy. And how might this affect my mother, living through yet another upset in her family? I had so many burning questions. Why had he picked me? Did he hope we would be happy in time? Or did he even care? Why didn't he marry one of the numerous young women he had been involved with? And why had his colleague encouraged him to do that in the first place? Ironically, maybe the next lawsuit against the university would be from me. I was seething and only wished Marcel would get home so I could face him.

Shortly after ten, he walked in the door, sweating profusely, with a crazed look on his face. The moment I heard the door I stood, hand on hips, ready to head him off at the pass. I wanted his immediate and full attention, but one look at him and I could see I would get neither. He brushed by me as if I wasn't even there and went directly to his whiskey. He poured himself a glass and took two big gulps. Then he looked up, noticing me for the first time.

"We need to talk," I said, but I doubted, from the looks of

him, that we would be doing any talking. He appeared in a state of fearful anxiety and shock. He didn't answer me, just took another gulp from his drink and then refilled the glass.

I made a coughing sound to get his attention, and when he finally looked my way, I announced in a calm and collected manner, "Marcel, I'm leaving you tomorrow. I know why you married me. You can stop the charade now."

He didn't answer me, just walked to the couch and sat nervously on the edge. I had had enough. I walked briskly to the office to find the letter. I stood in front of him and held it in front of his eyes. He just shrugged, infuriating me further.

"What do you have to say about this?" I demanded. He said nothing.

"What wise and prudent advice this was," I mocked. "Marcel, you should find some poor unsuspecting girl and get married. You know now we are doomed, don't you? No therapy can help this. I have decided to leave you. Tomorrow. I'll contact a lawyer in the next few weeks and we can finalize our divorce as soon as possible." He just sat, staring at me in silence.

"Did you hear what I said, Marcel? I'm leaving you tomorrow." Nothing. "Marcel! What the hell is wrong with you?"

"I was threatened tonight. Very real. Frightening," he murmured, staring straight ahead at nothing. He was far away, probably reliving the event.

Talk about a turn of events. I asked, "Where? On the street? Were you mugged? Did you call the police? Do you want me to call them now?"

"No, no police. It was a completely random act, and besides, I would never be able to identify the guy. I just want to forget it. Can you come over here and hold me, Rachel? Please?"

Incredulously, I asked, "Did you not hear what I told you, Marcel? And see that letter? I know why you married me, and I'm leaving you. Tomorrow. Daniel's things are packed, and I'll have my things packed by tomorrow. We're finished."

"Yes, I know. Just sit with me awhile and put your arms around me. I won't ask you to stay. I never should have married you. I'm just a lecher. You deserve better. I know you were sincere when you married me, and Rachel, to tell you the truth, at the beginning I was too. I thought maybe we could have a good marriage, but like they say, old dogs can't learn new tricks, and I guess you could say I'm a senior dog. Getting married was a new trick, and I just couldn't master it, adapt to being monogamous. I'm no good. I know that. But thank you for giving me a chance."

He walked up beside me and buried his head in my neck, and I could hear him crying. I put my arms around him and gently patted his back. I knew his crying wasn't for me.

*

Not having to drive Daniel to school the following morning, I was able to put all my attention into packing my things and getting away from Marcel. He had got up early that morning, showered, and made his coffee without saying a word to me while I stayed upstairs packing. He stopped at the door before leaving and called my name. I stood at the top of the stairs, looking down at him, and waited to hear what he wanted to tell me. Looking up at me, I could see the sadness in his eyes that reflected a measure of regret.

"I'm sorry, Rachel. I really am." He turned to leave, head bowed. *Oh well,* I thought. I felt one teardrop on my cheek, wiped it away with the back of my hand, and then grabbed my phone and texted my mother. *Good morning, Mom. I'm coming back to live with you today. I'll explain everything later.*

It was shortly after eleven, and I had two suitcases packed and one to go when I heard the doorbell ring. *Oh great,* I thought, *who could that be?* I hoped it wasn't the two Jehovah's

Witness ladies I had talked to the week before. They were really nice, and I had enjoyed our conversation and told them they could come back, but today was not the best day. In fact, it was the worst. I hoped they would understand I wasn't trying to be rude if I said I was too busy to visit. I decided to peek through the curtains and not answer at all. I was not in the mood to talk to anyone. What I saw was not two well dressed women with handbags but two policemen in uniform. I felt my heart rate increase and the hair on the back of neck stand on end. Had something happened to Daniel? I took several deep breaths to calm myself and then answered the door.

"Are you Mrs. Marcel Mancy?" the police officer asked with a sympathetic look. I croaked out a barely audible yes. I had difficulty speaking from the lump that had formed in my throat.

"We have some difficult news to tell you. May we come in, please?"

We sat together in the living room, and they proceeded to give me the shocking news. Marcel had died. More precisely, Marcel was murdered. Shocking news, yet sadly, all I felt was relief that nothing had happened to Daniel. I sighed deeply.

They watched me momentarily, I guess for my reaction, before continuing. Marcel had been stabbed to death as he exited his car in the university parking lot. The suspect was also dead. He had taken his own life, so there was no need for me to worry about any possible danger. When I asked them why someone had murdered him, they told me that was all the information they could share with me at that moment but assured me I was not in danger and gave me their sincerest condolences.

I was numb and lightheaded, as though I might faint. I took a couple of long, deep breaths then said, "Well, Officers, this is very bizarre. As you can see from the suitcases in the corridor, I'm about to leave the house. Permanently. Mr. Mancy and I were in the process of becoming separated and divorced. I'm not the person that will be dealing with this in the future. He has a sister who lives in Toronto, and she will be the person you need to talk to from now on. Let me get her number for you."

Interestingly, they weren't taken aback at the news of our separation. They took the number I had written on a piece of paper and wished me well. It was then, without them telling me, that I guessed why he was killed. A jealous boyfriend or husband had done it. And that was why the police were not at all surprised I was leaving.

It took less than a week for the whole story to hit the newspapers, nightly television, and radio broadcasts. The investigation revealed that a jealous boyfriend had confronted Marcel and the same man's girlfriend, with whom Marcel had been engaged in an affair, at a restaurant the evening before the murder and screamed threats at them before being driven out by the manager, who was told explicitly by Marcel not to involve police. The manager had no knowledge that pending lawsuits against the university were the reason Marcel wanted no police involvement. He now regretted not following his instinct and having the police arrest the man.

The following morning, the man went to his girlfriend's apartment and murdered her before she had a chance to leave. He then drove to the university and waited for Marcel arrive, whereupon he attacked him with a knife when he stepped from his car. Later that day, he committed suicide by jumping from a bridge at the Scarborough GO train station. Their pictures were flashed everywhere, and thankfully, because I was officially separated from Marcel at the time, I avoided being in the limelight. A picture of me appeared on page four of the *Toronto Star* for one day only. I was grateful, especially for Daniel.

Twenty-Five

I had been at my mother's place for three weeks when I started getting floaters and flashes in my vision. Lost vision, my punishment for being such an uncaring person and not burying my husband or even seeming to care that he was killed. And every night in my dreams, he appeared to tell me so. In some dreams we would be in his boat, enjoying a peaceful sail on a bright, sunny day, and he would turn to me and ask why I didn't call the police when he told me he had been threatened. Other times we were at a restaurant or in our living room. And he was beside me, as real as life itself. Not angry or irate. Calm and collected. Just curious. He would say, "Why, Rachel? Did you want me to die? Why, Rachel? Why, why, why?"

After repeating "why" over and over and over, I'd wake up in a sweat. When awake, I constantly I relived the night before he died. It was all I thought about. Like the restaurant manager, I wished I had called. I wasn't overwhelmed by regret, since my love for him had grown cold. But I questioned myself. Was I simply cold-hearted? And now I was going to go blind, because I deserved it.

My mother noticed I was becoming withdrawn, and after observing me grasp the counter for no obvious reason or hold on to a wall one too many times, she grew concerned and questioned me. I mentioned the floaters in my eyes but tried to brush it off. Like any good mother, she made an appointment with an optometrist, unbeknownst to me, and drove me there under the pretense of going grocery shopping. Parked in front of the office, I agreed to go in. After all, she was right.

My examination revealed no underlying eye disorder such as a torn retina. The very kind and wise optometrist asked if I might be experiencing any depression or anxiety. I admitted that I was. He then confessed that he was aware of my situation, since he had read about the murders in the newspaper.

"Well, I think what you are experiencing is anxiety-induced eye floaters, and while they are not common, they do happen occasionally to people who are experiencing anxiety and depression. My advice to you would be to try to treat the underlying causes of your stress, and that will go a long way toward reducing the floaters. Among other things that help might be making sure your diet is healthy, getting regular exercise, deep breathing when you feel stress, journaling, and, of course, talking to a professional grief counselor, or what I like even better is a good friend."

I took offense to his suggestion. What was he talking about? Had my mother told him my personal business? I was going to kill her when I left this tiny, windowless examination room, no bigger than closet, that was also beginning to stress me out, making me feel claustrophobic. Who was he to tell me I needed a grief counselor? I wasn't grieving. I was separated from Marcel. I was fine. Or was I? I thought of Lara. I needed to talk to her, my voice of common sense. She'd help. I would call her later.

The doctor continued, "Anyway, your vision problems are nothing to worry about and will go away as your stress decreases, but if they do not or they worsen, make sure you come back right away."

I drove home with my mother, head bowed, and I felt like a little child all over again. I glanced her way and was ready to ream her out, but instead I buried my face in my hands and wept bitterly. She just patted my knee and said, "There, there." We got back in the house, and I was going to my room to sleep but remembered what the doctor had ordered and grabbed the leash to walk Luna, who was always up for that. I was, quite frankly, a train wreck.

Luna and I walked for over two hours. She was dying of thirst and panting when we finally made our way back home and would probably from this point onward hide from me whenever I grabbed the leash. But, admittedly, the doctor had hit on something. The walk helped clear my head. I felt better, emotionally and physically. And not nearly as thirsty as Luna. Poor dog. Next time, I would bring a water bottle.

My mother prepared one of her healthy vegan meals that consisted of beans and beans and more beans. I wasn't crazy about it, but her health had markedly improved, so there may have been something to this way of eating. Plus, it was not completely tasteless and actually left me satiated. And my little picky eater, Daniel, ate every last mouthful. Maybe she was on to something. I practically had to bribe him to eat mashed potatoes and broccoli.

After we cleared the table, I asked her if she minded watching Daniel while I visited Lara.

"Giselle is coming by to visit tonight. I think she wanted to see you. I told her I was concerned. I hope you don't mind," she said nervously, afraid of my reaction, thinking I would be angry with her. And I was. I could feel my face redden. Was she going to tell everyone and their dog my business? I clenched my teeth. Then I remembered doing the same thing, entreating Giselle's help. I guess there is a fine line between meddling and caring. Maybe none of us get it completely right all the time, but I couldn't fault her for trying to help.

I took a couple of deep breaths, like the doctor had instructed, before answering. "No, of course not. I'd love to see her. She is my favorite aunt, after all."

Giselle breezed in shortly after seven and announced we were going out and I was to get presentable and put on some makeup.

"Where are we going?" I asked so that I could at least know what to put on, although I was pretty sure I would still settle on my faithful jeans and a white blouse, my favorite standbys.

"The band I manage, Black Dog, is having their EP release party tonight at Hugh's Room, and I'm bringing you as my date, my dear. It will be a blast. Their fans are nuts, and there will be many music industry professionals and music bloggers, plus local critics. It's all about promotion. Promotion, promotion, promotion. So, you could kind of say it's an important night. And I'm a little nervous. But that's just between you and me. To everyone else, I'm calm, cool, and collected. The epitome of professionalism."

And she was. Giselle glided through the room, and immediately upon entering, all eyes turned to see this beautiful woman. In addition to her height and gorgeous face and figure, Giselle possessed the perfectly unlined skin of someone who always wore a wide-brimmed hat and applied sunscreen judiciously before going outside. Her natural auburn hair shone magnificently in the yellow fluorescent lighting. We found our table midway through the crowded room and immediately upon sitting were approached by people Giselle knew. I observed with delight as she engaged in animated conversation with them all. No matter who talked to her, she smiled broadly and was gracious and polite, from the radio personality on the morning show to the band's roadies. She introduced me to everyone and remembered every person's name. When the band finally came on stage, following an opening act by a local comic, the room became electric.

The musicians performed with utmost passion and seemed

oblivious to the fact that the room was filled not only with diehard fans but also critics and media professionals that could either make or break them. They were consummate musicians and entertainers there to perform. They started the act with a cover of a Tragically Hip song and then two of their own older and beloved tunes. Next, they announced the six new songs from their latest EP. Back-to-back, the songs churned. The crowd was ecstatic, as was Giselle. A smile never left her face from the moment they took the stage until the stage lights dimmed.

The set finished with the band members being introduced by the lead guitarist and vocalist to the audience, who bellowed raucous cheers for each member. Then he expressed appreciation on behalf of himself and the band to all involved in making the evening a success, from the venue owner to the fans, and last but not least their wonderful and amazing manager, my Aunt Giselle, who never lost faith in them, even though she should have. Many times, he joked. To the absolute delight of the audience, they performed two more songs as an encore, and the music stopped. The night was amazing.

As the room thinned out, I thought it would be a good time to make my way to the bar and get a Perrier. Giselle had some more schmoozing to do, and I was parched from all the cheering that bordered more on screaming. I approached the bar and was waiting to get the bartender's attention when I felt someone tap my shoulder. Turning to the side and seeing no one, I looked back the other direction to see a very handsome face grinning at me.

"What's a nice girl like you doing in a place like this?" Justin asked cheekily.

"Hey, Justin. How are you?" I returned. It was really nice to see him. But only for a moment, till I came to my senses, remembering how things between us ended.

"Good, I'm doing good. I heard about your husband on the

news. I'm really sorry. That must have been awful."

"I wish I could say it was, but we were in the process of getting separated. I was going to be filing for divorce. So, I don't know what's worse, what happened to him or that I'm not destroyed by it." I gave my head a shake. "That's a stupid thing to say; obviously, what happened to him is worse."

"Yeah, that is kind of tough. I don't know what I would do if I was in your shoes. I'm really sorry, Rachel." He hesitated momentarily, then added, "And I'm really sorry for what I did to you too."

"Forget about it. I have. Listen, I better go. I think my aunt is about ready to leave." I saw her at the table surrounded by three people engaged in conversation, but I really needed to get away from him. Being close to him, talking with him, brought back the wounds he inflicted, as if they were fresh. I thought I might cry, and I didn't want a perfectly wonderful evening to end that way.

Justin grasped my upper arm and said, "Rachel, I didn't get married."

"What?" I asked. I was in shock.

"I didn't get married, and I wanted to tell you, but I heard you were married, so what would it have mattered if I was single? I called it off after us. I knew I would be doing the wrong thing. She was pissed, but I think she knew it was for the best. At least, I hope she understood. Anyway, I didn't tell you right away because I needed to give myself some space, take a good hard look at what I did and why. And I wanted to give you space too. And when I thought the time was right to contact you, I found out you were married."

I just stared at him, dumbstruck. I truly had nothing to reply.

Justin continued, "I've missed you, Rachel. I haven't dated anyone since you. Do you think you could find it in your heart to forgive me?"

I waited a moment before answering, and what came out of my mouth surprised even me.

"No, Justin, I don't forgive you. You hurt me very much, and I can only imagine how hurt your fiancée must have been. It could never work between us now." Justin looked at me in disbelief, then turned sharply to the bar, calling angrily to the bartender. I walked back to our table.

Giselle and I went to a Starbucks on the way home to wind down from the evening's excitement. We sat at the window table, decafs in hand. Suddenly, she lifted both fists in the air and quietly cheered.

"The evening went well, I take it," I said. For me too. It had been exciting and exhilarating and opened up a whole new world I never knew existed. I thought about Justin, too, how unexpected that was, and how I had stayed strong, saying no to his request for forgiveness. Maybe I was growing, after all. Although I felt so unsure of myself.

"Couldn't have been better. Unbeknownst to me, there was a representative from Sony Music there, and they want to sign Black Dog and want them to tour. New York, Chicago, San Francisco, Los Angeles, and, well, you know, all the big cities. No more small towns with only a hundred people in the audience. Everything is paying off. The guys have worked so hard for the last twenty years, and, frankly, they deserve it. They're so talented. Don't you think?"

"They have talent in spades. I'm surprised they haven't been discovered long ago. Have you been managing them for twenty years?"

"Yes, them and a few others that have actually made money, or I wouldn't have been able to stay in the business. I'm a talent agent, along with a manager of Black Dog."

"How did you start doing that?" I asked.

"You'll never believe it. The lead guitarist, Jeff, was my next-door neighbor, and the band was made up of his friends from school. They used to play every day in his garage, and I would watch because they were so good. But what I really wanted to do was sing. I wanted to sing in the band. So they let me, and I sucked. Really bad. I was a little disappointed when they said no but decided to use my energies in another direction. I determined I would make them famous, then set off to do that. I used whatever connections I had through family, friends, neighbors, and I even bugged teachers. I hounded radio stations and pretty well everywhere that I thought could be useful. And I found that I was good at it, not taking no for an answer. After I made a few useful connections for them and helped establish them, I applied for a job at a talent agency, and my reputation was now out there. I got hired, and that's how I became a talent agent. All because I couldn't sing." Giselle laughed cheerfully.

"That's amazing. You're so put-together. I envy you so much. How did I get to be such a screw-up? I feel like such a stupid loser. My bad first marriage and then doing it again. And what excuse do I have? It's not like I had a dysfunctional home, a child of divorce. I had two parents who loved each other and me very much. I shouldn't be such a screw-up. I only have myself to blame." I looked at her beseechingly. *Please tell me the answer.* I needed to know. And surprisingly, she did.

"Who told you your home was either normal or stable? Just because your parents weren't divorced and loved each other, it was far from a normal home. Is that all you remember about being a child? That your parents loved each other?"

"To tell you the truth, after Tommy died, I don't remember much. I remember my mother being a total wreck and my dad always trying to calm her. He loved her so much."

"Too much." I saw her give an eye roll.

"What do you mean?"

"He loved her too much and forgot about you. And because

you were such a smart and competent little girl, he was able to do just that. And yes, your mom needed the help, and I love her, and I know she has been through so much — she is very strong — but you kind of got lost in the fray. I hated to see how they neglected you. You used to get up every morning and make your cereal and go to school with no help at all. Don't you remember that?"

"No, I don't."

"I guess your memory is blocked. It must have been painful. Losing your brother and your parents at the same time. Anyway, that was why I tried, when I could, to come and see you and do things with you, but I was so busy. Just starting my career. I wish I could have helped more. I saw what was happening to you and just stood idly by. So, that was why, when I heard you were marrying your high school boyfriend, I wasn't surprised. In fact, in my opinion you fared pretty well. And I still feel that way. Just two bad marriages under your wings. Some people get into a lot more trouble and have to live with a lot worse problems. Why do you think there is so much alcoholism and drug addiction? It's all from people's dysfunctional childhoods."

"I don't know why that isn't making me feel better. In fact, I feel slightly overwhelmed. Giselle, I honestly don't remember things that way." I started wringing my hands and felt tears coming to my eyes.

"Oh, love, I know, I know. I hate telling you this. It's too much for you to take in. When I see how things have gone for you, I think of you as a baby bird who was pushed from the nest maybe just a little too soon. And had to learn to fly the hard way, all by herself." Tears were rolling down my face by now, but when Giselle saw that, she quickly added, "But you got it! Rachel, you survived. And no housecat or scavenger bird got you. And you'll master flight. You will. One day, you will be superb. I know it for sure. Yes, you had two bad marriages, but not all was lost. Look at that angel you have now."

"Daniel," I said. I was full-blown weeping by now, so I grabbed the napkin and blew my nose. Then I smiled, thinking of Daniel. And, all of a sudden, all I wanted to do was go home and kiss him in his sleep. "Giselle, thank you for a wonderful evening and for explaining so much to me that I didn't know. I feel sad for the little girl Rachel, but big Rachel can be better now. Now that she understands, now that I understand, so much more." I scooted my chair closer to her, threw my arms around her shoulders, and hugged her tight.

My mother was waiting up to greet us. Giselle came in briefly to tell her what a wonderful evening we had and to thank her for sharing me. My mother looked so sweet, smiling at us both, and then she reminded Giselle that the next outing was to be with her.

"The next outing is to Mexico. How does that sound?" My mother said it sounded great.

After saying goodbye to Giselle and goodnight to my mother, I walked upstairs to Daniel's room. I looked at him sleeping. His hair was damp with sweat, so I removed a blanket. I sat at his bedside, then, leaning in, I whispered, "Daniel, I hope I can do right by you. I'm going to really try. I'll probably mess up. But I hope it won't be so much that I won't be able to clean up the mess with just a little elbow grease. And whatever happens, I'll never abandon you."

I leaned in farther to kiss his forehead then stood. Looking back at him, I whispered, "Yes, I have you, my little angel."

I quietly left his room and went to bed, happy but sad, wiser but also feeling a little more vulnerable. It had been a long day.

ACKNOWLEDGMENTS

I want to say thanks to my editor, Allister, who even when critiquing me made me laugh. A thank-you goes to Laura, who read this novel without being coerced and whose input was invaluable. And to all my other voluntary readers who I appreciate beyond words.

ABOUT THE AUTHOR

Eunice Barnes was born in Toronto and has lived there her entire life. After finding herself divorced with four children at home and no marketable skills, she started a dog walking business, which pays the bills but allows far too much time for thinking. However, sometimes those thoughts turn into stories.

She discovered writing because of her love of contests that enticed her to enter a short story contest. And the bug was planted. Since then, one of her short stories has appeared in the anthology *Strange Love Affairs*, a poem was published in *Canadian Stories,* and a children's story was chosen as a finalist in an international competition.

She has written two other novels, an adult novel, *Who We Are Now,* and a middle grade, *The Adventures of the Backroom Rat*, awaiting publication. Eunice is currently working on finishing her third.

Look for Eunice Barnes on Facebook and as *eunicebarnesauthor* on Instagram and TikTok

If you enjoyed this book, please consider leaving a review on Goodreads, Amazon, or your retailer of choice.

Manufactured by Amazon.ca
Bolton, ON